The Lessons We Learn

HELL'S CHASER MOTORCYCLE CLUB SERIES

CHANDLER BEAN

ISBN: 979-8-9933539-0-6 (eBook)
ISBN: 979-8-9933539-1-3 (paperback)

Book Cover and Formatting by Books and Mood.

1st Edition 2025

To the people who told me to go for it.

Thank you for believing in me.

CONTENT WARNING

The Lessons We Learn contains content that may not be suitable for all readers. For that reason, I have put together a list of elements for you to look over, if needed, before continuing. This book has foul language, blood and gore, explicit sex/nudity, alcohol and drug use, kidnapping and murder.

Prologue

JENNA

My knees buckle under me as the knife slides from my bloody fingers. The sound it makes as it hits the hardwood floor rings in my head like a siren's song, pulling me into the darkness. I can hear the pounding of boots; doors being slammed and voices… his voice. *Focus Jenna, focus on his voice. He's here, it's over.*

But I can't move. Breathing even feels like an unimaginable challenge. Falling to the ground, my vision tunnels. The only thing I can focus on are my bloody hands. They can't be mine. A stillness calms my body as the cool air numbs the pain radiating from my abdomen.

"Jenna!" he yells in a gravelly voice, as if fighting to keep tears at bay. It's the last thing I hear before everything goes black.

Chapter 1

AXEL

FOUR MONTHS AGO

Bullets, blood and a shitload of anger follow us as we ride toward the clubhouse. The road in front of us is only lit by the headlights of our bikes, everything else is covered in inky black. I look in my rearview mirror to see Bear driving our black van. His expression is murderous and I bet if I check the faces of my brothers riding next to me, they will look the same. We ride into the darkness as if we are being chased by the devil himself, and maybe we actually are.

I've been a part of the Hell Chaser's for six years now, their Enforcer for five, and never have I been a part of a shit show like tonight. We've been driving for almost thirty minutes now and I have run through every single second of our drop. From the moment we pulled up to the warehouse everything felt off. The job was easy; meet up with the buyers, unload the guns, get paid and then get out of there. But instead, we were ambushed, masked men entered the building from all sides, guns blazing before we even realized anyone was there.

Lucky took the first shot to the leg; next one was to his shoulder before I was able to get him into the van. Bear, Jax and myself were able to return fire and somehow get out of there without any more damage.

My bike rumbles under me as I push her to move faster. I need to release this frustration, but until I'm back at the clubhouse this is the closest I'm getting.

All I want to do tonight is get drunk, find a club girl to take up to my room and forget about this shit for a few hours. Tomorrow I'll figure this out. Tomorrow I will find whoever thought they could fuck with us and slowly drain the blood from their bodies.

There's a party at the clubhouse tonight, a welcome-home-party for Knife. I take a moment to reel in my anger as I park my bike, giving Bear a head nod as he drives the van around back.

"Get the fuck out of the way," I growl at the clump of people standing in front of the door. This place is packed, I can barely get the door to open wide enough to pass through. One of the women from the clump looks at me and then quickly starts to pull her friends out of the way. No doubt she can probably feel the venom in my words.

My first stop is the bar.

Usually, I'm the happiest guy in this place. Booze and women are two of my all-time favorite things. But tonight, I'm not in the mood. I've never handled betrayal well, especially when it puts the people I'm supposed to protect in harm's way. I crack my neck, allowing the tension to flow out around me as I muster up the energy to welcome Knife home after being locked up in State for the last five years.

A palm slaps down on the middle of my back and I hear a hearty laugh I haven't heard in a long time.

"No shit, Axel, you're Enforcer now?"

"Been gone too long, Knife. That's old news." I can't keep the shit-eating grin off my face as we give each other a quick hug. "Good to see you, brother."

"Built like a bear and the biggest asshole I know; guess you were born for the job." His words are slightly slurred and from how bloodshot his eyes are I'm thinking Knife is making the most out of his first night of freedom.

"Hey, I'm about to go find Misty, but let's talk tomorrow. I got some shit to sort through with you," he says as he catches a glimpse of his old lady across the room.

"Okay, yeah, come by the shop, and we'll talk. You good?" Warily I watch for any signs that something might be off. I'm already feeling on edge from earlier and really could go without anything new popping up.

He looks back at me with a smile. "Yeah, man, all good. See you tomorrow."

Cal, Tank, and Mia are a blur behind the bar. The sound of beer bottles being opened and drunks yelling out their order fills my ears as I look for whoever is the least busy.

A flash of platinum hair whirls by me as Mia dances around, shaking her shoulder-length hair as she wipes a glass dry. Her large blue eyes scan the room, probably making sure no one gets out of line. She's tiny, standing right at five feet, but has this whole mama bear thing going on. Mia is Cal's cousin by blood but she grew up here with the rest of us. You would think she was everyone's little sister by the way she's constantly doted on.

I reach the bar just in time to catch the beer she slides towards me.

"Are you okay? You look pissed," she yells over the rowdy crowd. Letting out a long huff, I pick up the beer and chug.

"You could say that."

Her eyebrow rises as she gives me a *"want to talk?"* look. I can't discuss what happened during the drop with her so I decide to change the subject. I nod towards the craziness behind me.

"You okay back here tonight? If shit gets too crazy, come find me, and I'll have a prospect take you home."

She stops mid dance move and laughs at me. "Axel, you do know I can handle myself in here, right?" Mia puts her hand on her hip, "And anyway, no one is going to mess with me with the likes of you to scare them off."

She's right about that. No one would dare fuck with her here.

"Just promise me you'll come get one of us if you need us, okay?" I level her with a no-bullshit stare.

"Huh?" she leans a little closer.

"Just promise me you'll come get one of us if you need us, okay?" I say louder this time.

"Huh?"

"For fuck's sake, just pro--" Mia stands up straight and

smiles at me like she just won a jackpot. The little shit can hear me just fine. Sliding me another beer, she pats my hand.

"Fine, I'll—AHHHHH! Marley!" Her ear-piercing scream stabs my eardrums as she flies out from behind the bar.

Like he owns the place, my best friend and the number one pain in my ass, Blaze, walks into the party with his arm slung around his woman, Marley. He's been bringing her around a lot more and the other women of the club have immediately accepted her as if she is a long-lost sister, separated at birth.

I've never been one to care about who people bring around, but everyone recognized their relationship for what it is immediately. They're end game for each other, and that's not a pun because Marley is some insane tech genius. Blaze tries to pull Marley back as she practically flies towards Mia, but she's too quick.

"Getting slow there, old man." I chide him as he makes his way over.

As my best friend, he punches me in the shoulder. As my Vice President, his annoyingly smug gaze cuts to me.

"What the fuck happened today?" he gruffs as he nods to Cal for a drink.

"Someone must've got a jump on our drops." My fingers work aimlessly to get the wet label peeled from my beer bottle. The anger I felt earlier, seeping into my limbs again and leaving me aching to punch someone. "We're going to have to hold off on next month's run until we figure out what's going on."

It's a necessary step, and postponing won't set us back too much. The club has numerous other businesses around town that keep our coffers full and members financially set, but the runs are really big pay days. I can already feel the brothers breathing down my neck about finding who did this so we can get on with business.

"This isn't ideal. Not with the Reapers showing up more and more around town. We don't need another thing to worry about." His voice is low as he scans the crowd. "Handle it, fast. Let me know what you learn." Without looking at him, I nod in agreement.

I don't need a reminder that the Reapers MC are making appearances in our territory. A few days ago, two Reapers were fucking with Jones, a local grocery store owner who was just trying to close up shop. Not only were they in our territory, but they were blatantly fucking with people they know are under our protection.

Luckily, I was in a good mood and allowed one of them to crawl back to their clubhouse. Crawling because I set his piece-of-shit bike on fire after breaking his jaw. The other one, well now that I think of it, I need to figure out what I'm going to do with him. He's been tied up in the basement, and every day one of us works him over for information. Fucker's loyal, I'll give him that.

But I'm growing bored. I'll give him one more day before I start removing appendages.

That growing feeling of dread has me shoving the empty beer bottle away from me. They had to have something to do with what happened tonight. It's the only thing that makes sense.

"You find her yet? She flew off like she was on fire." Looking around him, I no longer see the spunky brunette and pint size bar tender jumping up and down like drunk sorority sisters.

"She's probably introducing Mia to Jenna." He scrubs his hand down his face and chuckles. "Mar brought her best friend, Jenna, with her tonight. I'm going to let them have some time together."

"How gentlemanly of you." Barely paying attention to him droning on about Mar, I wave to Cal for another beer.

"Marley just so happened to forget to mention I'm the vice president of a motorcycle club and that they were coming to a biker party."

"Oh shit." That catches my attention as two ice cold beers are placed in front of us. "Well, she's in for a wild night."

Placing my back to the bar, I take in the insanity of the clubhouse. Strippers dance naked on tables while brothers are drunk and strewn across every corner of the space. The people who chose to party here worship us as if we are gods, and that just spurs everyone on to do whatever the hell they want.

The Lighthouse, a more upscale strip club in town, supplies the women. It's club-owned and run by Fang, who, right about now, is probably upstairs enjoying a private show. That man is disturbingly good with numbers and can charm the pants off of any woman. He's turned what was a funky, drowning peep show into a classy, go-to strip club within a year of taking over.

Club girls make their rounds, desperately shoving their naked assets into the eyeline of any member that will give them the time of day. Some aren't even waiting to get upstairs as they give into their lust-filled obsession of sleeping with one of the brothers.

Unless you're a part of this world, being here might be a

shock.

"What's her name again?" I ask nonchalantly, wondering if I'll run into her tonight.

"Jenna." He says flatly, turning to glare at me. "Try not to fuck this up. She means a lot to Marley and I don't need you and your little dick fucking it up for me." Sauntering away, he flips me the bird and a little bit of the weight I've been carrying comes off my shoulders.

"For your information, my dick is huge!"

Chapter 2

JENNA

"Why is your hair blue? And why is there so much construction paper... and is this a laminator?" The rustling noise I hear coming from the living room is now barreling towards my room.

"Jenna, can you hear me?" Marley, my roommate, waves her hand in front of my face as I lay partially comatose on my bed. Is it possible to lose all ability to make decisions and answer questions all in one day? I smack her hand out of my face and resettle myself into the comfortable lump I had established.

"My hair is blue because Aiden Creston decided that the best way to get my attention during my art lesson was to hurl his paint tray at me. The construction paper is for a science project I need to prep and the laminator is for my new insurance card. I want it to be pretty."

"Oh my god, when did my best friend die and this 60-year-old woman inhabit her body? Laminating your insurance card?" I keep my eyes closed but can picture Marley standing above me with a disgusted look on her face. "That's it. Get out of bed, you're coming with me!"

I decide to stay as still as possible, maybe if I act dead, she will leave me here to rot. Today has been the longest day of my life. My feet hurt from not having a moment to sit and I can't get the ringing in my ears to stop from thirty tiny humans screaming "Ms. Waters!" at me.

"Come on Jenna, get dressed! We don't want to miss out on all of the fun! The party started an hour ago," Marley screeches from her perch on the bathroom counter.

I've been listening to my best friend and roommate simultaneously blast Chappell Roan and get ready for the past thirty minutes while I have been mulling over the options of calling in take-out or taking a chance on whatever mystery frozen meals we have in the freezer.

"Marley, trust me you don't want me there. You're meeting Max. I'll just be in the way." My not-so-subtle way of announcing that being her and her new boyfriend's third wheel sounds less than exciting.

Although her excitement for this new boyfriend has truly piqued my interest. Since meeting Marley freshman year of college, I've only known her to date around and "see what life has to offer." Whatever that means. I swear she dates enough for the both of us.

But never once has she dated someone for more than a month tops, never wanting to be tied down. I listen to the lull of Pink Pony Club and watch her throw clothes out of my closet as she picks through my excellent collection of cardigans.

Something has changed since Marley started dating Max. It's been three months since they met, and I have yet to hear any mention of a red flag or, in a normal 'person's view, a mildly yellow flag. She once stopped dating a guy because his haircut was too close to a mullet.

My eyes hurt from how hard I roll them in their sockets, knowing that I actually do want to meet the guy who has wormed his way into my best friend's heart.

Lifting my head I run my gaze over my trashed room. Who knew someone so tiny could cause so much chaos? Marley holds up a black dress I wore to a funeral once and a lime green cocktail dress I wore to my junior prom with an over-exaggerated look of disdain. She shakes her head at her options and throws them haphazardly back into the closet.

"Come on Jenna, you never want to go out anymore and I miss spending time with you. I also really want you to meet Max and his friends." The soft thud of her body against the bed has mine bouncing slightly. "They are great... and not bad to look at, if you know what I mean. Maybe you'll have a fun hookup." She says, wiggling her eyebrows.

I'm definitely not one to be out on the prowl looking for a quick hookup, but I do need to get out of my bubble. My days are starting to blend together.

"A quick hookup? Well, shiver my timbers why didn't you say that in the first place?" I shimmy my shoulders for extra affect as Marley throws her body to lay next to me. She giggles as she lightly nudges me with her shoulder.

"Come on Jen, we never get to spend time together

anymore. I miss you and don't make it weird but I really want you to meet Max." She wiggles closer and we lay there in a cozy silence, her in her tiny party dress and me in my "Read More Books" shirt.

This year I started teaching at one of the local elementary schools in Cranson Creek, quickly realizing that being the new teacher means I'm the one who gets volunteered for everything. Dances, pep rallies, PTA—you name it, I'm always the teacher chosen to be there.

That, on top of trying to get a handle on new curriculum and planning lessons, means I'm at work until 7 or 8 p.m. some nights. I barely see my best friend anymore before I'm eating dinner, taking a shower, and climbing into bed for the night. Every day has become Groundhog's Day. If it wasn't for the fact that I love teaching so much, I'd consider changing careers.

Being twenty-six and always busy with work or constantly exhausted isn't doing great things for my nonexistent love life.

Mar's phone dings between us and I watch as she runs her hand across the comforter at a ridiculously fast pace. We're the same age but she knew early on that her future was in technology. Now she owns her own tech business and I can't for the life of me actually tell you what she does every day. But I've always envied her ability to make her own schedule and create a stress-free, easygoing work environment for herself.

With a deep breath, I unglue myself from my bed. "Fine, I'll go. But I'm wearing something comfy, and you need to promise me that I'll be greeted with a drink upon arrival to said party."

"Done!" Marley flies off the bed, engulfing me in a rib-crushing hug. Her hair whips me in the face and I think I momentarily go blind from how much of it lands in my eye.

"Just please lose the cardigan… and the granny sneakers. This is a party, after all."

I look down at the shoes I did extensive research trying to find. The best sneaker for arch support, is what I had typed into the search engine. Placing my hand on my heart, I look her right in the eyes and feign disbelief, "How dare you talk badly about my granny three-thousands." I look back down at my shoes again. Assessing them from an outside perspective, they really are ugly.

"Okay, fine I'll change them."

She flashes me with a megawatt smile and practically skips out to our tiny apartment kitchen. Minutes later, I can smell the coffee before she hands me a cup.

"Here. Get going, missy. We leave in thirty!"

I step into the brightly painted bathroom. It's the cheeriest color of yellow and a stark contrast to my waning energy level. Turning on the shower, I slip under the warm spray. This is going to be fun…right?

Ugh, I don't even believe me.

Marley drives like a Bat Out of Hell towards a side of town I'm not as familiar with. We both recently moved to Cranson Creek, so I'm still learning the area. Music blasts from the speakers, and we sing our hearts out to every pop song that plays. Even though I would never admit it to Marley, I'm happy she dragged me out tonight. I need a night with my girl.

"Where is this party at Mar? I don't recognize anything here." I say, while turning the radio down. She quickly makes a sharp right turn off the main street down a dirt road.

"Okay, don't freak out please." She squeaks as we drive closer to a tall gate with barbed wire swirled on top. My stomach tightens as I look over at my sweet, smiling best friend.

"Marley May Janson, where the hell have you taken me?" I glare at her as she keeps driving, never once looking over at me. We roll up to the gate and a man with a very large gun steps out of a small house-like booth. Slowly he bends down and rests his forearms on the windowsill, coming eye level with both of us. My palms start to sweat and the coffee in my stomach churns.

What is this?

"Hey Marley, Blaze is waiting for you in the parking lot. Who's your friend?" The large man drawls as he juts his chin in my direction.

He's actually quite handsome with shaggy blonde hair and a short beard, but the giant gun strapped to his chest brings me right back to reality.

"This is my bestie, Jenna!" She says with that smile still plastered on her face. Is she crazy? Does she not see his gun? Or the barbed wire? And who the hell is Blaze? Weren't we here to meet Max?

The giant man smirks at me. "Pleased to meet you, gorgeous. Go on in you two. Enjoy the party."

With that, the gate slowly opens up to a large parking lot filled with motorcycles and cars. A huge black industrial building sits at the back of the lot and a few other garage-like buildings sit on either side. People mill around the parking lot and buildings, seemingly oblivious to our arrival.

Marley slowly drives into the lot but maneuvers around cars to a specific spot, almost as if she has been here before.

"Okay, last time I ask, Mar. Where are we and who is Blaze? Where's Max?"

Her face is bright red by the time she actually turns to look at me. It only turns that particular shade when she's nervous. Marley releases a heavy breath.

"We are currently at the Hell Chasers' Clubhouse and this is a welcome home party for one of the brothers. Blaze is Max's road name and F.Y.I. you are only allowed to call him Blaze when we're around his brothers or actually anywhere, really. And he's the Vice President of the motorcycle club." She finishes so quickly I barely have time to process the information

I look around the lot and upon further inspection notice almost all the men are wearing black leather vests with patches on the back and front. Turning back to my best friend, I take a moment to center myself before I explode. I mean, what the hell is she thinking bringing us here? I try to take steady breaths and count to ten slowly, but it doesn't work.

"What? You brought me to a biker clubhouse without giving me a warning. Marley, take me home!"

Out of nowhere, a man taps on her window, startling both of us.

Before I can get a look at the guy, Marley squeals and practically leaps out of the car, jumping straight into his arms. The two of them latch onto each other's mouths and for a moment my heart squeezes for Marley. She looks so happy with this man, something I can't say I've seen before.

After what feels like ten full minutes of having to watch them play tonsil hockey, the tall man sets my best friend down.

"Jenna, get out of the car, let's go have some fun. I didn't tell you because I knew you would say no," Marley says into the open car door.

Well, she has a point.

She turns back to the man standing behind her watching our interaction with curiosity, "This is Blaze, well Max, but remember, we call him Blaze." She says as she raises her eyebrow to drive home the point.

The man standing next to Marley practically bends in half to address me in the car. "Hi there, you must be Jenna. And based on your facial expression, I'm guessing you're surprised to be here?"

"You could say that," I grumble, pulling the door handle a little too hard, trying to take my frustration out on the car and not my friend. Stepping out of the vehicle, I once again scan the crowd around me, immediately noticing I am extremely overdressed.

Every woman here is dressed in either a micro skirt or booty shorts and a tiny cropped top. And those are just the women who'd chosen to actually wear clothes.

Tonight, I had decided to wear a tight, black long sleeve shirt tucked into distressed light wash jeans that frayed right above my ankles. I'd paired the outfit with strappy black heels and dainty gold jewelry. I'd left my auburn hair down and wavy, and stuck to light make-up. I'd felt confident in this outfit when I left the house, it showed off my slim but curvy body in the best way. But now, I feel like a fish out of water.

As if Marley can read my mind, she comes up next to me, grabs my hand, and whispers in my ear, "Jenna, you are by far the hottest woman here. You are dressed to perfection. Anything else wouldn't be you."

She's right. I straighten my shoulders, raise my chin, and turn. "Mar, I think one of my stipulations was that there would be a drink waiting for me."

As if right on cue, Blaze whistles and a tall skinny kid comes running with a beer. He can't be more than 19 years old and I just stare at him in confusion.

Marley barks out a laugh as she catches sight of the shock on my face. "He's a prospect." She says, waving her hand in the air. She makes it seem like I am supposed to know what the hell that means.

I take a long drink from the ice-cold beer and let it wash some of my nerves away. If nothing else, I will be getting a good buzz out of tonight.

"Hey, where's the bathroom?" I ask Marley as we make our way into the party.

Marley points me down a small, dark hallway to the right of the entrance and promises to meet me at the bar when I'm done. I make my way towards the bathroom, trying to dodge drunk party goers along the way. Behind me, a loud screech of Marley's name catches my attention. Of course, they all love her here. She fits perfectly anywhere she goes. Me, on the other hand? I'm not so sure this is my scene.

The bathrooms are located at the end of the small, dark hallway because, of course they are. The first tall black door is cracked open with the light off, so I walk in expecting an empty restroom. The moment I flick on the light, a very large man fills my vision, specifically his muscular butt. For a moment I think I'm hearing things but nope, a woman's moans are coming from between his legs. I quickly glance down to confirm she's kneeling in front of him. I should turn around and walk out, but for some reason I can't get my feet to move.

"You either join, or get the fuck out." The man says without turning around. His voice is low and gravely, giving the distinct sound of someone who's an avid smoker.

I shake my head, trying to get my brain to focus on why I really came down here, and quickly turn around, heading into the other restroom. No way am I joining whatever that is. I'm pleased to see that this restroom is sparkling clean and very well-stocked. There are folded towels next to the sink and good smelling hand soap and lotion out for use. Not everything here scares me, I guess. I go about my business, taking a few extra minutes to enjoy the quiet and center myself.

Walking back to the party, I decide to keep my head down and avoid making eye contact with anyone in the hallway, just in case anyone saw me walk in on the couple in the bathroom.

When I finally find Marley, she's sitting towards the end of the bar and waves her hand in the direction of a woman behind the bar.

"Jenna, this is Mia. She is Cal's cousin and is one of my favorite people here. You'll love her!" I shake Mia's hand and smile at her. She's a small woman, but what catches my attention are her eyes. They are so warm and caring. Something about her makes me feel instantly welcome.

"Want something to drink? I'm one of the bartenders for the night." Mia mentions while heading back to grab a bottle of liquor. I walk around Mar and hop on the stool right where the end of the bar meets the wall, hoping that if I stay as far away from the party as possible, everyone will leave me alone.

"Yes please! Something strong and fruity and keep them coming. Someone didn't mention that this was a biker party, so I'm currently too sober for this situation." I glare at Marley, making it evident who I'm talking about.

Mia's head falls back, letting her platinum hair wave behind her as she lets out a long, loud laugh. "Wow Marley, way to shock the girl. "

Marly just raises her shoulders, as if lying to get me here isn't a big deal. "You going to be okay here with Mia? I'm going to go find Blaze. But I don't have to if you aren't comfortable."

I shake my head and shoo her off. "Go, spend time with your man. But I do want to actually meet him when I'm not in a state of panic," I say, gulping down the drink Mia puts in front of me.

Marley smirks at me and mock salutes, "Aye, Aye, Captain."

I watch as she walks off towards Blaze, who's on the other side of the bar. I notice he tracks her movements through the crowd, making sure she's safe until the moment she gets to him. Hmm, maybe I do like this guy.

As I look out across the large room, my jaw slightly drops as I take in just what kind of company I am currently keeping. Women, practically naked, are dancing all around the room, some even on top of men in the middle of open areas. I'm definitely out of my element here. Running my hands back and forth on my jeans, I try to focus on just making it through the evening. But the smell of smoke, weed, and alcohol is so heavy that all I feel like doing is bolting. I turn back to Mia who gives me a knowing look and smiles before turning to the man next to her.

"Cal, this is Jenna. She likes strong and fruity drinks, so if I'm not here, you keep them coming, okay?" Cal quickly glances at me and then returns his focus back to what he was doing, only to immediately turn back to me. He looks eerily familiar, like I've seen him before.

I watch as he stops what he's doing at the bar and walks over to me with a huge grin on his face, "Well Teach out on a school night I see." And that's when it hits me, I have seen this man before. In the pickup line, after school, on the days I have line duty.

"Hey now, don't give my teacher title away. I want to seem somewhat cool tonight," I joke. "I remember seeing you during pickup. Does your child go to Cranson Creek Elementary?"

"Yep, my daughter, Sarah, is in preschool there. I didn't think you'd recognize me. There are always hundreds of parents there to pick up kids." He studies me for a moment as I fidget under his curious gaze.

"Well, not all parents are tall, muscular, and good looking." Wow, maybe I need to slow down on the alcohol. I push my drink a little further away from me and try to avert my eyes from Cal, who now stands with his arms crossed over his chest, smirking at me.

I don't even know if he's single. I mean, of course he's not. I've seen him and Sarah's mom come to pickups together.

"Oh my gosh, I'm so sorry," I reply, feeling heat creep over my cheeks. "I shouldn't have said that, especially since you're in a relationship." I don't know why I keep talking, digging myself deeper into embarrassment. Don't get me wrong, he's handsome but really not my type, so I should just close my mouth.

"Why do you think I'm in a relationship?" he cocks his head, his smirk transforming into a full-blown grin.

"Well, Sarah's mom comes with you to pickup. That might be the tipoff," I say shyly.

"That is Sarah's mom, but we aren't together. We never actually were together when she got pregnant, but shit happens and she's a great mom, so we're friends." He shrugs and then starts making a drink for the guy next to me.

I blow out a steady breath, happy to be steering the conversation in a different direction.

"So, I have some questions if you have a moment... about all of this." I wave my hand in the air as a way to convey what I'm talking about.

He smirks. "I would be surprised if you didn't. Shoot."

"Okay, what is a prospect? And what is a road name? Why is there barbed wire outside? And a guy with a gun? And—" he stops me by holding his hand up.

"Alright Teach, one thing at a time," he says with a chuckle. But before he can answer my question, he's called to the other side of the bar for a drink order.

"I'll be right back to answer your burning questions." He

says as he quickly walks toward the men who called him over. I scan the party for Marley, hoping to see how much longer she wants to stay when I lock eyes with the most handsome man I have ever laid eyes on. His dark brown eyes catch mine and for a moment I can't look away, can't break the spell that's bound me to him.

"Alright, a road name is a name you get when you join the club... Teach? You listening?" Cal asks as he waves his hand in my face. I blink a few times and drag my attention back to Cal.

"Yes, I'm listening. So, a road name is...?" I try to give him my full attention as he explains "MC Life" to me. But I can't help but notice the gorgeous man now headed towards the bar.

Chapter 3

AXEL

About an hour after getting to the clubhouse, I am finally buzzed and relaxing. It's almost time for me to call it a night, pick a club girl and head up to my room. But I'm enjoying spending time with my brothers. Bear, Savage, Blaze, and Marley are all sitting with me at a table in the back. I'm not particularly interested in being in the middle of the party, and neither is anyone else at our table.

"I'm going to get another round, anyone want anything?" I look around to everyone shaking their heads, then move toward the bar. Making my way through the crowd, I catch sight of Mia and Tank flying around, slinging drinks as people line up.

Where the fuck is Cal? I look over to the end of the bar and see him talking to a woman I haven't seen before—and damn, I would remember her. She's gorgeous, with long, wavy auburn hair framing a delicate face. I can barely tear my eyes away from her face to look at her body.

She's wearing a top that looks painted on, showing all her delicious curves. She's sitting, but you can tell her body is fit and strong. There's something about her expression that makes me wary, like she's unsettled here at the clubhouse. She's definitely uncomfortable and occasionally looks around with eyes bugging out of her head when she catches sight of a naked woman or someone lighting up a joint. She's too good to be here and too beautiful to be sitting at the bar alone.

Cal is heading back to help with drink orders when I holler, "Hey, Cal, can I get a whiskey?" He nods my way. I like Cal—recently patched and loyal as fuck. He makes a good brother.

"No problem, Axel. How's it going out there?" He gives a subtle hint that the question is about more than the party, but we don't talk club business in front of anyone outside the club, and this mystery Angel is definitely a new face.

"Fine. We'll talk tomorrow," I say as I glance at the woman sitting at the bar. She turns to me, and I catch sight of the brightest green eyes I've ever seen and full lips that would look glorious wrapped around my cock. Fuck, my dick is pressing so hard against my zipper I think it might burst open if I move. She's hands down the most gorgeous woman I've ever laid eyes on. She blushes and quickly turns away the moment I catch her staring.

I smirk, I know I'm pretty good-looking, but damn, does it feel good to catch her off balance.

I lean in so she can hear me over the loud music, but that's a mistake—she smells like lavender and vanilla with a hint of liquor. I'm intoxicated just off her scent. *What the fuck is happening?*

I never go out of my way to talk to women or even care enough to notice what scent they have. Women come to me, begging to be the one I take upstairs for the night. But something here is different. She is different.

"Hi, I'm Axel. I've never seen you around. You here with someone?" She better not be here with a brother, or we're going to have a problem.

"Okay, now is that one of those road name things, or are you really named Axel?" she hiccups with a giggle—a fucking giggle. That sound warms my heart. "Because Cal has been teaching me all about the MC life, and I think I understand the road name stuff... maybe?" She gives me a shy smile, but her eyes are bright with excitement and wonder.

"Axel is my road name, babe," I move closer to her. "But you never answered my question. You here with someone?" She looks around the bar as if searching for them, and I drop my head. She's here with a fucking guy.

"There! Marley!" She waves over my shoulder, but Marley and Blaze are too caught up practically having sex in the corner to notice her. "I'm here with my best friend, Marley," she explains.

Oh shit, she's the teacher.

"Ahh, so you're the one who got conned into coming to a biker party."

She looks at me with those mesmerizing eyes, unsure how I know that information, and it makes me laugh. Fuck, she's something else. "I'm friends with Blaze."

She tilts her head and runs her fingers over my patch. "And

you're the Enforcer," she says as she looks up at me through long lashes. I stare at her for a moment. Most people won't come near me because of who I am and what I do, but here she is running her fingers over my cut like it's the most natural thing in the world. "I can honestly say I'm not sure what you do. Do you enforce laws, or…?"

"Kind of. I enforce our code and protect the club. People who try to fuck with us or don't follow the rules deal with me." I say in all sincerity. I take my position seriously and would lay my life down for those I've promised to protect.

"Hmm, seems dangerous." She sighs and drops her hand from the patch. I instantly miss having her hands on me.

I shrug and take a drink of my whiskey. "Can be." I want to be honest with her. I feel like she's someone I can bare my truths to, and that scares the shit out of me.

"Shit, I haven't even asked you what your name is." I wait for her response.

She giggles again. "My name is Jenna. Nice to officially meet you." She goes to shake my hand. I can't believe it. We've been having a conversation with our faces mere inches away from each other, and she goes to shake my hand.

"Pleasure," I take her hand in mine, but when she tries to let go, I don't. I can't.

Chapter 4

JENNA

I AM FEELING the full effects of the four "strong and fruity" drinks Mia has made for me. So, when my hand is captured by the most handsome man I've ever laid eyes on, I feel like I can barely breathe. I let my eyes rake over Axel, enjoying everything I see. His jet-black hair contrasts well with his olive skin, his hands are littered with tattoos, and I am curious just how many he has hidden under his shirt. His dark chocolate eyes pool with desire as he draws small circles over the back of my hand with his thumb. He stands so much taller than me—even in my heels, I probably only come to his shoulder. His muscles ripple under his long-sleeve Henley. Gosh, I want to lick every inch of his body, and that is a problem.

I can't do a one-night stand. My heart won't let me. The last time I tried, I ended up dating Jack for three years, and he turned out to be the world's biggest jerk. So no, sadly, the incredibly hot, hunky biker will not be getting into my pants tonight.

He leans in to brush a piece of my hair behind my ear. A shiver races down my entire body. How can one touch affect me like that? Noticing my reaction, he moves closer, so close I can taste the whiskey on his lips. But he doesn't try to kiss me. He just waits patiently.

Axel is waiting for me to make the first move. The part of my brain that hasn't yet been drowned in alcohol screams, *No, red alert! This will not end well!* But the rest of my body screams, *Yes.*

"Fuck it." I lean forward and crush my lips to his. His hand slips to the back of my neck and holds me in place as he slowly ravages my mouth. He smells like pine, tobacco, and all man, and I am screwed.

He starts to trail kisses down my jaw, moving toward my neck, where he lightly bites down. It shoots a lightning bolt between my legs. The need for his hands on my body is almost unbearable, but I need to stop this. Just as I'm about to pull away, he gently pushes his thigh between my legs. I open for him without pause. He moves closer and presses himself into me, and I can feel his arousal. Holy hell, does it feel amazing. My head feels like it's in a fog, all my senses being taken over by Axel.

"Okay, let's slow down," I say breathlessly, though it sounds more like a moan than I intend. Axel kisses back up my neck and gives me one last peck on my lips.

"Phone," he says gruffly.

I blink up at him, unable to move as he entrances me with

his stare. His eyes are almost black with want, drawing me to him in a way I can't explain. He gives me a half-smirk when he realizes I'm frozen. Without thinking, I draw my bottom lip into my mouth and dig my teeth into the sensitive flesh, trying to savor his taste.

He slowly moves his hand up to my face, pinching my chin with his thumb and pointer finger, gently drawing my lip out. He stares at my lips, probably swollen from our kiss.

"Bite that lip again, and I will haul you upstairs and fuck you until you can't do anything else but scream my name," he rasps in a sexy growl. But he has to be joking, right? No one talks like that.

I almost do it again just to see if he's bluffing, but ultimately decide against it. Something about this man screams danger. He smirks when he realizes I'm not going to tempt him.

"Angel, give me your phone." He doesn't look away as I slowly grab my phone out of my purse, which sits on the bar.

I unlock it and hand it to him. He navigates his way to my contacts and adds in his phone number. The thought of seeing him after this sends my stomach into knots with excitement, but I know that will never happen. After last summer, I promised myself to focus on work and my goals—never again letting a man distract me from what I want. And this man is definitely distracting. Not to mention he's a member of the area's most notorious motorcycle club.

I don't care how attracted I am to Axel; I can't let this be anything.

After my encounter with Axel, I need to cool off. He'd been called over to a table by some other men in those leather vest things—cuts, I think Cal called them. I'm relieved I don't have to awkwardly make an excuse to leave. I wave at Mia to let her know I'm going to step outside for some fresh air and to let Marley know where I've gone if she asks.

"She went up to Blaze's room with him a little while ago. I wouldn't count on seeing them anytime soon," Mia shouts as she races around the back of the bar. "But I'll tell her. Hey, do you want me to go with you? I could use a break!"

I smile. "I would love the company."

We snake our way through the crowd and out the door I entered earlier tonight. The cold air washes over me and calms my racing heart. I'm acting crazy. He's just a hot guy at a bar—a guy I won't be seeing again if I can help it.

I hear an annoyed huff come from Mia. "I totally forgot my jacket at home, and dang, it's cold out here!"

She isn't wrong. Even though it's mid-June, the weather still feels like winter. It's the worst. When Marley and I chose Cranson Creek to move to after college, we didn't even think to worry about the weather. We both had job offers in the same town, and we weren't splitting up. I am also shaking from the cold.

"This might have been a bad idea. Want to go back inside?" I say as both of us hug our bodies with our arms. She chuckles, and I can see her breath in the air.

"Yeah, probably," she says as she turns for the door. She stops before her hand reaches the handle and turns back to me. "But before we do, I have to talk to you first." She narrows her eyes, examining my face. Her expression quickly softens. "I saw you talking to Axel a little while ago, and I have to tell you that I've never seen him look at a woman like that before." I stare at her in confusion. Why would she be telling me this? I barely know him—actually, I don't know him.

"Oh, Mia, it was just a liquor-filled make-out. Honestly, he's probably forgotten about it by now." I laugh it off, waiting for her to drop the conversation and walk inside.

"No, I don't think it was, but I could be wrong," she shrugs, crossing her arms. "Just hear me out. Axel is like my brother, and he deserves someone like you. I can already tell you're a good person. But be careful." And with that, she walks back inside.

"Ominous much?" I mutter, watching her tiny form disappear into the crowd as the door closes behind her.

I am left standing outside with her words swirling around in my head. What in the world is Mia talking about? I am not going to be a part of this world. It could be the tequila not sitting well, but I'm left with a bad feeling in my gut. I look around the parking lot—it's quiet, and there are only a few people out here braving the cold. I take a deep breath, steady myself, and head back inside.

Chapter 5

AXEL

"Axel, I'm calling Church first thing in the morning. I want to hear your ideas on what we're going to do about our problem." Our president, Prince, says to me as he takes a drag of his cigar.

Prince and I had been friends long before I decided to prospect for the club. We met in the third grade. I was the kid that was constantly in trouble, getting into fights, pranking the school. Prince was always right there, having my back. We've been hellions from early on.

When we were twenty, Prince's Dad was taken out by a rival MC. Prince and I had gone out the night before getting as drunk as possible, like we usually did. We'd been patched members of the club for about a year and thought we were invincible. I'll never forget the look on Prince's face when Tango called to tell him about his dad. Prince would never admit it, but I know he still feels guilty for not being with his dad on that run. That night, everything changed for us. Instead of the easygoing lifestyle we had come to enjoy, our days are now filled with responsibility.

Prince easily stepped into the president's role. Always calm and levelheaded, he is exactly the president this club needs. I sit back in my seat, eyeing his disheveled look. He's pissed about the ambush tonight as much as I am. Ever since his dad, runs have been choreographed to a T. We haven't had a problem in years, which makes this that much more serious.

"Got it Prez, I'll be ready." I look around the clubhouse for Jenna. I could tell she was feeling overwhelmed, so when Prince and Jax called me over, I let her have some time to herself. But I don't plan on that lasting.

"Who are you looking for, man?" Jax says as he gets a lap dance from Cherry. He obviously isn't too impressed if he's focused on what I'm doing.

I'm not about to let the guys know I'm looking for a fucking chick. I need to be focused on our work, but I can't shake her—she messes with my head in a way I can't explain.

"Just doing surveillance. Can't be too careful at these parties," I say as I glance at my brothers. Prince nods at me in approval as I stand to walk away.

"Remember—Church, 9 a.m. Make sure Blaze knows," Prince calls after me as I give him a nod and head toward the bar. Walking through the mob of people, I see Blaze coming in from outside.

"Hey, man, have you seen Jenna?" I ask. Blaze usually doesn't pry or dig any deeper, but the look he gives me tells me he has questions.

"Why do you want to know? Got the hots for Teacher?" He punches my arm and laughs.

"Shut the fuck up. Do you know where she is or not?" I'm getting slightly annoyed with this conversation and just want to find the girl who's fucked with my head.

"Her and Marley just left. It's a school night. Someone has to be up bright and early to mold young minds," Blaze says as he uses his hands to pretend like he's molding clay.

Fuck, I was planning on taking her to my room and getting to know every inch of that perfect body so I could get her out of my head. Because that's the only thing that can come from this. It could never be more than sex. She's too good for me, too pure for this life. But damn what a fun ride we would have in the sack.

Right at that moment, a hand slides down my shoulder and around to my belt. I look down to see a skinny hand with long black nails that look more like claws clasping the front of my jeans. Sapphire is my usual girl. I would normally let her come upstairs, we'd fuck, and then she'd get out while I caught some sleep before Church. But it doesn't feel right tonight. I just need to sleep this day off.

The club girls are a group of women who provide comfort to club men when they require it. The girls are treated well and taken care of, but some of them are just bad apples. Sapphire was great when she started—young, hot, and in school to become a nurse. She came here knowing the job and was fucking great at it, but one day the light went out in her eyes. She dropped out of school and started running with a few of the women over at the strip club who are into some nasty shit.

I've been meaning to figure out what happened. Find out what the hell she's thinking, but I don't have the time tonight.

"Hey, Ax, why don't you let me take your worries away?" she says in a soft voice. Blaze cocks his head and raises an eyebrow at me.

"Nah babe. Go find Savage. He'll be happy to show you a good time." I brush her hand off and head to my room. I turn to leave, looking back to see Sapphire with a pouty look on her face and Blaze laughing.

I walk up the stairs that lead to the second floor. This is where members have their own rooms to crash in. Mine is near the end of the hallway, right next to Blaze's. I unlock the door and slam it shut behind me. I'm over today, but shit, I need a shower.

Walking into my bathroom, I strip off my clothes and step under the waterfall shower. Fuck, it feels good to wash the day off me, but I can't stop thinking about that teacher and the way her lips fused to mine.

I place my hand on the shower wall to balance myself, and with the other, I wrap it around my pulsing cock. I close my eyes as I start pumping, seeing those bright green eyes stare up at me through long lashes and those fucking lips I wish were wrapped around my dick. In no time, I'm cumming harder than I have in a while. I need to fuck this girl out of my system—and fast.

I finish my shower and head back into my room, not even bothering to put on clothes. I fall into bed and pass out.

Chapter 6

JENNA

It becomes increasingly clear to me that the Hell Chasers don't have early morning day jobs, or they wouldn't be partying on a Thursday night. I can't believe I had been so stupid as to drink five mixed drinks. I mean, I can handle my liquor pretty well, but those were the strongest little devils I've ever had. Clearly hungover, my head pounds from all sides, and I feel like if I try to move, I might vomit. This is why I usually limit myself to two drinks—I'm fine while actually drinking, but the mornings after are hell.

I drag myself out of bed, shoving sunglasses over my eyes as I leave my cave of a bedroom and make my way to the coffeepot. Like always, Marley had set it when we got home last night so that it started brewing right at 6:00 a.m. The welcoming smell of my favorite blend hits my nose, and my mouth pools with saliva in anticipation of the first drink. I pour myself a cup and head to the bathroom.

Flipping on the light, I peer at myself in the mirror, feeling pretty proud. Even in my inebriated state, I managed to complete my entire skincare routine and put my hair in overnight curlers before bed. I want to give Drunk Jenna a hug for saving Sober Jenna a ton of time getting ready this morning. Although I'd done my due diligence in the beauty department last night, I still woke up with horrendous dark circles under my eyes. Each one screams for concealer.

I do a light makeup look, fluff out my hair, and go to get dressed. Usually, I have my morning routine down to twenty minutes, but today I feel like I'm moving at a snail's pace. I'm never drinking again...

"Morning," Marley groans, trudging out of her own bedroom. Her normally perfect, straight brown hair is sticking up in all directions. She's wearing an extremely large men's t-shirt that practically drowns her small frame—a motorcycle stretches the length of her chest. Must be Blaze's. She didn't drink last night since she promised to be our designated driver, but staying up until 3 a.m. really did a number on her. She always needs a lot of sleep to be a functioning adult.

"Morning. Thanks for driving last night, you little liar," I say, eyeing her from my room as I pull my favorite green dress down over my body.

"Okay, first of all, I didn't lie. I just didn't tell you the whole truth," she says as she walks over to get a cup of coffee. "And besides, I saw you having fun." She pokes her head back around the corner and looks at me with a knowing smile.

"It was alright," I smile back at her. As I look up at her,

I catch sight of the clock on the wall behind her. Shoot, I'm going to be late.

"Can we chat about last night when I get home? I'm going to be late if I don't leave now."

"Of course, go! But don't think you're getting out of this conversation," she says, shuffling back to her bedroom.

"I wouldn't dream of it," I mumble as I run out the door.

I make it to school with minutes to spare. Luckily, I never leave work without having all my lessons and materials ready to go for the next day. Really, all I have to do today is teach the lessons, and I can be back home in my bed in no time.

I've been looking forward to having a weekend at home, cuddled up on the couch, ordering my favorite Chinese takeout, and watching sappy romantic comedies. A good rot day is just what I need.

I'm writing today's date on the board when I hear a small knock on the door. I walk through the rows of desks, straightening name tags as I go. I take pride in my classroom and the attention to detail I put into the space. I believe my students deserve a calm and welcoming environment. I open the door to a tiny blonde holding a to-go coffee and a pastry bag. I kneel down in front of her—I recognize Sarah right away.

"Ms. Waters!" Sarah exclaims with the sweetest smile. "My Uncle Axel told me to bring these to you. He says you'll need them this morning." She holds out the large coffee and what appears to be a breakfast sandwich. My stomach growls as I look at the welcome treat. In my hurried race out the door, I forgot my travel mug full of coffee on the counter. I try not to think about how incredibly thoughtful this is and will the butterflies in my stomach to stop flapping. Why hadn't Axel just brought these himself? He probably knew I wouldn't have taken them from him. Again, I barely know the guy.

The bell rings, and kids start filing into classrooms. I grab the drink and food from Sarah and smile at her.

"Thank you for bringing these to me. Now head to class. Have a great day!"

She skips off to class, leaving me in the empty hallway. I try to shake off the surprise breakfast from Axel and focus on teaching today. The gesture is sweet, but I don't want to dwell on it too much. Maybe he's just being friendly and does this for all the girls he makes out with. I roll my eyes at myself for even thinking that.

Axel is the type of guy who only does things with a purpose, and I'm just not sure what purpose that is yet. I just know I need to stay far away.

Chapter 7

AXEL

PRINCE BANGS HIS heavy metal gavel against the table, signaling the beginning of Church. This is where officers of the club meet. We all sit around a large wood table with the Hell Chaser's emblem carved into the center—angel wings set on fire by the flames beneath them. To outsiders, this might seem strange—bikers forming a meeting—but this is our place to discuss club business and make decisions. Church is sacred. If you miss one of these meetings', there's hell to pay.

I look around the room at my brothers, all ready to go to war over the Reapers encroaching on our territory, but we have to make a plan first. I've seen clubs wiped out after making quick reactions to shit like this. We need to be calculated and methodical in our approach.

"Alright, I hope all you fuckers had your fill of fun last night because it will be your last for a while." Prince looks out across the table, making eye contact with each of us. "We have shit to handle," he snarls, nodding toward Blaze, who is sitting to my left.

"We caught a few Reapers hanging out down near the diner. Both acted like it was their fucking territory. Jax and I dealt with them and sent them packing, but I don't think they plan on staying away," Blaze explains as he leans forward. "Jax thought he saw one of 'em dealing, so that adds another level to this shit." He shakes his head. We got out of the drug business a few years back when Prince took over. Shit was ruining our community, and he wasn't going to stand for it.

Blaze snorts and shakes his head like he's remembering something funny, but when his eyes lift, I see a fury in them, one I haven't seen in a long time. Something else happened.

"One of them mentioned us needing to watch our backs— the normal shit-talking we always hear—but this time, it was different. He started talking about the old ladies. Even fucking mentioned Marley by name to me." He slams his fist on the table in a rage. "By the time I went to strangle the motherfucker, they were hightailing it out of the lot."

I understand his fury. No one threatens one of us or the people we care about and lives to talk about it. The tension around the table visibly thickens as the men in this club with old ladies sit a little taller. What the fuck are the Reapers playing at, coming after the women of the club? It's an unwritten rule that women and children are off limits, but it seems the Reapers aren't playing by the book.

It's only been a few months, but I can see that Blaze loves Marley—we all do. This won't fucking stand.

"I'm putting someone outside her apartment 24/7. And all of you with old ladies might want to do the same." Blaze looks at me, and I nod. It's my job to arrange security, and I'll figure it out for everyone.

"Where are we with this, Axel?" Prince asks from the head of the table.

"I have Ace looking into all surveillance cameras around town to make sure we deal with any trespassing in Cranson Creek. He's also digging for any dirt he can find on their Prez, Red. Guy's a lunatic—he's into some shady-ass shit. I'm having my guys do private recon as well." I'll make sure this problem is dealt with. Red is a slimy asshole I've met a time or two. "I also want to throw out that I have a bad feeling the Reapers have a hand in us getting ambushed last night. This can't all be a coincidence."

"I agree. This all smells like shit. Let me know if you need anything. But keep up with recon." Prince states and then continues with the meeting.

Thirty minutes later, we've gone over all club business. "Anything else we need to discuss?" he asks. Everyone shakes their heads.

"Wait, I've got something," Knife says from the other side of the room.

Shit. It's weird having him back after all this time, but Knife is probably one of the most loyal brothers we have in the MC. I'd trust him with my life. Usually members who aren't officers in the club aren't allowed in church meetings, but with him being an officer before going to prison, we have welcomed him back into the fold.

Prince nods, giving him the floor.

"First of all, I want to thank each of you for being there for Misty and the girls. I know this shit wasn't easy for them, but all of you stepped up when I couldn't," he says sincerely.

Knife and I are the same age, prospected together, and got patched in on the same night. We were still running drugs at that time, and shit was getting tense with the Feds.

We had to make a shipment, but with the DEA and ATF breathing down our necks, it didn't seem possible. Knife, being the crazy motherfucker he is, made a deal with our Prez to help set up a new pipeline. He met with Roman Semenov, the head of the Russian mob. How he got that meeting, we'll never know. Things looked promising until they weren't. Semenov had a rat among his men, and the Feds raided the warehouse where Knife and a few of Semenov's men were meeting. They found the smallest amount of dope during their search and decided to throw the book at Knife and both of the Russians.

Knife took the fall for the whole operation, never naming anyone from the club. He was sentenced to ten years with the possibility of parole for a tiny bag of dope. But that's what happens when you're part of a biker club—the Feds will try to get you on anything they can. Knife served his time and got out in 5 years.

But Knife had a lot to leave behind. He and Misty had been together since freshman year of high school. We always gave him shit for being in so deep with a girl before truly experiencing club life and the women that came with it, but he didn't care—he loved Misty. He'd claimed her in front of the club almost immediately after patching in, and they've been together ever since.

A month after he was sentenced, Misty found out she was pregnant with twin girls. They were devastated he couldn't be there for the birth or the first years of their lives, but that's what happens when you come from this life. There's always a possibility you'll end up in prison or six feet under.

The club stepped up and supported Misty in any way we could. The old ladies are just as close as the brothers of the club and were with her through it all. Honestly, though, Misty is a supermom. She never complained or was frustrated with the situation, just raised her girls and made sure that everyone was taken care of.

Every man at the table nods at Knife.

"It's what we do, Knife. They're family. You don't have to thank us," Prince replies.

"I know, I get it. But I just had to say it," he says in an almost uncomfortable tone. "I don't like talking about my emotions and shit, but what you guys did for my family, I'll never forget it." He pauses for a moment and then looks right at me. "Now, let's kick some Reaper ass!"

The room erupts with fists pounding on the table and men voicing their support.

Prez pounds the gavel, ending our meeting. I'm already heading out the door when it dawns on me—Jenna mentioned she's Marley's roommate. If the Reapers go to the apartment, they'll both be in danger. I've only just met her, but the thought of Jenna in danger makes my blood boil. I'll rip the limbs off anyone who lays a hand on that Angel of a woman.

"Who did you put on Marley's apartment?" I snarl at Blaze.

"Cal and Jax are taking shifts," he states like it's a no-brainer. He's texting on his phone, a cigarette hanging from between his lips as if he had gone for a smoke but got distracted by a text.

Honestly, those two are who I would've chosen as well. Jax is ex-Marines, and Cal is an underground MMA fighter who's also one of our best shooters. I nod at Blaze, even though he hasn't looked up from his phone, and walk out of the room.

I find Cal outside straddling his bike, getting ready to leave. "I want a text every hour giving me a report on what's going on. A full fucking report." I look at him with a *don't-even-ask* look.

He smirks and whistles. "You've got it bad for the Teach, huh? First the coffee delivery, and now this?"

"Leave it alone, Cal. Just do it."

"Yeah, Axe, no problem. If she's important to you, I'll make sure to fill you in." He starts his bike and drives out of the lot.

"She is," I mutter to myself.

Looking up at the sky, I know I'm royally fucked. The good thing is, no one saw her at our party except for Chasers, so I'm sure she won't be linked to us—besides rooming with Marley. But I can't take any chances.

Chapter 8

JENNA

THE BELL RINGS, signaling that the school day is officially over. The classroom looks good, but I'm making sure to put everything in its place and leave it ready for Monday morning. Plopping myself down into my chair I get to work on all of the tasks I haven't been able to get to throughout the day. Answering emails, planning and prepping my lessons for the following week, calling parents. I'm on a mission to get this all done, so I won't have to take it home with me and ruin my weekend plans of doing nothing.

By the time I finish, it's 7:15 p.m. The sun has set, and the night janitor, Mark, has started cleaning my classroom for the evening. I take that as my signal to head home. Packing my bag, I wave to Mark and make my way out the door.

"Have a great weekend, Jenna. See you Monday!" he says in a cheery voice. Most of the time, I'm the only teacher he sees, since his shift starts at 5 p.m.

I turn to reply, "You too! Tell your wife and that sweet baby of yours hello for me." With that, I'm on my way to the car, finally free to spend my weekend however I want.

Once I'm outside the front doors of the school, the cold air instantly hits my skin, leaving goosebumps all over my body. This morning, in my hurry, I quickly threw on my favorite green maxi dress, a white cardigan, and my cute sneakers— fashionable and comfortable, but not suitable for this type of weather. I start walking faster to my car, the only one still left in this creepy parking lot. The flickering lights around the parking area give me an anxious, visceral feeling I can't shake. I glance around the lot, making sure I'm alone, and relax a bit when I don't see anyone in sight.

I almost drop my keys when the loud sound of a motorcycle roars up the street, startling me. That's weird—why would anyone be at the school this late at night? Maybe it's Blaze and Marley, or Cal needing something for Sarah? But that bad feeling sits heavy in my stomach, so I get in my car and lock my doors just as the motorcycle pulls around to the front of the building.

I sit and watch, unable to get a good look at the man's face when he takes off his helmet, but I focus on what's on his back. I take a moment, examining the name and the large image of a Reaper with blood dripping from its mouth, covering the back of his leather vest. It looks nothing like the vests Axel and his club were wearing last night. I take out my phone and dial Marley. The man pulls out his phone and looks to be making a call as well, seemingly unaware of my presence just a few yards away.

Marley answers on the second ring. "Hey, Jen, where are you? It's late, and I already ordered Chinese!" I can imagine her doing a little happy dance at the thought of food.

"I'm still at school, but Mar, I just got into my car, and a guy on a motorcycle who looks to be part of a motorcycle club pulled into the parking lot. I'm the only one here except for the janitor. Do you have any idea why he'd be here this late?" I say, staring at the man. He's just hung up his call and is getting off his bike. "His cut says Reaper MC on it. Do you know him by chance?"

The gasp on the other end of the line sends a shiver down my spine. Marley's voice comes through the phone, deathly serious. "Jenna, stay in your car and don't get out for any reason. Matter of fact start driving here, now!"

I clench my hand into a fist, trying to focus my anxiousness on something else. I hear Marley talking to someone, but it's not me.

"You're really starting to freak me out," I say as the man turns and catches sight of my car. The parking lot is dimly lit, so I'm not sure he can even see me.

"Hey, Teach, can you hear me?" It's not Marley on the phone anymore; it's a voice I don't recognize. "Jenna, my name is Jax. I'm from the club. Can you tell me what you see? What's going on?"

My throat catches as the man smiles in my direction. Shit, he can totally see me. I look down at my door handle, making sure it's locked, and glance around for anything in my car I can use to protect myself. I find a stick of deodorant and a phone cord. I make a mental note to remedy my ill-equipped car in the future.

The man sets his helmet down on the seat of his bike and starts to saunter over to my car.

"He's coming over to the car. I'm going to put you on speaker and set my phone down, okay?" I do what I say without waiting for a response and set the phone face down on my thigh so the man can't see the light from the screen.

"Jenna, goddammit, don't open your door. Drive away," Jax roars through the phone.

But it's too late. The man is at my window.

The man is a giant—he must be 6'4" and looks like he works out at least three times a day. His biceps are bigger than my head. He bends down, and I notice his extremely greasy long brown hair tied up in a bun and a scraggly beard that really needs to be tended to. He looks at me with eyes as black as the night, seemingly empty, and a smile that makes my stomach churn.

"Hi, Miss. I hope I didn't scare you. I'm just looking for someone. Think you can help me?" he says in a deep, scratchy voice.

I take a deep breath to stop my voice from shaking. "I'm sorry. Everyone's gone home for the night. You might want to check back on Monday." I'm happy about the window between us, but it honestly doesn't feel like enough separation.

"Well, shit. I knew it was a little late but thought I'd try anyway," he says as he scratches his scruffy chin and stands to his full height.

I should start my car, say goodbye, and leave, but something inside me is extremely curious about who he's here to see.

"Who are you looking for? Maybe I can tell them you were looking for them on Monday," I say as sweetly as possible.

He eyes me for a minute and then nods. "Her name is Jenna Waters. You know her? I guess she teaches here."

I think my heart stops in my chest. Why in the world would this man be looking for me? I've never seen him in my life. *Think, Jenna. Think. Keep talking so he doesn't get suspicious.*

"Oh yeah, I know Ms. Waters. I'll let her know that Mr...." I pause for his name.

"Death," he states.

"Uh... that Death was here to see her." I give him a big smile, shoving my keys into the ignition to get the hell out of here.

"Wait, can you give her a message for me?" he says. I nearly groan. All I want is to go home and forget this whole creepy exchange ever happened.

"Sure, what's the message?" I ask, watching as he bends back down so his face is level with mine in the window. Catching sight of his cut, I notice a patch similar to Axel's—Enforcer.

"Tell her to let her new MC friends know the Reapers are moving in, and if they don't want a war, they'll leave our fucking brothers alone," he snarls at me. I gasp at the venom he spews with every word.

"Oh, and Jenna," he says with a straight face, obviously catching on to my lie, "you really shouldn't be out here alone this late at night. Never know what could happen." With that, he taps my window with his knuckle and saunters back to where he parked. I can't breathe, my hands are shaking and I feel like I'm going to throw up. How the hell did I get wrapped up in all of this?

In less than 24 hours of Marley taking me to that party i'm accosted by a terrifying stranger who is using me to send his threatening messages? Of course, because this is what happens when you hang out with bikers.

"Jenna!" Jax's voice roars through the car. I grab my phone off my lap, staring at the call I completely forgot about.

"I'm okay. Did you hear all of that?" I say, my voice still shaking. God, I hate how scared he made me.

"I heard it all. I already called the club. Are you okay to drive?" Jax's voice is a mix of worry and annoyance.

"Yeah, I think I'm fine," I reply softly, though I need a moment to process what just happened.

"Okay, get to the apartment *now*. Don't make any stops. You hear me?"

I take a deep breath, counting my breaths until they even out and I feel like I can drive again. "I hear you. Be there soon."

The line goes dead, and I sit in my car in silence. What the hell have I gotten myself involved in? I shake my head, trying to pull it together, and put the car in drive. I need to get out of here.

I drive in silence until I'm in front of my apartment building. While looking for a parking spot, I notice four motorcycles parked in front of the door that leads up to our apartment. Part of me doesn't want to go up. I want to get far away from whatever mess I've been dragged into.

I park, turn off the car, and hear my phone chime in the

passenger seat.

Axel: Where are you?

Clearly, he's already heard about my new "friend" Death. I'm not in the mood for Axel right now. I already have to go into my apartment and deal with the other members of his club. I lightly bang the back of my head against the headrest and curse myself for even thinking I was going to have a chill night in with Marley. The universe just loves to watch me squirm. My emotions are all over the place, so I settle on sending a short text to let him know I'm safe.

Jenna: I just pulled up to my apartment.
How did you get my number, stalker?

I hit send and rest my head back on the seat. I just need a few moments to myself before facing the onslaught of questions waiting for me inside.

Just as I relax, the door to the apartments flies open, and a large figure barrels out, heading straight for me. What is it with large men accosting me in my car tonight?

The figure gets closer, and I realize it's Axel… here at my apartment, looking extremely pissed.

"Open the door, Angel," he orders even before reaching my car.

I hesitate but ultimately unlock the door and get out.

"Okay, before you get all macho-man on me, you should know I did nothing wrong. I literally just walked to my car—"

Before I can finish my sentence, Axel's hands are on my

body, and his mouth is fused to mine. This kiss isn't sweet; it's intense, soul-crushing.

After the evening I've had, I don't want to fight Axel or push him away. I melt into his body, letting his embrace soothe my frayed nerves. When I try to pull back and catch my breath, Axel pulls me closer. Having his arms wrapped around me makes me feel like they can protect me from anything or anyone.

He finally moves back just enough so our foreheads are touching. I take a deep breath of his masculine scent and try to focus on what I was saying before he interrupted me. "Scared me tonight, babe."

I blink up at him, confused. We've known each other for less than 24 hours, so why is he so worried about me? And what's with all the pet names?

"I'm fine. Really, he just scared me. But I'll be okay, I promise. You didn't have to come here. You can go—I just need to get inside and wash today off," I say in a rush, trying to downplay everything. Whatever this is right now between us is what got me in this mess in the first place.

Axel's eyes flare with fury. "You think I'm going to leave you here without me? Absolutely not. They know who you are now. You're a part of this because of the club. The Reapers think you have ties to us and showed tonight that they're willing to go to any length to get what they want—even harassing you at a fucking school." His jaw twitches with rage as he tries to keep his cool.

I place my hands on his chest and look up into his eyes. His jaw ticks again as he turns us towards the apartment building.

Tucking me into his side, he puts his arm over my shoulder, keeping me close to his body.

I let out a breath, feeling some of the tension leave my shoulders as I lean into him. My brain is telling me that I need to pull away, put some distance between us, but my body isn't quite following along.

"Thank you for being here. I know you don't know me, but having you here is calming my nerves. I can't explain it, but there's something about you," I sigh as we walk through the door.

"Yeah, babe. I feel it too." He kisses the top of my head and lets out a rough sigh. "When I got the call that you were in trouble…" He shakes his head like he's trying to get rid of a bad thought. "Shit, I had to make sure you were safe for myself." Axel looks down at me with his piercing eyes.

"Well, I'm fine. Truly I am," I say, smiling to lighten the mood. "But what I don't understand is—why me? I only just heard about you guys yesterday. I'm not a part of the club,"

"Babe, that's something I'm going to figure out. I'm sorry I didn't have someone with you. Fuck, I didn't think you were someone they'd connect to us, honestly," he says, his expression darkening for a moment before shifting the conversation. "Come on, your food just got here."

He chuckles as my stomach growls loudly, making me realize how hungry I really am.

Chapter 9

AXEL

Marley and Jenna devour their take out while she explains in detail the events of the evening. I can't fucking believe their enforcer would scare someone who has no real affiliation with the club. It doesn't make any sense. This just puts all of us on high alert. The Reapers are trying to prove a point. There isn't anyone who is safe.

When we finish, Jenna heads to take a shower, and my brothers and I make a plan on how we're going to set up security. Tonight, I'm taking the shift at the apartment. I can't believe the anger I felt when I got the call that Death messed with Jenna. It shocked me how intense my protective feelings were and before I knew what I was doing, I was flying down the highway towards her apartment. When I get my hands on their enforcer, I'll make sure he never gets near her again.

Blaze insists on staying too, so I guess we're both spending the night. It's unexplainable, but I can't be away from Jen right now. Jax and Cal leave the apartment and I turn around just in time to see Jenna come out of her bedroom. She's wearing the tiniest shorts, every inch of her legs on display. On top, she's in a tight white tank top that lands just above her belly button, showing off a few inches of her toned stomach, and a very oversized cardigan that hangs loose around her shoulders. The whole outfit leaves nothing to the imagination—it's obvious she's not wearing a bra. She brushes her wet hair as she makes her way to the kitchen and fills the teakettle with water. Catching a glimpse of her face, I notice her forehead is wrinkled, and she seems lost in thought.

I walk up behind her. "Hey, let me do that for you," brushing my chest against her back as I reach around her. My hand slides around to take the kettle, and she nearly jumps out of her skin, obviously not realizing I was in the room.

"Shh, it's okay, babe. It's just me. Why don't you go sit on the couch? I'll bring your tea out when it's ready." I tuck a piece of hair behind her ear, out of her face. A light blush creeps up her heart-shaped face—it's cute as hell.

"Thank you," she mutters with a shy smile, heading toward the couch.

Marley and Blaze have already turned in for the night, so no one's going to bug her. If she wants to watch movies all night, I'll gladly keep her company. If she wants to sleep this day off, I'll be right here on the couch, keeping watch. What the fuck is happening to me? I sound so weak, so caught up. But I'm learning it's only when it comes to this woman.

After a few minutes, I round the kitchen island and head

to Jenna. She's lying down, cocooned in a fluffy blue blanket. I set the mug in front of her on the coffee table and sit down with her on the large L-shaped couch. I drop into the seat next to where she's resting her head on a pillow, trying not to disturb her relaxed state. She moves slightly so she can look up at me.

In one quick motion, Jenna tosses the pillow to the other end of the couch and rests her head on my thigh. She turns back to the TV and inhales a deep breath. I don't know why I do it, but I start running my fingers through her silky red locks. She hums in appreciation as her eyes flutter closed.

"You do this for all the girls?" Jenna says in a lulled voice.

I chuckle at her half-asleep state. "No, darlin'. Just you." My chest tightens, knowing this woman is everything I want. I've never thought about settling down or meeting someone I could see myself being with forever. But after just a few hours I already know that she would be it for me.

But I can't let this happen. I can't drag her into this life or taint her further with the dangers and secrets that plague us daily. Jenna is a light, someone who makes this world better just by being in it. Jesus, when she got out of her car tonight, she looked like Mrs. Honey herself dressed in bright colors, ready to teach the youth of America. I sigh heavily as I continue to play with Jenna's hair. I quickly realize I'll do anything to keep my world from touching hers again. Tonight, is already more than she should have been involved in.

"You're going to break my heart," she says out of nowhere in a whisper so soft I almost don't hear it. She freezes, as if she hadn't meant to say it out loud.

I peer down at her; her eyes are still closed. I still my hand, resting it on the side of her face and tilting it up to mine. She slowly opens her eyes. Her green eyes pierce me, holding me in place.

"Jenna, the last thing I would ever want to do is hurt you," I say, hoping my tone conveys the promise. "And let's be real. I would probably be the one getting my heart ripped out by my little miss sunshine, fuck I haven't been able to stop thinking about you since last night." I sound like a pussy, but I don't give a shit. She ponders my words for a moment, then moves her body to grab the remote from beside her, muting the TV. Whatever she's about to say, she wants my full attention.

"Let's make a deal," she says, tilting her head to the side. God, I'd do anything for that face.

"Depends on what it is, Angel," I reply, giving her my full attention.

"Tonight, let's just enjoy this, us, whatever this is. And tomorrow morning, we part ways, and that's it," she says in a serious voice. "I know it's inevitable we'll probably run into each other with Blaze and Marley being together, but we can just say hello and go on with our lives." She stops, waiting for my response. "It's not even like we really know each other."

I take a second to study her face. She's serious. I know what she's saying makes sense for us. Jenna is trying to protect herself. Part of me feels proud she's guarding her heart; the other part of me hates the idea.

I cup her face with my hand, the contrast between my tanned, tattooed skin and her untouched, silky, porcelain face reminds me of just how different we are. I can't drag her into harm's way, no matter how much I want the chance to get to know her.

"Deal," I say in a voice that doesn't sound like my own. It's strangled with uncertainty, and I almost second-guess my response. Fuck, this may be the worst decision I've ever made.

I take one last look at her angelic face, then pull her toward me. If this is the only night we get, I'm going to make a memory that lasts me a lifetime.

Chapter 10

JENNA

I KNEW AXEL would agree to the terms, I mean we've practically been dancing around it since the moment we met. But I can't help but feel like this is just asking for disaster. Never the less, I do feel a sense of relief when he makes the deal with me. This way we can relieve this tension between us and then move on. I feel an intense connection to him, one that I know will consume me if I let it. His mouth ravages mine as I snake my body up to his. He grabs the back of my knees and places me on his lap so that I straddle his body. Instantly I feel him beneath me and grind myself down, trying to find some relief for the throbbing between my legs.

I pull away, only slightly, placing my forehead against his and take a moment to think. I'm fighting an internal battle; this agreement allows me to have him just for one night and then walk away with no attachments. But the other part, probably the more sensible part, is screaming at me that this never ends well for me, especially since the feelings I'm having for this man are intense and I barely know him. Hell, I don't know him!

I can't tell if it's the emotions from everything that unfolded this evening, or if I am losing my mind. But all I want is Axel here with me, to protect me, hold me, make me feel alive. And those feelings scare the shit out of me. *Gosh Jenna, just have sex with the extremely sexy man under you and leave it alone.*

Fuck it.

I grab the hem of my shirt and pull it up and off of my body. The cool air makes my nipples pebble and stand at attention. Axel's eyes drop to my chest, and I bite my bottom lip in anticipation. He looks up at me with a fire I hadn't seen a moment ago. A sly smile slides onto his face as he runs his thumb across my lip.

"What did I say about biting that lip?" he says. Barely giving me time to respond — let alone think — he drops his head and takes one of my nipples into his mouth. I drop my head back, letting my hair fall behind me. He expertly sucks and licks, torturing my other with small and gentle tugs. I can barely breathe it feels so good, but the need to have his mouth somewhere else is becoming unbearable.

"Tell me what you need, Angel," he says between sweet assaults on my sensitive breasts. I try to answer, but my brain has turned to mush. He pauses and plants his hands on my hips, stopping me from grinding on him. I squirm with the need to move.

Kissing up my chest, to my ear, he holds me in place,

seemingly driving me insane.

"Talk to me, Jen. What do you need?" Axel slowly makes his way back to my breast and draws a circle around my nipple with his tongue. Drawing a hiss of pleasure from my lips.

"I need your mouth… on me," I choke out, suddenly embarrassed by the need in my voice. I'm usually more confident than this. In my last relationship I did most of the talking but Axel throws me off. He's so sexy I can barely keep it together.

"Here?" he says as he kisses my neck.

"No," I pant. He moves further down my body to the middle of my breasts and nips me gently.

"Here?" he says again, the smirk on his face making my stomach pool with warmth. How is he so devilishly handsome?

"No." I watch as he draws his head away from my body. "Hmm" he says as he begins to stand, I momentarily latch on to him before I realize he already has me up in the air. I'm amazed by how effortlessly he can carry me. I'm not exactly the smallest woman; I'm toned and healthy but still have significant curves. Being carried like I weigh nothing is incredibly hot.

Without hesitation, he starts walking us out of the living room and down the hallway. Once in my room, he kicks the door shut behind us.

"Don't want to worry about being walked in on," Axel moves quickly for such a large man and drops me on the bed where I bounce from the short fall. I crawl up the bed so that my back is pressed against the pillows.

"What? No voyeur kink I should be made aware of?" I joke. Unashamed that I am openly staring at him as he begins to get undressed.

"Babe, I usually don't give a fuck who's watching. But you, you're all mine. For my eyes only."

I have no quippy come back. Something about him being possessive of me sends electricity through my body. I like a man who knows what he wants and keeps it for himself.

Axel strips off his boots and pants, then takes off his shirt. I nearly moan when I see what he has been hiding from me. His body is gorgeous. Muscles ripple under large tattoos that cover his torso. A thin gold chain hangs from his neck and a small ring from the chain. I focus in on the petite ring and a flash of green catches my eye. I wonder whose ring it is, feeling slightly jealous at the thought of it belonging to another woman. But then I remember that isn't my place, this is a one-time thing and I really shouldn't care.

He runs a hand through his luscious, black hair. His eyes roam my body, taking in every inch on display. Someone else might feel embarrassed to be so exposed but I love my body and feel confident in my skin.

"Do you have any idea how fucking perfect you are?" he says in a gravelly voice.

I offer a smile and lean forward so that I am on all fours in front of him. "I could say the same to you." I whisper as I run my tongue across his abs, right above the hem of his boxers. He lets out a small whistle while grabbing a fistful of my hair. He holds me in place for a moment, his hold tight and the slight sting on my scalp makes me want more. Within seconds, Axel releases my hair and flips me onto my back.

His hard body moves with mine, our faces only inches away. "Just one night?"

"Just one." I reply.

He nods, but holds my gaze. I squirm under his watch, wanting to continue what we've started. I don't want him to get any ideas and think this is anything more than a one-night stand. Reaching down, I cup him through his boxers. With my free hand, I grip the back of his head and pull his lips to mine. Immediately the heat between us grows and I can't take it anymore. Axel must feel my need. He kneels between my spread legs and slides my shorts and underwear from my body. Axel trails his hands up my thighs until he reaches my center. Painstakingly slow, he runs his finger between my lips, my body bucks when he makes contact with my clit.

"Fuck baby, you're so wet. Is this all for me?" He locks eyes with me as I nod, biting my bottom lip. Honestly, I don't think I have ever been this turned on. He moves his finger down and circles my entrance. I moan, unable to control the noises leaving my body.

"Axel," I beg just as his mouth latches onto the sensitive bundle of nerves and he plunges his fingers inside me. My back bows off the bed, allowing him full access to me. He expertly moves his tongue while pumping his fingers in and out. I writhe in pleasure as I try to grab my sheets for support. All of the pent up want that has been building inside me since meeting Axel last night comes crashing down. It takes no time at all for me to feel like I'm going to combust. His motions turn faster and more intense. All I can do is scream out his name as my orgasm rips through my body setting my limbs on fire. Axel's tongue slowly moves through my folds as my body convulses through my release.

"That's just the beginning, Angel." He speaks into my skin as he kisses, nips, and licks his way up my body.

"Do you know how good you taste?" Axel's eyes meet mine. I feel heat creep up my cheeks as I see my arousal glistening on his lips and chin. I can't help the shy smile on my face as I turn away from him. He is so sexual and owns everything he does with confidence. I'm not used to all of this dirty talk; I don't know what to say.

"Don't you do that," he says as he turns my face back to him. "You are the sexiest woman I've ever laid my eyes on, and everything about you turns me the fuck on." He leans down and kisses me with a passion I have yet to find with a partner. I taste myself on his tongue and fuck, it's hot. I deepen the kiss, wanting to make this moment last a little bit longer.

Axel leans down next to my ear. "I need to be inside you. I need to fuck you hard and fast. You okay with that?" My body tingles with excitement.

"Yes, Axel." I reply.

"Fuck, I love the way you say my name," he groans as he rolls off of me, standing up and walking to his discarded jeans. "Shit, you have a condom?" he asks, it's obvious neither of us had prepared for this.

"Oh, uh, no, I don't have a condom." I say, feeling slightly annoyed we may not be able to finish.

He takes a moment and looks at me thoughtfully, "I'm clean, just been tested. You on the pill?" he asks.

I've been on birth control since freshman year of college, but I've never had sex without a condom. I consider it for a moment and look at Axel trying to decide if this is a good idea.

He walks back to the bed, I am now sitting on the edge of the bed and he leans down so we are face to face.

"Babe, you don't have to do anything if you're not feeling it."

How can this incredibly rugged and tough biker be so sweet and caring? Last night at the bar, I watched as everyone moved out of his way like he was the devil himself. I know that outside of this space, Axel is not all rainbows and sunshine, but a dangerous man. It makes me flush, thinking that he might only be this way with me.

"I'm on birth control and I'm clean as well." I say with confidence, leaving out the part where I haven't had sex in over eleven months. "Come here Axel, I need you."

The corner of Axel's lip twitches, taking his time he steps out of his boxers. He springs free from the confines of his briefs; my mouth begins to salivate as I stare at the gorgeous man in front of me. He's huge, in every way possible, and all mine for the night.

I quickly move to be in front of him, wrapping my hand around his throbbing cock and exploring his length, pulling a moan out of him. Axel's hand travels to the back of my head; he grabs my hair slightly pulling back so that I have no choice but to drop my head back, exposing my neck to him.

"Turn around," he says in my ear. It's a command, and it has me instantly dripping wet. I turn around and bend over for him, arching my back so that my ass is up in the air. I'm his for the taking. Axel places himself at my entrance. I wiggle at him, needing him to hurry. Slowly he enters me, allowing me to get used to his size before he goes any further. My breath hitches as I try to allow my body to fully relax. Fuck, he is huge. Behind me I hear Axel let out a slow hiss, "Angel, you're so fucking tight. You're like a vice wrapped around my dick."

I can't speak, not yet. He starts to move slowly in and out, the feeling is mind blowing.

"Oh my God, Axel, you feel so good. I've never felt so...full." I moan into the pillow, allowing it to swallow my admission. Without warning, he pulls out of me and I'm suddenly spinning around at lightning speed.

Axel grabs ahold of both my legs, pulling them up so that my ankles rest on his shoulders. Without warning, he slams into me, my body welcoming him easily. My body feels like origami and he has folded me so that I am taking every delectable inch of him. The position change has his pelvis rubbing my clit as he pumps into me, sending me careening towards my second orgasm.

"Babe, I am extremely close," Axel says in a clipped tone. "I want you to look at me while you cum. I want you to know exactly who's fucking you." I open my eyes and look at him. How the hell he thinks I could forget whose inside of me is beyond me. At this point I'm not sure where I end and he begins.

He's staring at me with a heat in his eyes that sends goosebumps over my skin. The look he gives me feels like it's meant for a lover, not a one-night stand. The connection I'm feeling has my heart racing and I break eye contact to try to remain unattached.

Axel draws back, slamming into me with so much force I know I'll feel him for days afterward. I arch back as my second orgasm tears through my body.

"Eyes here baby," Axel holds me in place. Locking eyes with me as my body loses control. My walls tighten around him as my release takes over. I feel Axel's body tense above me as he calls out my name.

When I open my eyes, it's to see Axel's gut-twisting smile.

Chapter 11

AXEL

WRAPPING JENNA IN my arms, I pull her under the covers and hold her there, not ready to let go.

"Sleep, Jenna. If tonight is the only night I have with your sweet body, I'll be waking you up in a few hours for round two." I murmur to her, already half-asleep myself.

"Sounds perfect," she responds with a small smile. Within minutes, her breathing evens out, and a light snore fills the silence. I'm glad she's finally getting some rest. I asked Cal for a report on her daily schedule—this woman works her ass off. Settling in, the warmth of her skin relaxes me, and I fall asleep faster and harder than I have in a long time.

I wake the next morning when the first hint of daylight filters in through the large window in Jenna's room. I've never been able to sleep in—it sucks, but I never waste my mornings. Lying on my back, I savor the feeling of her wrapped around me. Her head rests on my chest, her legs intertwined with mine. The sheet has slipped down to her waist, leaving her beautifully toned back exposed.

I woke her up two more times during the night. Each time, we had sex, talked, fell asleep, and repeated. She's perfect. All night, her body was so responsive, the sound of my name on her lips as she clamped around me in ecstasy is on constant replay in my head.

My chest tightens as I think about another man being with her, waking up to her warmth wrapped around him. The thought makes my blood boil, but I know the arrangement I signed on for. She needs someone who doesn't have blood on his hands, someone who doesn't bring danger just by being in her life.

She starts to stir, her face rubbing against my chest. Her brow furrows, and she mumbles as if caught in a bad dream.

"No, no, no!" she cries, each word louder than the last.

My pulse quickens at the desperation in her voice. I shake her shoulders, calling her name to wake her, but it doesn't work. I shake her harder.

"Jenna, wake up!" I say firmly.

She shoots upright, gasping for air. I pull her to my chest, running my hands over her back.

"You're okay. It was just a bad dream," I say into her hair, pressing a kiss to the top of her head.

Her body relaxes against me, but a moment later, she

stiffens. I wonder if this is from last night, she probably hasn't dealt with anything like that before and it can scare some people.

"Tell me what your dream was about," I say calmly.

"It was just a bad dream, Axel. It happens sometimes," she says, her voice shaky as she slowly moves away from me. The action a stark contrast from the woman who couldn't keep her hands off of me last night.

I want to pull her back and never let her leave. *Holy shit, what kind of spell has this woman put on me?*

She stands, pulling an oversized t-shirt and a pair of shorts from her drawer. I hate it. I want her naked in bed with me, but I know that's over.

"Um, you can hang out if you want. I'm going to get coffee and make some breakfast," she says, turning to leave. *What the fuck just happened?*

"Wait," I call after her. "Come here."

She turns back, hesitating, but then walks over to the bed. I take her hand and pull her into my lap. She rests her head in the crook of my neck, and I breathe her in.

"Where do you think you're going in such a hurry? We can't part ways with a weird fucking 'see ya later,'" I tease, mimicking her voice.

She laughs softly. "I'm sorry. I just thought it would be easier to make a clean break. Last night was— " she pauses for a moment searching for the right word. "Amazing." she admits, still not looking at me.

I move so she has no choice but to meet my gaze. Her tousled, wavy red hair and puffy, sleep-worn face make her look even more beautiful. I drink in the sight of her.

"Don't look at me like that, Axel," she says slapping my chest. "We are not having sex again, no matter how magical your dick is." She laughs. She has some sass. I'll give her that.

"My real name is Dane," I blurt out. I have no idea why I tell her that, but I need her to have that part of me.

Her hand runs down my arm, landing on mine. She intertwines our fingers, staring at them for a moment before looking back at me. "Dane is a great name. It suits you," she says with a smile, leaning in to kiss me quickly. I try to deepen the kiss, but Jenna pulls back with a sly smile.

"Tsk, tsk" she waggles her finger at me. "See you around, Dane." I watch her stand to leave. But I grab her hand, pulling her back. That is not the kiss we're leaving on.

Now she's full blown giggling as I lock our lips together. She opens to me, letting me taste every inch of her. That's my girl.

When we finally pull apart, I brush my thumb across her cheek. "Angel, always know that I'm here for you. I don't care if we're friends or not—you mean something to me. Got that?"

"Yes, I understand. Same goes for you, okay?" she replies. Fuck, she looks at me like she really means that.

I chuckle softly. "Yeah, babe."

She stands once more and heads to the door. When she opens it, I catch sight of Blaze and Marley standing in their doorway, grinning like idiots. It's obvious they heard everything last night.

Jenna doesn't look back. She squares her shoulders, lifts her chin, and closes the door behind her. I fall back onto the bed, scrubbing my hands over my face.

It's time to deal with the pieces of shit threatening our town and our club. I get dressed and walk out the door.

Chapter 12

JENNA

THE NEXT SIX days fly by as my focus stays on wrapping up the school year. Summer break is so close I can taste it. I pack the last of my bags, taking my personal belongings home for the next few months. Across the room, the door opens, and Jill's kind face greets me. One of the second-grade teachers at our school, I've seen her around a lot but haven't had time to get to know her. She replaced another teacher that oddly, up and left, three-fourths of the way through the school year. Today she is wearing a bright yellow dress dotted with sunflowers that flows around her, and her short, wavy brown hair falls around her face with one side tucked behind her ear, showcasing her numerous piercings. She looks effortlessly beautiful.

"Hi, Jenna!" she says in a cheery voice, walking into the classroom.

"Hey, Jill. Enjoying the last day of school?" I ask with a

smile.

"Oh my gosh, yes! I feel like this school year dragged on. Now, I'm ready to have some fun," she says with a mischievous smile on her face. Jill walks over and begins helping me place my things in boxes.

"I'm sorry I didn't come over to chat with you more. You seem like someone I'd really get along with," she adds with an apologetic look. "It's been crazy taking over for Mr. Meyers on such short notice."

"Oh, stop. Don't apologize. I was so busy I didn't even try to hang out with anyone, anyway." I snort as I move a finished box to the back counter.

As Jill walks beside me, I notice a small tattoo behind her ear—a rose with petals falling from the flower and a word written in some kind of chicken scratch. I open my mouth to ask her what it says, but she continues talking before I can.

"Well, if you're up for it, I'd love to get to know you! My friends and I are going to Tipsy in two weekends. I know it's weird to plan this far ahead, but everyone's busy this weekend and next. I wanted to ask you to join us," Jill says with a smile, waiting for my response.

Tipsy is a club in the next town over. A few of the teachers were raving about it last week, talking about the drinks and the atmosphere. I hesitate, unsure whether to accept her offer. With the school year ending, I'll have time for fun, but I don't really know Jill or her friends.

"Um, I'm not sure, Jill. That's really nice of you to offer, but—" I say warily.

"Come on, it'll be great! You'll be with me the whole time," she says, batting her long lashes.

I think about it again, maybe Marley can come with me. But remember Marley will be in California that weekend for some major tech unveiling she's been talking about for weeks.

Jill doesn't break eye contact with me while waiting and I start to feel awkward not giving her a response.

"Okay, yeah, I'll come," I sigh, giving her a half-smile.

"Yay! You won't regret it. We're going to have such a good time! I got your number from Mrs. Adams so I'll text you the details." Jill waves goodbye and leaves, her cheeriness contagious.

For the first time, I feel excited about making some work friends. This year has been lonely, trying to figure everything out on my own and only having Marley to complain to. She's a great listener, but she doesn't understand the ins and outs of teaching. I finish collecting my stuff, turn off the lights, and lock up for the summer.

Two weeks later, as I drive to the club, Axel occupies my thoughts. The last time I went out for the evening, I got more than I bargained for. We haven't talked or seen each other since he left my apartment three weeks ago. Cal and Jax took shifts watching the apartment for a few days, but with seemingly nothing happening, two prospects took over their duties. Cal explained that prospects are men who aren't fully patched members of the club yet, but are proving their loyalty. They prospect for a year, hoping to earn their place in the club.

Over the last few weeks, I've learned a lot about MC life, and I'm still unsure how I feel about it. Part of me understands the family aspect of the club—the need to have people who always have your back. But the constant danger and tension I have seen, seems like it would become too much.

Thanks to Mia, I've met a few more women from the club. She invited Marley and me to dinner with some of the "old ladies," as she calls them.

I met Sierra, who's Jax's wife, and Cali, who's with Gunner. I haven't met him yet, but he is the Hell Chaser's Road Captain. Again, more terms I really am not familiar with.

I wasn't sure what I had expected when meeting the women, but they are probably the most welcoming people I have ever met. Sierra works as the office manager for one of the MC's mechanic shops, using her accounting degree. Cali, surprisingly, is one of the top attorneys in the county. I thought she was joking when she told me, seeing as how she was with a man who is in a biker club, but she just shrugged when I mentioned it. "My work and home life don't usually cross paths unless the club needs my help. I'm on retainer for that," she said nonchalantly.

I'm impressed by how smart and interesting these women are. After dinner, we planned a girl's night for next week when Marley is back. The girls want to wait until the situation with the Reapers dies down. All three have someone from the club assigned to protect them, which they don't seem to mind, but I struggle to understand why I need the same level of protection.

Even though Death tried to scare me, I've taken precautions. I carry pepper spray on my keychain and keep a taser in my car. Both make me feel safer. I've also signed up for women's self-defense classes starting tomorrow. I hated how scared that man made me feel that night, and how unprepared I had been. I was able to get Marley to sign up too. Blaze was very on board about the idea and helped me convince her it was needed.

He comes by most nights, bringing dinner and spending time with Marley. I don't mind having Blaze around, but I always find myself looking to see if Axel is outside or walking in behind him. I hate that I look for him, it was a one off and I need to remember that. Gripping the steering wheel, I try to focus on the excitement of meeting new friends tonight, though I wish Marley were with me.

Pulling into the parking lot, I find a spot close to the front. Tonight, I'm wearing a skin-tight, mini black dress with a plunging neckline that shows off a lot of cleavage, paired with little black stilettos that make my legs look incredible. I've had this dress in the back of my closet for almost a year now with nowhere to wear it. This club is known for being sexy, so I chose to finally put it to good use.

Before I go in I decide to call Marley. We haven't checked in yet today and I'm almost about to talk myself into just heading home. The phone rings a few times before Mar picks up.

"What's up?" She says like she's a California surfer dude. "Shouldn't you be hanging out with all the cool teachers by now?"

"Hello to you too, weirdo." I laugh. "I'm sitting in my car outside." I take a deep breath, staring at the caller id on my dashboard.

"Jenna, I know it's hard stepping outside of your bubble. Especially with how hard you've been working. But this will be really good for you. Having people at work who can support you is important. You can't be the lone wolf forever."

I roll my eyes. She's right, but I just wanted to commiserate with my best friend for a moment.

"I'm going in." I state. "I'm hanging up now."

"Wait!" Marley screeches into the phone. "What are you wearing? Please tell me you aren't wearing your work clothes." *Jeez, you wear one "Reading is fun!" shirt to a bar and now you can't be trusted to dress yourself?*

"Black mini dress and heels if you must know." I say with my hand moving in closer to the disconnect button.

"Back of the closet black dress?!" Her voice is filled with disbelief and I have half a mind to just finish the job and hang up. "Wow, you are going to be literally the hottest person there!"

I shake my head laughing, "Thanks Mar, I'm going now, love you!"

"Okay, text me when you're home, please! Love you!"

"Will do" I reply. With that the car is plunged into silence again. But now my confidence to get in there has been renewed.

Stepping out of my car, I can already hear the music pounding inside. I move quickly to the door, show the bouncer my ID, and enter the dark building. Neon strobe lights flash, and fake smoke covers the floor. There is a bright white dance floor in the center of the room and it is packed with people. On one side of the room there are large booths; on the other, a massive bar. Straightening my shoulders, I push through the crowd, texting Jill to find out where she is. She responds quickly, and I find her at a booth tucked near the back.

The black velvet couch curves around a small table littered

with drinks and bottles of alcohol. I sit down next to Jill, who nearly spills her drink as she turns toward me. She's plastered. How long has she been here? I'm already feeling like I want to go home. Not only did I get dressed up, but I also drove twenty minutes out here for *this*? I pushed that feeling to the back of my mind, I had come here to have fun so I could still get a drink and maybe dance a little.

"Jenna! You made it!" Jill slurs.

"Yes, thanks for inviting me," I say, waving at the table. "Looks like you guys already got started."

She giggles and gestures to a guy behind her. "It was all Max, When I got here, there were shots and drinks waiting for us!" She starts naming everyone at the table: "That's Sabrina, Alex, Gracie, Conner, and Max!" She's practically screaming inches from my face and I actively have to try to fight the urge to lean back.

I nod politely, giving each of them a tight smile. They all seem just as drunk as Jill. I'm not in the mood for small talk, but I remind myself I came here to have fun.

"I'm going to get a drink," I shout over the music.

"Oh yay! I'll take a Cosmo!" she screeches back at me. I almost roll my eyes at her. I will be bringing back water in a martini glass; she won't know the difference.

I stand up and take note of my surroundings. In order to get to the bar, I need to walk through the dance floor. Great. Sweaty bodies gyrate around me as I try not to bump into anyone. Almost to the bar, a large hand wraps around my bicep. I take a deep breath, ready to tell some jackass to fuck off. I really am not in the mood for pushy men trying to get me to dance. I whip my head around, only to see a man I never thought I was going to see again. Jack.

The irritation I was just feeling has now turned to dread. What the hell is Jack doing here of all places? His ocean blue eyes are the same, but everything else about him has changed.

We've only been broken up for a little over a year and a half, but in that time physically, he has become a whole new person. His once perfectly combed blonde hair is shaggy and tousled. A barely trimmed beard is taking the place of the clean-shaven face I once knew. My gaze travels down his body. Jack has always been extremely fit and still is, but he is dressed completely different. He no longer dons a suit, but a pair of dark wash jeans and a white t-shirt. I watch as his eyes cast down my body, and I can't help but hold my breath.

"Jack?" I stare at him in disbelief.

"Jenna," he says with a mischievous smile.

He points toward the bar with his chin. "I'm headed to the bar. Want to grab a drink?"

I nod and start to walk in front of him. His hand drops from where it was holding my arm, and I feel the air woosh out of me in relief. I don't like him touching me.

Reaching the bar, Jack orders himself a beer and me a Blackberry Mojito. I feel annoyance bubbling up inside me like hot lava. Who does he think he is—ordering for me? I pause and count to ten; it is still my standard order, so I let it go. I stare at his profile, still surprised that he is here. The thought of returning to Jill crosses my mind, but she probably won't realize I'm gone.

"Long time no see," he says as he moves closer. I can

smell his spicy cologne around him, the same cologne that he always wore. My stomach twists, and I catch myself rolling my ring around my finger nervously. That scent alone brings back memories I would rather bury deep inside. Jack and I had been together for three years. In the beginning, I thought Jack was the person I was going to marry one day. But as the years went on, he became controlling and constantly wanted my attention to be on him and not on anything else. Now, after extensive sessions with my therapist, I know he is a narcissist and would play mind games and guilt trip me into complying with his needs. He always needed to be the center of my world, and if he wasn't, he would lash out with cruel words and sly comments. After arguments, he would slither back to whisper sweet nothings to me. I was young and thought I loved him. I couldn't have been more wrong. Our relationship became a game of who could be more codependent and quickly turned toxic.

Of course, this caused me to draw back from work, family, and school. I ended up falling behind and needed to stay at the university for an extra year.

The day after graduation, I showed up at Marley's door and told her I needed to get out of my relationship. I needed to start fresh and not look back. She didn't even blink. Within a few weeks, we were settling into our new apartment here in Cranson Creek. Marley has always detested Jack from the moment she met him. She'd told me, "Something about him just doesn't seem right, Jenna." Over the years, Marley had mentioned her worries a few more times, but didn't push it. I think she was waiting for me to come to my senses.

When I left, I wrote Jack a letter explaining my need to break things off. I left it for him on our kitchen table—not my best idea in hindsight. Jack spent the next month messaging and calling me, trying to grapple with our breakup. Many of his messages were apologies and promises that our relationship would be better if I came back. Then his messages turned angry, and he lashed out with evil and harsh insults. Same story, different day. I blocked his number after that month and haven't heard from him since. Until now.

I offer him an anxious smile. "How have you been?"

"Pretty good. I live here now," he says as he looks at me. "Got a job working private security."

"What happened to business school?" I ask in a curious voice. Private security was a big jump from his original plan of owning his own business.

He shrugs, and an angry look passes across his face. "After you left…" he starts, but shakes his head and stops himself. "I needed a change," he says matter-of-factly. The DJ changes songs, and the sea of people behind us erupts in excitement. I wait until the noise level isn't deafening before responding. In that moment, Jack turns to the bar, avoiding eye contact with me.

"I'm sorry for leaving the way I did. I didn't think there was another way," I say in a low voice. He turns to me with a look that sends a shiver down my spine. It is almost as if his anger from the past year and a half has come flooding back and he's fighting with everything he has to control it. But as quickly as it is there, it is gone again; he hides it behind a cool exterior. I blink at his rapid mood swing.

"I get it, darling. You were doing what you thought was best. Hey, I ended up finding my family after you left, so I'm in a good place now." He takes a swig of his beer and places it on the counter. Jack's parents passed away in a car accident a few years before we got together. It was heart-wrenching, and for a long time, I was his only family. I am glad to hear that he has found people he's become so close with.

"That's good, Jack," I say as I sip my drink. The rum settles in my stomach, sending a warm sensation through my body.

"So, what are you up to now?" he says, keeping the conversation going. I open my mouth to answer, but all of a sudden, the atmosphere in the room changes. The hair on the back of my neck stands up, and the warm sensation I had felt turns to lead in my stomach.

Jack's face turns to stone as he leans off the bar, staring at something behind me. I slowly turn and catch sight of Blaze walking through the crowd. I turn a little more and see Jax. For a moment, I think I am imagining things. Why would they be at a club?

Blaze glances over in my direction, but it doesn't seem like he saw me as the two of them continue to stride to their destination. The look on both their faces tells me they aren't here for fun. I avert my gaze, trying not to attract attention to myself. I know that if one of them sees me, they will probably be shipping me back to the apartment. I was told to stay close to town and to check in with Cal. I have done neither tonight. Cal and I have become pretty good friends the past few weeks, seeing as how he was forced to spend most of his time with Marley and me. He would be pissed to know I didn't listen to directions very well. Now I understand why; it seems like something is happening tonight.

As if on cue, my phone vibrates in my bag. I reach inside, and my heart begins to pound. Axel is calling me. I silence the call, knowing I won't be able to hear him in the club, and send a quick text.

> **Jenna: Out with a friend. I'll call when I get home.**

I hit send and clutch the phone in my hand, waiting for his response. I look up at Jack. His posture seems defensive, and his eyes don't shift away from the men making their way to the back of the building. He shouldn't know who they are. Why does he care?

"Are you okay?" I ask in a calm voice.

Jack turns back to the bar and downs his beer. He quickly orders another and then turns to me. I catch sight of Prince walking up the stairs that lead to what I assume is the VIP area, a few other men wearing cuts following behind him. I recognize a few of them, but many are unfamiliar to me. What are the Hell Chasers doing here?

I tilt my head back down to my drink, trying not to think about it. The MC runs so many businesses I wouldn't be surprised if this is one of them. I take another sip of my drink and long for the comfort of my apartment. Slipping on a warm set of pajamas and watching trashy TV sounds way better than being here. My head is pounding from the loud music, and I am ready to head home. This run-in with Jack is not helping my already frayed nerves.

Just then, a pair of hands land on the bar on either side of my body, encasing me in my seat. I stare at the tattoos that cover the hands in front of me. They're the same hands that a few weeks ago were all over my body. I don't need to turn around to know whose hard body is pressed against my back. *Axel.*

Chapter 13

AXEL

Two days ago, Prince got a call from the Reapers president. He asked for a sit-down meeting to discuss heightened tensions. I didn't feel good about it, but the Prez has the final say. He agreed, but only if we met in neutral territory. The club Tipsy isn't owned by either MC, and the management owes the Hell Chasers a favor, so we chose it as the meeting ground.

I walk into the club on high alert. The place is packed. Everyone seems too drunk to notice that we are here. Prince is doing the real business, but many of us came in case something goes south. The probability of that happening is high, seeing as they are already less than cooperative. Being out of our territory makes my palms twitch; there are too many unknowns.

I'm just getting off my bike when my phone rings in my pocket. It's Cal letting me know Jenna hasn't checked in tonight. My heart thunders in my chest, and a surge of protectiveness shoots through my body. The feeling makes me uncomfortable. Jenna isn't mine, and she can't be. So why the hell do I feel this way? I shake my head in disbelief. Tonight isn't the night I need to deal with this shit.

I hang up with Cal and immediately call Jenna. Her phone goes straight to voicemail. Where the fuck is she? Just then, I get a text from her saying she is out with a friend and she will call later. Is she fucking joking?

I quickly ring up Ace and ask him to track Jenna's phone and send the location to Cal. He will go get her and take her home. I take a deep breath. Knowing that Jenna is just out with a friend gives me momentary relief from the possessive, protective feeling surging through my body.

I need to deal with whatever is happening inside first, then I'll find her and remind her that she needs to take her safety seriously. We don't have round-the-clock security on all the club women for no reason. Jenna isn't technically a club woman, but they threatened her as one, so we decided as a club that she would be under our protection until we feel she is safe.

I step into the dark building and make my way toward the back. A large staircase leads to the VIP area the manager has cleared for our meeting. I see Prince and the guys making their way up and decide to take a quick scan of our surroundings. The second floor is covered in what appears to be black mirrors, but really, I know they are two-way mirrors. The VIP area gives the illusion of being in a secluded, untouchable area.

Swerving through the crowd, I catch sight of bright auburn hair at the bar. I keep walking, thinking nothing of it, then halt in my tracks, turning again. I take a closer look, and my heart slams in my chest. Jenna is here.

Fuck, she is here in a club full of Reapers. I can't help but take note of what she is wearing. Her perfect body is wrapped in a black dress that is painted on. The front of her dress stretches open to reveal a generous helping of cleavage. I instantly want to rip my shirt off and shove it over her torso.

Usually, I would be ogling a woman's chest if she put the goods out there like that. But she is hands down the most gorgeous woman in here, and every man within a ten-foot radius is checking her out. I want to slam my fist into the face of any fucker who looks at her. Something about this woman really sets off my inner cave man.

Her long, wavy hair beckons me to wrap my hand around it and take what is mine. Show everyone in this bar who she belongs to.

Mine? Belongs to? What the fuck is wrong with me?

I need to get Jenna out of here and call Sapphire to meet me at the clubhouse after we are done. Some other pussy will help get Jenna out of my system. I want to roll my eyes at myself. I know full well I haven't been able to get my dick up for the last few weeks for anyone but Jenna. And right now, I'm sporting a healthy rod in my pants.

I start to make my way to her when I realize she isn't alone; she is talking to some asshole who is way too close to her for my liking. I stop and pull my phone out to send Blaze a text.

Axel: Got a problem. Jenna is here.

Blaze: Shit, what is she doing here?

**Axel: Not sure. I'm going to get her out
of here.**

**Blaze: Okay, I'll handle things here.
Check in when you're done.**

I text Cal, letting him know Jenna is with me and he can
go home for the night. I know Sarah is at her mom's tonight, so
Cal has some rare free time.

I put my phone back in my pocket and head for Jenna.
She doesn't even see me approaching her as she stands at the
crowded bar. It pisses me off; she needs to be more aware of her
surroundings. I put my arms on either side of her, enclosing her
in front of me. I press myself to her, needing her body against
mine. I feel her go rigid at first, but then she melts against me.

I lean into her ear, "Hey, baby." I say so only she can
hear me. She turns in my arms, a surprised look covering her
gorgeous face. I stare into her mesmerizing green eyes and
breathe in her scent. Her just being this close to me soothes my
soul. She is slowly wrapping herself around my heart, and she
doesn't even know it.

Before she can respond, the man she is talking to postures
and glares in my direction. "What the fuck, take your hands
off of her, Chaser," he says in a demanding tone. I don't even
move, just raise my eyes to glare at the pathetic man standing
in front of us. He obviously doesn't know who the fuck I am or
he would be long gone by now.

Jenna whips her head around to him, almost as if forgetting
he is there. "Oh, Jack, it's okay. This is my, um, this is Axel," she

finally gets out. I smirk at her and nod at the fucker who thinks he can step up to me. I let it go, seeing as how my mission is to get Jenna out of here as quickly as possible.

"I'm her Axel," I say with a *fuck-you* smile. That earns me a sideways glance from Jenna.

The blonde-headed man stares at us with disgust, and it makes me want to bash his face into the bar. Who the hell is this guy? Jenna turns around to face me once again, my hands still on either side of her.

"What are you doing here?" she says curiously.

"I could ask you the same thing, Angel," I say, eyeing her as she glares at me like I'm not allowed to question her. My little badass. Most grown men cower when I level them with my anger, but Jenna just puts her hands on her hips and reciprocates my glare. She hasn't been afraid of me since day one and something about that makes me happy.

"For your information, I'm here with my coworker and her friends." She points a perfectly manicured finger in the direction of a table across the room. I look over my shoulder to see a group of people so plastered they probably won't remember half the night. I move so that my face is directly in front of hers.

"We will talk about this at your apartment, but right now it's not safe for you to be here. I need to get you out of here." I think she will respond best to the truth. I don't want to scare her, but I need to get her somewhere safe. She looks up at me through her long black eyelashes. Even in her heels, the top of her head only comes up to my shoulder.

With hands still on her hips, her shoulders relax a bit.

"Okay, but I want to know what's going on when we get out of here. You're making me nervous," she says as I drop my hands to her hips, pulling her to me. The smell of lavender and vanilla wafts around us. God, I miss her. These past few weeks have been torture for me; I can't get her out of my head. She sighs against me, and for a moment I wonder if she's been wrestling with the same feelings.

"Let me pay my tab, and we can go." She turns and gives the bartender a wave. He races over to her. Jenna hands him her card and then looks up at the blonde asshole, still staring at us, stunned. I haven't forgotten his presence, just don't give a fuck. My hands never leave her body.

"It was nice seeing you, Jack. I think I'm going to head home," she says, giving him one of her beauty-queen smiles. He looks from her to me. It's obvious he wants to say something, but wisely keeps quiet. I can't put my finger on it, but something is off about this guy. I will have to ask Jenna about him later. We head toward the door. I keep her smaller hand in mine as I lead us out of the crowded club. Exiting the front, I feel her shiver and pull her into my side.

"Where's your car?"

"It's right there," she points to her compact black SUV in the front row. We start to walk that way.

"How much have you had to drink?" I question her, studying the side of her perfect profile. She lets out an annoyed chuckle. "I barely had half of my drink. I'm okay. Promise."

I nod at her in approval. "Good. Now I need you to drive to your apartment. I'm going to ride behind you."

She shakes her head and sighs. "Why? I'll be fine, Axel.

You must be here for something important. Don't worry about me."

I stop abruptly and pull her in front of me. "Jen, you are important." I stop for a moment, unsure if I should continue and let her know I've been keeping a close eye on her for the last few weeks. "I worry about you every day. Now, you are going to get in the car and drive home with me behind you. I won't be able to focus without knowing you're home safe," I say in a gruff voice. She blinks at me for a moment, then smiles.

"I missed you too," she says as she closes the gap between us.

Before I know it, she is in my arms, and my lips are on hers. I trace the seam of her plump lips with my tongue, and she opens for me, allowing my tongue to explore every inch of her mouth. She fits so perfectly against my body I want to keep her there forever. She pulls away. "Okay fine, you can come home with me," she says with a small laugh. I can't help but smile at her. "But only if you– " she stops talking as shouting rings out behind us. I move Jenna behind me and take the gun out from my waistband. I feel her shuffle behind me, trying to see what is happening. With my free hand, I reach back and squeeze her hip. "Jenna, be still," I demand in a low voice.

She grips the back of my cut as I catch sight of what's happening. I need to get Jenna into her car without bringing attention to us.

Chapter 14

JENNA

"WHAT THE FUCK do you mean you ain't starting shit? Why else would you have come here?" a man whose voice I don't recognize yells. Axel pulls me behind his large frame, and I struggle to see around him. He pulls a gun from the back of his waistband, and I instantly freeze. Why does he need that?

"Shut the fuck up, Stab. You need to back off before this gets ugly. You don't want to start this war," another man says in a low growl. That voice I do recognize. I peek around Axel's shoulder. Blaze and another equally terrifying man are face-to-face. They look like they are going to tear each other limb from limb. The other man, who I now know is named Stab, starts to laugh—a slow, creepy laugh that makes my skin crawl. Not even a second later, the man pulls out a gun and rests the barrel on Blaze's temple. *Great more guns.*

I panic. Blaze has spent the last week staying at our

apartment with Marley. I wasn't sure about him at first, but I have come to realize that he actually is great. He takes the time to show how much he loves and cares for Marley, and that makes him okay in my book. I lightly gasp at the sight. Axel's hand still rests on my hip, and he gives me a reassuring squeeze. I have been so focused on the two men arguing in front of me that I hadn't noticed the crowd that has formed around them. Both Hell's Chasers and Reapers are surrounding both sides, guns drawn, waiting for someone to make the first move. Blaze stands calm at the center of the storm.

Axel slowly starts to walk me back toward the cars. Part of me wants him to stop, to not draw any attention to us. But he is the expert in this situation. I slowly move with him, keeping my body as close as possible to his. In what feels like only a few steps, my back is pressed to the cold metal of my car.

If I wasn't so close to Axel, I probably wouldn't hear him say, "Wait for me in the car, Jenna. Lock the doors." I slowly unlock the driver's side door and slide onto the soft leather seat. Axel keeps his back to me the whole time, staying focused on what is happening with Blaze. Before he closes the door, I look at the back of Axel's cut and say a silent prayer. I didn't tell Axel, but the nightmare I had the morning after we slept together was about him. And right now, it's all I can think about.

I'm standing in the middle of a large, lush green yard. My white dress pools around me. Looking out into the orange and pink sunset, I feel content and safe. I slide my hands down the soft, buttery fabric and adjust my veil that sits at the back of my head. My thick auburn hair is pinned back on one side, the rest cascading down my back and shoulders in soft curls. My dress is an off-the-shoulder A-line wedding dress that accentuates my large breasts and small waist. A modest slit shows off my right leg and my gorgeous sparkly pumps.

I look down again, admiring my almost glowing gown, but now I have a large bouquet in my hands. I faintly hear a man off to the side of me and look around to see that I am not alone but in the middle of a wedding. My wedding.

Gazing out across the never-ending rows of people, I find Marley front and center next to my parents. They look so excited and happy, tears falling from their faces. I look off into the distance again. The same sunset seems to have paused in place, leaving the perfect golden hue over the ceremony. I follow the gorgeous view to the man standing in front of me—Axel.

He is the most beautiful man I've ever laid eyes on. His broad, muscular form is perfectly fitted in a dark navy suit. His face is completely clean-shaven, and he smiles at me with the most adoring look. His chocolate eyes are illuminated by the soft orange glow of the sunset. I am now noticing that there are hints of blue throughout his irises. My breath hitches in my chest. I'm marrying Axel, the man who has set my world on fire.

The voice I heard only slightly before is loud and present. A minister is standing to the left of me and is asking me to repeat after him. I recite my vows and slide Axel's ring onto his finger. Perfect fit. Then he turns to Axel, and they begin to go back and forth. The vows sound almost angelic from his mouth as he promises to love and cherish me. But as Axel continues to speak, blood starts to drip from his lips, and he becomes increasingly pale.

"Axel, stop. What's happening?" I say in a voice that doesn't sound like my own, a voice that only comes out as a whisper.

Axel drops to his knees, and I can now see blood pouring from his abdomen. I drop with him, screaming to the crowd of people around us, "Help him! Please, someone help him!" I feel hot tears leaking from my face as I grab onto the man in front of me. Axel's body falls into me, and I hold his head tight to my chest.

I look up to my parents and Marley. They are all still smiling and showing the same excitement as before. What's happening? Can't they see Axel is hurt?!

All I can do is rock with Axel, holding him close and soothing him with words of promise, "You're going to be fine! Look at me!" I say as I feel his body go limp against me.

"No, no, no!" I scream. This isn't right. This can't be happening. That's when I woke up.

"Please be safe. I'll wait for you right here," I say to Axel, keeping my voice down. I want to grab him and pull him into the car with me, not let him rush into danger. But I also know this is a part of his life, the life I now find myself in.

Without looking back at me, Axel responds, "I'll try, Angel. Keep your head down and don't open the door for anyone but me." He then starts to walk back to the crowd as the front door of the bar bursts open. Prince steps out with a deadly look on his face. I am too far now to hear what is being said, but within seconds, all hell breaks loose.

Chapter 15

AXEL

HAVING JENNA HERE makes this messy, makes me messy. I can't turn back and look at her in her car. I know that if I do, I won't be able to do what needs to be done. The club always has to come first, before anything else. I try to shake off the sinking feeling in my gut. Never once have I ever thought about putting anything or anyone before the club. I need to put as much distance as I can between Jenna and me after this is over. I want to punch myself. How the fuck am I supposed to do that when it has been hell staying away from her these past few weeks? *You have to do it*, rings in my head. *Jenna needs someone who can give her a white picket fence and a stable life.* This lifestyle isn't right for her. I'm not right for her.

I take small, light steps toward the center of the crowd now forming in the parking lot. Before I make it to Blaze, the front door slams open. Prince saunters out with a dangerous smirk on his face. He looks calm, but his eyes glow with disgust and anger.

If Jenna wasn't here, I would be excited at the idea of getting my hands dirty with Reaper blood. It's the reason I was made Enforcer. I protect my Prez and club and make anyone pay who threatens either. I'm not ashamed of what I do. I know what has to be done, and I'm good at my job.

"This is how you show us fucking respect at a meeting you set up?" Prez turns around. I can barely make out the figure of a man standing in the shadow of the doorway. I keep my body moving forward, getting myself into the center of the mob. A bright red beard and bald head are illuminated by the outdoor lights as the man Prince talks to steps outside. He has a snake tattoo that wraps around his neck, the head of the snake placed next to his mouth. I haven't seen Red since he was made VP a few years back. After their Prez was killed last fall, he took over. The Reapers have been going down a bad path since.

"We may have had a meeting, but we never came to an agreement. You don't want to give me what I deserve, then there is no respect," Red spits out. A devilish look crosses his face as he turns back to go inside. "Finish this," he calls out over his shoulder. He isn't even going to fight with his men. A fucking pussy is what he is.

Within an instant, the parking lot descends into chaos, the Reapers come from all sides, boxing us in. This whole thing was a setup.

I shove my gun back into my waistband and take down the first Reaper I see. I feel the change happen the moment my fist connects with his chin. I am no longer Dane but Axel—

the Enforcer for one of the most notorious one-percenter Motorcycle Clubs. The sound of bone breaking and the feeling of blood coating my hands brings me to life in a way most wouldn't understand.

My vision tunnels as I take out everyone in my path. Then I catch sight of the man I have been looking for, Death. He had threatened my club; he had threatened Jenna. He had signed his death warrant. I turn and start in his direction when a Reaper launches himself at me. I move my body, allowing myself to take the hit with ease. We are on the ground grappling when his head comes down on my brow in a crack. I feel a sharp sting and then hot liquid slithers down my face. *Motherfucker.*

I maneuver my body so that I am perpendicular to his torso. He is big, but doesn't have nearly as much training as I do. I place my legs over his chest while pulling his arm up to my ear. The snap of his shoulder and the sound of his scream is music to my ears. *Fucker wanted to play, so let's play.* I stand, grabbing my Glock from my waistband and pointing it at his head. The look in his eyes tells me he's accepting his fate, dying protecting his piece-of-shit club. Instead of killing him, I slam the butt of the gun against his temple. I'm not going away for murder tonight. I whistle for a prospect who has just beaten the shit out of a Reaper, and he runs over without pause.

"He leaves with us, *alive*," I grind out. Shiny is a newer prospect, but I can see he will make a good brother. He looks at the man and then back to me.

"We need him for information," I explain. Not that I really fucking need to. Prospects should do as they're told without question or explanation. Shiny nods and lifts the man's limp body from the pavement.

I smirk when I see my target once again. The Reapers' enforcer has quite the reputation. He is what horror stories are built on. I had asked Ace to look into him, see what shit he is into. You name it: guns, drugs, human trafficking. This guy is a psycho with no conscience, and that makes him extremely dangerous. I will be doing a service to the public by putting a bullet between his eyes.

The Hell Chasers are in no way good guys. We run guns and launder money through our more legit businesses. We are outlaws; normal laws don't apply to us. But the moment I learned about the trafficking and selling of drugs near Cranson, I knew this needed to be dealt with.

Death catches sight of me and turns to give me his full attention. He smirks, much as I am, but his eyes say it all. They are hollow, dead, unaware of the monster he is.

Almost to him, I hear bikes from all directions and shots blasting around us. I look up to see a brigade of Hell Chasers storming the area. Pride swells in my chest as my brothers make their way to us. I drop my head to avoid the shots.

When I look back to the spot where Death stood, it is empty. My blood boils as I look around the lot, catching a glimpse of his bike as he tears out of here. I almost go after him, but tonight we hadn't driven our bikes. We had taken two SUVs to not attract attention. I curse myself for not bringing my hog.

"Let's get the fuck out of here," I hear someone shout behind me. Looking back, I see my brothers racing to their bikes or hopping into cars. I move my eyes to the only vehicle

I care about.

The black SUV sits in the same spot, but now the windows are gone, only shards of glass hanging onto the window panes. Much like most of the cars that surround us. I can see a body on the front of the car, boots staring me in the face and Cal looking at me with fury in his eyes. *Fuck*.

Chapter 16

JENNA

I LEAN FORWARD in the driver's seat as far as I can and try to keep my breath steady. All I can hear is shouting and glass breaking. My mind races with all the things that could be happening outside the car. Who am I kidding? I know exactly what's happening out there, and none of it is good. I'll do as I promised, though—I'm going to stay right here and wait for Axel, even though every part of me is screaming to put the car in reverse and hightail it out of here.

My car shakes with an extremely loud thud, followed by a loud cracking sound. The sudden movement has me ducking my head and shrieking into the otherwise quiet car. I look up to see a man on my now broken windshield, his lifeless eyes staring at me. Instantly, I lean over the passenger seat and throw up any remaining contents in my stomach. I hold back tears threatening to fall down my face. This is insane—I need to get out of here.

Without thinking, I pick up my phone and call Cal. Over the short time he had been stuck doing surveillance for us we had developed a friendship, and I trust him. He picks up after the second ring.

"Teach?" he says in a groggy voice.

Shots pop around me, my body tensing with each one. "C-Cal," I reply, trying to calm the shake in my voice. The tears I was trying to keep at bay spill onto my cheek now.

"Jenna, what's wrong?" I can hear rustling in the background. "Axel said he was with you. Where is he?"

"I don't know," I say, steadying my voice. "We were leaving the club when a guy got into it with Blaze. Everyone came outside, and the man—well, biker... Reaper—pulled out a gun." I look up at the man still staring at me through my windshield. God, I hope I'm making sense. "I'm in my car, but Axel went back." I pause, still trying to gather myself.

"And now there is a fucking dead guy on my car," I say as my voice breaks. *Damnit, Jenna, hold it together!* I have never been one to use expletives but I think this moment calls for it.

"Okay, take a deep breath. I'm going to call the clubhouse and get guys there. Where is your car?" he says in a calm but deathly serious voice. I consider telling him again about the dead person on my car, his level of concern for the situation not matching my own.

"I'm in the front row, a few cars left of the entrance." I look up to see a fury of men. "Cal, please hurry. This doesn't seem right." Looking up, I can tell there are way more Reapers than Chasers. "There are twice as many of them here." My heart sinks in my chest.

"Fuck." I hear a motorcycle start and can barely hear Cal's next sentence. "Keep your head down, Teach. We're coming." Then the line goes dead.

I look back toward the front of the club; it's turned into a full-on brawl. I've never seen so many people fighting— punching, kicking, and throwing bodies through the air before. I run my hand along the door, making sure it's locked, and start looking for Axel. I can't find him in the sea of fists and leather.

My chest tightens, and I dig my nails into my palms. I try to tell myself that the only reason I'm searching for him is to make sure my friend is okay. But in my gut, I know I can never just be friends with Axel. This right here is what I should have been prepared for. Entangling in his world means getting dragged into violence, and I don't think I can handle this. For Pete's sake, my daily tasks include deciding what craft pairs well with my daily read aloud. Not what dress pairs well with blood.

I don't know how long I've been waiting, but out of nowhere; I hear the rumble of motorcycles in the distance. It sounds like thunder tearing through the dark night. Men start yelling, and more shots ring out. Glass shatters around me as my windows burst from the outside in. I drop my head down and don't look up again. I hear boots hitting the asphalt as and men shouting around me while motorcycles roar to life only to become quieter as they fly into the distance. Everything becomes eerily silent. I try to move, but my body is frozen in place. Seconds that feel like years pass as I stare at the back of my eyelids, holding my eyes shut to block out everything around me. A silent buzz seems to wrap itself around me as I focus on my chest, rising and falling.

I barely register a hand entering my car through the now shattered window. They unlock the door and rip it open. Strong hands touch my shoulders, and I flinch back.

"Fuck, Jenna, it's me," Cal says in a gruff, concerned voice. I open my eyes and stare at my feet. The floorboard of my car is littered with shards of glass… and drops of blood. Looking up, I see the man on my windshield has now started to leak blood into the car and I don't think I will ever be normal again. *How can this just be normal to them?*

"Teach, look at me." This time, his voice is commanding. I slowly unfold myself and turn to him. His eyes meet mine, and I see them soften.

"There she is." He smiles, but I can't return the expression.

"Hey, you, okay?" Quickly, his face darkens with concern. My body starts shaking uncontrollably.

"I don't know what's wrong with me," I whisper, looking at him for help.

"Christ, you're going into shock." Cal takes off the sweater he's wearing underneath his cut and shoves it down over my head. He rubs his hands up and down my arms in fast motions. His sweatshirt engulfs me, giving me a false sense of security from the hell around me.

"Jenna, I need you to focus on me and my voice, okay?" he says in a tone similar to one used to comfort caged animals. I nod at him and try to copy his long breaths. After four deep gulps of air, the fog starts to lift from my brain, but my body still isn't cooperating. Just then, a large figure appears behind Cal. I look up to see Axel staring down at us. *He's okay.*

Cal looks back at me with a frown on his face. "I'm going to grab you some water," he says, moving to leave. As he walks by Axel, he says something to him, but it's too low for me to hear. Axel's jaw twitches at whatever Cal says, but he never takes his eyes off me.

I take note of his injuries. His beautiful face is covered in cuts and bruises. Above his left eye is a gash that's leaking blood all over him. Speaking of blood, he's practically covered. If I knew any better, I would run for my life. But I know deep down that Axel would never hurt me. I still want to be wrapped in his arms and have some sense of protection. *What the hell, Jenna? You should be running from this man, not making him your solitude.*

Axel drops to his haunches in front of me, just as Cal had been. I bring my shaking hand up to cradle his face, careful not to touch anything that's hurt. His large, calloused hand comes up to cover mine, as he leans into my palm. The look on his face is still serious, and I know the man before me is an Axel I've yet to meet.

"You're alive," I say in a small voice, trying to will myself into staying calm. I hadn't realized how scared I was for him, for all the men I've come to know.

"I'll always come back to you," he says as he brings my palm to his mouth. He places a soft kiss on each of my knuckles. Staring at the sweet gesture, I catch sight of my hand, which is covered in small cuts. I take a moment to look at each one and then let my gaze return to Axel. His eyes follow mine. I see his jaw tick once again, and a flush of rage passes across his face.

He slowly looks up at me. "Babe, I know there's a lot of shit we need to sort through, but we have to get out of here." Just then, I hear sirens in the distance.

Looking around, I'm now aware that the motorcycles I had heard were Hell Chasers. Dozens of them are in the parking lot waiting for us and my stomach churns at the sight. I should be nobody to them. Axel's arms wrap around me as he picks me up out of the car. I quickly grab my purse and phone before I'm hefted into the air.

"Wait, stop, what are you doing? I can walk, you know!" I protest.

"Hush, I need you close. And you are shaking like a leaf," Axel says in my ear.

Even though my brain is telling me this is absolutely ridiculous, I stop wiggling and settle into him. I need him close as well. A sudden wave of exhaustion crashes over my body.

I rest my head in the crook of his neck and breathe in his soothing scent. I close my eyes, trying not to take in more of the scene around me. I already know the face of the man on top of my car will haunt me for the rest of my life. I don't need to add any other gruesome images to my memories.

I feel Axel step up into a vehicle. Without setting me down, he settles into the backseat with me on his lap. I look around the interior of the seemingly brand-new SUV. Noting that we're not the only people in the car. Eyes land on me from all directions. Jax, Bear, and Blaze fill the silent car. Blaze finally speaks from the front seat.

"Are you okay?" His eyes scan me.

I shake my head. "No, I'm not." my voice cracks as I take in all their faces. They're all bleeding and bruised. "Are you okay?" He gives me a quick nod in the rearview mirror and pulls out of the lot onto the dark highway.

I've only seen Blaze with Marley; he's usually kind and lighthearted. That is not the man sitting in this car. It seems like these men are each two different people—the every day, caring men they are with their families and friends, and the bikers who rule the county.

"Listen, Jenna, what you saw tonight—" Blaze begins to speak, but Axel quickly cuts in.

"She's not going to fucking talk, Blaze." I furrow my brow at the exchange. *Talk to who?*

I try to move out of Axel's hold, but his hands tighten around me. I focus my glare at Blaze in the mirror. "You're worried about me talking to the police?" I scoff. "Honestly, Blaze, if I was going to talk to the police, it would have been the night the Reaper's enforcer came to my school. Or when an outlaw motorcycle club decided my apartment needed 24/7 protection." The fear inside me turns to searing rage. I feel the anger bubbling out of my pores. The stress and anxiety of the last few weeks finally rise to the surface. How dare he turn this on me?

"Jenna, I just have to make sure," Blaze says in a curt voice, like he has a right to question my loyalty. But they need to remember that they pulled me into this. I didn't come running to them.

I lean back against Axel's chest, not wanting to be a part of this conversation anymore. I can't trust myself not to lash out at Blaze and say something I can't take back. We'll talk about this another time.

The silence in the car conveys more than words. Tonight, a war has started. No longer is anyone safe. I take a deep breath and stare out the black window.

Chapter 17

AXEL

Jenna fell asleep about ten minutes ago. Her body finally relaxes into me, and her breathing evens. She probably is crashing from an adrenaline dump and will feel like shit when she wakes up. I study her small form; she sits across my lap and buries her face into the crook of my neck. I finally take a deep breath.

She is safe.

From the moment I saw her in that club, my insides had felt as if they were being ripped apart with worry over her. I close my eyes and try to even my breathing. How did I let this happen? She somehow entered my life and burrowed into my heart without even trying. I rub my hand up her back with featherlight strokes, careful not to wake her. Cal's words from earlier ring in my head.

"She called me. That's how we knew to come. She's tough, but she needs you right now."

Jenna saved our asses tonight, and she doesn't even realize it. That's why it pisses me off so bad Blaze even questioned her.

Gunner took a bad shot to the shoulder, and Max—a new prospect—took a shot to the leg. Other than that, we had come out unscathed. Both men were rushed back to the clubhouse where Doc was waiting for them. Doc used to be an ER doctor before he retired and comes anytime we need his medical assistance.

"Axel, what do you want to do with her?" Blaze asks from the front seat.

"She's coming back to the clubhouse with me until this gets figured out." I keep my voice low.

Blaze nods, still staring out onto the street ahead. "Marley is on her way back now; she'll be staying with me." His neck muscles tense. "I won't take any chances with her. I'm going to claim her in Church."

Holy fuck. Claiming a woman is like marrying her in the eyes of the club. It gives our women protection and security from other clubs or danger. Blaze is taking a big step, making her his. I can't help my smirk; Blaze deserves this.

"Good for you, brother. She's a good woman and keeps you in line."

For a split second, Blaze's eyes meet mine in the rearview mirror. Jax and Bear fell asleep in the back around the same time Jenna did, so we're the only ones hearing this conversation.

"I know you're going to do whatever you want, but let me make myself clear." He turns the steering wheel and seems to melt back into the seat. *Oh, here we fucking go.*

"Jenna isn't like the club girls that hang around. She isn't just some chick you can fuck and walk away." He says while staring out the front window. "She has become close with some of the brothers and fits in well with the women. We all like Jenna."

I glare at the back of Blaze's head as he speaks. Who the fuck does he think he is? And who the hell does he think I am? I know damn well Jenna isn't some club girl looking for strange. She's the opposite of every other woman I've ever met. She's courageous, witty, and gives me a run for my money. She's a ray of sunshine in any room she enters and makes even my grumpy ass feel at ease around her. But Blaze has no right to concern himself with my relationship. I don't say shit about the women in his life, so he needs to back the fuck off.

"She means a lot to Marley, and over the last few weeks, I've learned why. Jenna is not like us, Axel. So don't do this if you're just going to treat her like a club slut."

That's the last straw. "Blaze, you have no right to fucking tell me what to do. If I want to fuck Jenna and that's it, then that's my business. If I want more, that's also my business, not yours. Stay out of it." I need to set the record straight with Blaze. He has no business questioning my intentions. Blaze is my best friend, and I've never seen him try to protect someone from me, but for some reason, he feels he needs to protect her. Which pisses me off because I've never led a woman on or treated her with anything but respect. But something he doesn't realize is I don't think I can let her go.

"See, that's where you're wrong, and this is the last thing I'll say about it." He now glares at me in the rearview mirror. "Fuck this up, and I'll beat the shit out of you. Walk away now, and I can put a prospect at her door. She'll be safe."

The safest place for her is with me. I go to speak, but an ugly, visceral feeling creeps its way through my body, rendering me momentarily speechless. Am I being selfish?

I can't be what she needs me to be. I can't be the man who works a safe job and comes home to her every night at 5 p.m. so we can live a happy little life with a white picket fence and a fluffy dog. But this primal urge to hold onto her and never let her go—to have her body, to ruin her, to make her mine—had grabbed ahold of me and hasn't let go.

"Drive to the clubhouse," I growl at him. A small part of me likes the fact that my brother is protecting Jenna as if she's already family. I know she's safe with the club, but I can't let Blaze think he can fucking parent me. "If you ever question me or threaten me again, we're going to have a fucking problem." I don't care that he's my VP or my best friend. I spit the words out as if they're laced with venom, ending the conversation.

We drive into the compound. Blaze, Jax, and Bear exit the vehicle. Before closing his door, Blaze turns to me with a hard glare before his gaze drops to Jenna, softening a bit. He quickly closes the door and stalks into the clubhouse, leaving Jenna and me alone, wrapped in silence.

I bring my mouth down right next to Jenna's ear, speaking softly so as not to startle her. "Baby, wake up. We're here."

I would carry her inside, but knowing her, she probably wouldn't be a fan of that idea. Jenna likes to be independent, which is one of the things I like about her.

She stirs, her face scrunching with annoyance and then smoothing back out as she nestles into me.

"Leave me alone," she says in a pouty tone.

I can't help the small chuckle as I rub my hand down the side of her face. Brushing my thumb back and forth across her cheek, I sit her up so she has to wake up.

"Angel, you need to wake up." Her eyes pop open as if realizing she's still asleep in the car. Jenna softly rubs her eyes with the palms of her hands and then looks out the car window toward the compound.

"Wait, why are we here?" she asks, looking puzzled.

I take a moment, memorizing her gorgeous, relaxed face. Because in a moment, she's either going to be understanding or super pissed.

"You're going to stay here at the clubhouse with me until we figure out what our plan is for the Reapers."

I watch as her face quickly morphs into an annoyed grimace. "If it makes it any better, Marley is going to be staying here too. She's on her way back now," I blurt out. I don't know why I try to soothe her annoyance. She is staying whether she likes it or not. It's not safe for her to be anywhere else.

"I'm sorry, but you can't be serious. I want to go back to my apartment... tonight. I am not staying here," she growls with aggravation. "Axel, this is ridiculous. I need to go home. I need to figure out what to do about my car. I need to take a hot shower." She finally looks at me with tired eyes.

Jenna begins to chew on her bottom lip in an anxious movement, making my dick kick to life in my pants. I can't help myself. Whenever she's near me, my cock is insatiable.

"Your apartment isn't safe right now," I say, letting out a deep breath. "I'll deal with your car, and you can take a shower upstairs in my room." I run my fingers through her soft, fiery locks. "Just let me take care of everything tonight, and we can talk it all out in the morning."

She lets out a dejected huff. "Seems like you've thought of everything."

My only response is a quick wink before I reach for the door handle. Her hand lands on mine as I pull the handle.

"Wait, what about that guy on my car? What about the whole fight tonight? Won't you all be arrested? Wait, will I be arrested?" Her voice sounds frantic as the reality of tonight settles in. "Axel I'll lose my job!"

I wrap my fingers around her hand, trying not to touch the small cuts that cover her delicate skin.

"Jenna, none of us are going to jail. Don't worry about any of this," I say in a calm, commanding voice. I want to say that the Hell Chasers have the sheriff and a few deputies on the payroll. None of this is blowing back on the club; we weren't even in Chasers' territory when it happened. But she doesn't get to know that information. Frowning, she nods and lets my hand go.

I open the door, letting the cold air whip us in the face. I fucking hate this weather. I wrap my arm around her and pull her into my side as we walk to the clubhouse. Once inside, my brothers all nod toward us as we make our way to the stairs.

"Church in an hour," Prez bellows from where he sits at the bar. Jenna looks up at me, and I can't help but smile at her confusion. Her eyebrows scrunch together in the cutest fucking way. Glancing around the room, I don't miss the glares the club girls are shooting Jenna's way. It pisses me off because they have no claim to this club, no claim to any member. I make a mental note to deal with this shit tomorrow. Tonight, all I want is to wrap myself around Jenna and sleep.

Chapter 18

JENNA

ALL EYES ARE on us we make our way to his room. Walking through the common space feels like walking the plank. I keep my head high and try not to let the glares and eye rolls get to me. What is that about? I don't even know any of these girls. I've come to the clubhouse a few times with Marley and Cal since my one night with Axel, but none of the women ever gave me a second look. Now it seems I'm the star of some twisted show. I only see a few of the guys but they are too busy doing other stuff to really pay us any mind. What happened tonight was big.

Stepping onto the second floor, I'm shocked by how many doors line the long hallway. This clubhouse is like Mary Poppins' bag—just when I feel like I've seen it all, an entire second wing pops up. Axel leads me down the hall until we stop in front of a large mahogany door with the number four nailed to the front. Fishing his keys from his pocket, Axel opens the heavy door and gestures with a slight nod of his head for me to enter.

Pausing, I take a moment to rethink complying with his plan for me to stay. What is Axel thinking? I can't stay here... with him. This is a disaster waiting to happen. We had a deal. I ultimately decide I've made it this far, so turning around isn't an option.

No going back now.

I drop my shoulders and walk into his room, immediately smacked in the face with his delicious scent. I revel in it for a moment, letting it cocoon me like a soft blanket. To my left, I see a bright white bathroom with black honeycomb tiles on the floor. In the back of the bathroom is a generous glass shower, making me yearn for the hot shower I've been promised. The idea of washing away all traces of today from my body sounds fantastic.

Axel's hand softly lands on the small of my back, making me almost purr at the connection. *No, stop. Remember the deal*, my inner voice snarls at me.

Honestly, who are we kidding? For some reason, Axel and I are always being pulled to each other, whether we like it or not. I don't understand it, but just having him near makes me feel whole, as if nothing and no one could harm me. Axel's gentle touch burns my back as he guides me further into the room. He doesn't look at me, but the small tick of his jaw lets me know he isn't unaffected by this moment, either. The intense energy between us is almost palpable, sending lightning through my body at his slight touch.

Light gray walls and black leather furniture adorn the room. The space is well put together but not at all what I expected. A twinge of guilt fills my chest at the realization that I've judged Axel based on the fact that he's a biker. I thought I'd be walking into a gross, thrown-together dorm room, but instead, I stand in the center of a lavish apartment.

Axel's bed sits at the far wall of the room, its grand black leather headboard and ginormous size taking up most of the space. All the bedding is black, like his furniture. The only hint that this room is Axel's is his boots by the front door and the motorcycle magazines on the bedside table.

"Is black your favorite color?" I ask, still snooping around the room.

"Prince's ol' lady was a part of renovating the club house. She wanted everything to look nice but also feel like it was ours." He says, eyeing me from where he stands. Axel watches me cautiously and I wonder if that's because I'm in his space or because he thinks I might fall apart.

That makes a lot of sense. Everything is so organized and orderly; you can tell that the space was well designed. I instantly feel relaxed in this room; the comfort of Axel is everywhere, and it's a welcome reprieve from the evening. Masculinity and control—exactly the two words I would use to describe Axel's style.

The shrill sound of Axel's ringtone slices through the silence like a sharp knife. He gives me a wary look before pulling his phone out of his pocket. I decide to walk toward the window on the other side of the room to give him space. Glancing back at Axel, I note how tight his jaw is clenched and how intense his focus is on the screen. Part of me wants to ask him what's wrong but I know I probably won't be able to handle any more bad news tonight.

I turn back to look out the window. It's dark, and I can't really make much out except for the moderately sized rectangular patio that sits behind the clubhouse. I spot some of the members out around a fire pit, lost in conversation. Others sit at one of the picnic benches, smoking. Even from up here, I can feel the tense energy everyone is carrying.

I sense the moment Axel comes up behind me, as if my body seeks his out. I feel his feather-light touch brush my hair back as he slowly leaves a trail of soft kisses from my shoulder to my ear. Lightning once again strikes through my body, and I force the moan threatening to escape my throat back down.

"I have to make a call. Go ahead and take a shower. I'll set out a towel for you," he says as he intertwines his fingers with mine and leads me to the bathroom.

I move with him, our bodies moving in sync, when I realize I only have my purse, which is filled with cash, mints, and my phone.

"Wait, I have nothing to wear." Looking down at the large sweatshirt that Cal gave me and heels, it's clear I wasn't expecting an impromptu sleepover tonight. Without missing a beat, Axel walks over to the tall dresser next to his bed and grabs a white t-shirt. He hands me the shirt and kisses the top of my head as if he's done it a million times before. He's being so sweet with me right now, and I can't help but swoon a little. I love this side of Axel, the man only I get to see.

"Go." He turns me by the shoulders and gives me a quick

pat on my butt. I shiver at his gruff voice, and my core clenches as his hand kneads my backside for a swift moment before he's gone.

I walk into the bathroom, close the door behind me, and lean my back against the cool wood before remembering why I came in here. I glance at the mirror as I walk to the shower, expecting to see myself, but the woman looking back at me is one I don't recognize. I stop and confront my reflection; my face is pale, and dark circles have formed around my bloodshot eyes. I could seriously use a makeup wipe and about ten hours of sleep.

Pulling Cal's sweater over my head and shimmying my tight dress down my body, I examine the bathroom. There's nothing on the counters, and the black towels are perfectly folded and draped on the towel rack next to the sliding glass door. It is sparse, just like the bedroom. Axel could leave tomorrow, and no one would ever know he lived here.

Sliding the large shower door open, I notice the rectangular shower head is mounted directly in the center of the ceiling. A rainfall shower. In this moment, I'm extremely grateful Axel had me stay. *This is going to be glorious.*

Stepping onto the matte black tiles, my feet relish in the amazing feeling of the heated floor underneath them. The handle for the shower is placed on the back wall. The moment I turn it on, the room fills with warm steam, and a downpour of water falls from the ceiling. Heaven is a word that comes to mind. I wish I could truly enjoy this moment, but the anxiety and panic from today still courses through me. I feel nauseous and gross. I move so that the water is perfectly overhead, bowing my head so the hot water sears my scalp and neck. I can instantly tell the water temperature is too high, but I feel like I need it to be scalding. I want to fry the violence and grimy feeling of today off my body.

"Jesus, babe!"

I nearly jump out of my skin at Axel's voice. I've been so lost in my thoughts that I hadn't noticed him come in. Opening my eyes, I catch sight of his perfectly toned, extremely naked body reaching over to the handle on the wall. I barely register the temperature change as I stare at the large tattoo that covers his back. A black-and-white skull sits in the center, flanked with long black wings that start from right below his shoulder blades and land at his hips. The wings look as if they've been singed by flames. Across the top of his back, the words *Hell Chasers* stand out in bold lettering. Across the bottom, in the same style, reads *Till Death*. My gaze travels over his body, memorizing every delicious piece of him. His toned, olive skin glistens in the steam, my body tingles with need. This man doesn't even have to touch me, and I'm putty in his hands. Glancing over his shoulder, he catches me staring, awestruck by his godlike form. My brain tells me to look away and stop being so creepy, but my body decides against it.

"Did that hurt?" I say in a breathy voice. Maybe he'll think my staring is purely innocent interest instead of horny lust. Axel walks past me, grabbing the bottle of shampoo from a square built-in shelf on the wall. When he turns back, he's squeezing some into his hand. Slowly, he massages the thick liquid between his fingers. The motion seems so sexually charged that I think I'm starting to go insane. He's just rubbing shampoo between his fingers. I mean, honestly, Jenna, get a grip.

"Hurt like a bitch, but I was so drunk I really only felt the pain the next morning," he says in a dangerously sexy voice.

"And the other ones? Were you drunk for those, too?" I let my eyes trail down the obscene amount of black-and-white ink that covers his chest and arms. A smile pulls at the corner of his mouth. "Not all of them, but many." Axel's body now stands behind me. All I can focus on is the sizzle of electricity I feel between our bodies. Well, that's not the only thing I feel between us. His dick is as hard as a rock, and right now, it's resting on my ass.

"Relax, Angel. I can hear you overthinking."

Without warning, he begins washing my hair, delightfully scrubbing my scalp, and massaging the shampoo into my thick mane. Letting my eyes close and my head drop back, I give in to the peaceful moment. Never before has a man washed my hair or touched me in such a loving way. I keep my eyes closed as he rinses the shampoo from my hair and conditions it.

"Turn to me." Axel's voice is low, almost strained. Turning slowly, I blink open my eyes to look at the sex god in front of me. Water drips down from his brow and slides over his delicious lips. He moves his hands until they're holding my hips in place. He puts slight pressure on each side of my hips, a way of telling me to move backward without words. Axel matches my steps and walks forward with me. I yelp at the sting of the cold tiles against my back. Never once does Axel take his smoldering brown eyes off mine.

Axel slowly lowers his head until his mouth rests at the base of my neck. He slides his mouth up as he kisses, sucks, and bites the expanse of my sensitive neckline until his lips finally meet mine. I nearly come undone from that action alone.

"I've missed this perfect fucking body." He speaks into my lips as the shower becomes a blur. A quick, possessive kiss is all I get before I'm spun around to face the wall. I place my hands out in front of me, steadying my body against the cool tile, such a stark contrast to the heat of my body. Axel wraps my hair around his hand, pulling slightly so my head dips back, exposing my neck to him. My chest heaves in the air as my breaths become fast and erratic.

Axel palms one of my heavy breasts in his hand. "Mmm, look at these fucking tits." Slowly, he starts his delicious torture, rolling and flicking my tender nipple between his fingers. A moan escapes my throat as my body melts into goo at his touch. My brain feels like it's short-circuiting from the pleasure surging through it, but this isn't part of the deal.

"What about our deal, Axel? We were supposed to be a one-night thing." I'm surprised I'm able to get the words out so clearly. A moan leaves my lips as his hold on me becomes tighter.

"Fuck the deal," he growls in my ear, never letting up on his sweet assault of my breasts.

"I'm not a good guy, Jenna. I should let you go. But, fuck…" His breathing becomes shallow and quick against my back. "I don't know if I can."

His hand travels down my stomach, beautiful tattoos splayed against my skin. Before his hand gets where I so desperately need him, he pauses. I almost groan with annoyance. The only sound around us now is the sound of the shower and our breathing.

"Tell me what you need, baby." I almost want to roll my eyes at him. Here we go again. Why does he always need to push me out of my comfort zone? Why does he need my words when my body so clearly conveys my want?

"Dane…" I pause, wanting him to continue his downward movement. He still holds my hair in his hand, not letting my head move from its position. His mouth rests on the corner of mine, but he doesn't kiss me.

"Angel… Tell me, or—"

"Fine!" I say in a loud, exasperated voice. I can't handle this anymore, and honestly, I don't care if he knows how badly I want him. I can feel his smile as a deep, sexy chuckle comes from his lips. Part of me wants to gouge his eyes out from how frustrated I feel, but the other part of me becomes sad at the thought of anything harming him.

"I want you, all of you. Inside me… now."

"Mmm, there she is, my perfect, dirty Angel." He speaks into my lips as he turns my head to the side. His mouth crushes into mine as his hand finally dips between my legs.

"I don't think you know how fucking hard it makes me to know you're this wet before I even touch you," Axel grunts.

"Oh, I can tell," I giggle, feeling his thick cock poke me in the back. Axel smirks and starts to rub my clit so perfectly that I feel my legs giving out from under me. Steadying me to him, Axel keeps his unrelenting pace. I involuntarily whimper when his masculine moan catches me off guard. He's so sexy. I need more, I need him.

"Not yet, babe." Axel says.

I freeze for a moment. Did I say that out loud?

Axel stops his torture only for a moment as he grabs the back of my knee and pulls my leg up so that my folded leg is pressed against the shower tiles next to me. This gives him full access to my entrance and without pause, he slams into me. My body tries to adjust to him, but he's so big. Axel peppers the side of my neck and shoulder with kisses as my body relaxes around him. He slowly, tormentingly, pulls out so only the head of him is still inside me, then slams back in. His hips move seamlessly, methodically pushing me off the cliff and into bliss.

"Touch yourself, Jenna," Axel huffs out between pumps. "I need you to cum with me, babe."

I move my hand between my legs and use my fingers to rub firm, tight circles. I lean my head back into his hand and let out a half-moan, half-scream. Stars dance in my vision as tingles start to spread through my body. My orgasm slams into me, and it takes everything I have not to collapse.

"That's it, baby. Fucking cum all over my cock," Axel growls, his words shoving me over into ecstasy. My body tightens and contracts around him. Axel pumps into me faster and harder, still holding me in place as he chases his own release. Two more pumps and his muscles ripple along my back. God, he's so hot.

Axel pulls out of me, still gently holding me as I turn to face him. His mouth crushes mine in a kiss that makes my body heat again. *Down, girl,* my inner voice chants at me.

Pulling me back under the water, Axel grabs the body wash and washes us both. My mind races to keep up with him and his ability to switch from biker badass to sex god to the sweet romantic now standing before me.

Once he's done, he turns off the shower and opens the steamy door. Axel steps out first and grabs a towel from the rack, holding it open for me. Wrapping the soft bath sheet around my body, I realize it's heated—of course it's heated. Although this man is rugged and tough, he sure likes to be comfortable. Axel looks over to his phone on the counter. The screen is lit up with a litter of notifications.

Anxiety once again sits in my stomach like a lead ball as memories of what happened tonight flood my brain. I find a moment of reprieve to be sucked back into the drama of this motorcycle club.

He pulls me close and kisses my forehead. "There's an extra toothbrush and toiletries in the drawer over there," he points to a deep pull-out drawer in the vanity. "Get dressed and get into bed. I need to deal with this." He nods toward his phone.

"Should I even ask why you have an entire drawer dedicated to female toiletries and overnight supplies?" I quip. "A lot of overnight guests?" I joke, but there's a piece of me that feels jealous at the thought.

Axel turns to me with a deadly serious look on his face. "Angel, if you want to have that conversation, then we'll have it, but not here and not now."

I think a vein pops out of my head from the amount of discipline I use to stop myself from asking, *What in the actual hell does that mean?* Did I just have hot shower sex with a man-whore? Wait, does he have a girlfriend? That would honestly explain all the eye daggers the women downstairs threw my way.

Before I can respond, he's already wrapped a towel around his waist and walks up to me, so I have to look up to meet his gaze.

"Whatever you're thinking right now, stop. It's nothing like that. Just… it's a long story, okay?" he asks, as if looking for my approval.

But honestly, none of that makes me feel better. This started out as me joking with him, trying to have playful banter, and has turned into something serious.

"Sure, but I want to talk about it when you're ready, okay?" I make sure to look him in the eyes.

He gives me a nod and smooths some hairs down on my head.

"But I do have one question I want you to answer now, because I can't continue *this* without an answer." I signal between us.

"Okay," he replies, eyeing me warily.

"Are you with someone?" I ask, bracing myself for an answer.

"Is that what this is about?" He stills, and I hold my breath in anticipation. *Great fucking work, Jenna, you're a homewrecker.*

Axel lifts my chin and places a soft kiss on my lips. "Babe, I don't know what the fuck happened to me, but you are the only woman I can think about. Not only am I only hard for your tight body, but I actually want to spend time with you, hear your thoughts and opinions." He shakes his head and turns to walk out of the bathroom, still holding the towel around his waist with one hand.

"So, no, Jenna, I'm not with just somebody. I'm with you,"

he says with a smirk.

I gape at him and his obscenely handsome face.

I'm with you.

My world starts spinning around me as I take his words in. He feels it too—this uncontrollable draw between us. We've only known each other for a little over three weeks. And most of that we weren't even together. So, how can we feel this strongly for each other?

A sinking feeling settles within me. This isn't normal. Maybe we need to slow down and let this take its course. Something that burns this hot and bright is bound to fizzle out sooner rather than later. Right?

Chapter 19

AXEL

I flip through my messages; almost all of them are from Shiny, letting me know the Reaper we took is at the warehouse and filling me in on cleanup. I roll my shoulders, excited to get my hands dirty and get some information out of him. Realizing I have a missed call from Bear, I hit his contact and put the phone to my ear. Jenna is still in the bathroom; our last conversation plays back in my head. The look on her face leaves me worried. Had I been too honest with her? She looked like she was going to run for the hills.

Fuck, get your shit together, Axel. There's no time to sit around and have a fucking feelings circle.

Honestly, the toiletries are from my sister. She and her asshat of a boyfriend are on again off again and when she needs a place to crash, she stays here and I find one of the guest rooms to stay in. But Jenna questioning me about the girls I've slept with leaves a bad taste in my mouth. I don't want her worrying about anyone else. She should know how strongly I feel for her.

With her still occupied in the other room, I'm able to talk freely on the phone.

"Axel," Bear answers in an almost groggy tone. Most of us are pissed off and tired, but we won't be able to sleep until after Church.

"Yeah, what's up?"

"How's Teach?" he asks. I pause. Is this what he's really calling me about? But it wouldn't surprise me. Bear has always been very protective over women. He was married a few years back but when things went down with Knife, she was collateral damage from the fallout with the Russians. He's never been the same and I don't think I've actually seen him talk to another woman except for the old ladies.

"She's fine, Bear. Was that all you called for?" I reply in a short tone. I need to get dressed and get downstairs for Church.

"No, we've got a problem down here you might need to see for yourself. Gunner's lost his shit; we need to call Cali," he says as I hear a commotion in the background.

"I'll be down in five." I hang up with more force than needed. Tossing my phone on the bed, I move to my dresser and pull out a pair of dark jeans and a long sleeve flannel. Jenna walks out of the bathroom as I sit on the edge of the bed to put on my socks and boots.

"You're leaving?" she asks, giving me an unsure look. She's wearing nothing but one of my shirts. It's so big on her it falls just above her knees. Her hair is still wet and falls around her face in deep red waves. She's the most gorgeous woman I've ever seen. It takes all my willpower to keep putting on my shoes and not pull her into bed with me.

"I have to go deal with something before Church. You'll be fine here. I'll have someone bring you food." That look of confusion wrinkles her perfect features again at the mention of Church.

"You guys go to church in the middle of the night?" Jenna asks curiously.

I smirk to myself. "Angel, this isn't the type of Church you're thinking of." I finish lacing up my boots and stand in front of her. Nothing stands between me and her naked body except for the thin material of my shirt.

"It's what we call a club meeting. All the club officers meet to discuss business."

Her eyebrows raise for a moment, and then her eyes latch onto mine. "Huh, I thought I had entered some extremely religious biker club."

I rub my hands down her silky arms, feeling goosebumps erupt in their wake. It's nice to know I affect her just as much as she affects me.

"Thinking about bolting?" I raise an eyebrow at her.

"Only about a dozen times," she jokes and turns to walk over to the bed. "I mean, it would make more sense as to how this brood of large bikers has welcomed an innocent teacher into their lair... human sacrifice." She wiggles her eyebrows as she says the last words.

I watch as she pulls the covers back and settles herself right in the middle of the bed. I've never let a woman actually *sleep* in my bed before, but I don't know if anything has felt more right. I grapple with my feelings, trying to suppress the surge of possessiveness that once again consumes me. Every time I look at her, I know she's made just for me. Her curves fit my hands so perfectly, her face delicate but strong, and she's braver than most grown men.

"Nope, sweetheart. Whether you want to acknowledge it or not, you fit right in here." I let her think I'm talking about the club. Honestly, she does seem to fit right in with the club. Sierra, the office manager at my garage, couldn't stop blabbing about how great Jenna was after some dinner with the girls. Even Cali, who almost never likes anyone new, seems to enjoy her company. But really, there's an unspoken truth: she fits perfectly here with me.

"A gorgeous, smart, pain in my ass. What more could I ask for?" That coaxes a giggle out of her. The sound makes my chest tighten. I love it when she laughs.

"Ugh, I knew I was destined to ride a motorcycle!" she says with gumption.

Something about the thought of having her ride on the back of my bike has my dick throbbing. Shit, I need to get downstairs to deal with business so I can come back and bury myself in her for the rest of the night.

She yawns and stretches her arms out in front of her, beckoning me forward. She's adorable.

"Be safe, okay?" she whispers into my chest.

"Always," I say into her hair.

She leans back, and I can't help but leave her with a breath stealing kiss.

"Bed, now." I tuck her in and watch as she fights to keep

her eyes open.

I walk to the door. "If you need anything, text me." Without a look back, I'm out the door.

Coming down the stairs, I hear shouting and chairs scooting around.

"We've got a fucking rat! I don't care what the fuck you have to do, but we need to find the fucker and make them pay!"

I can't see anyone yet, but I know that voice belongs to Gunner. Crazy bastard has a slug in his shoulder and is still yelling about club business. Stepping off the last step, I'm met with an absolute shitshow.

The first person I see is Cali, standing off to the side in a dark purple pantsuit and sky-high heels, her arms crossed against her chest. Her platinum blonde hair is pulled back into a perfectly slicked-back bun. She exudes power when she needs to, but her face is painted with worry. She's staring at Gunner, who's standing between Jax and Bear. Both men flank his sides, keeping him upright. He's slurring his words, and it's clear Doc gave him some hardcore pain medicine.

"Can you please take him up to his old room?" Cali says, pinching the bridge of her nose.

"No problem, Cali. I'll have the guys help you get him back into bed," Prince says as he walks toward her.

I make my way over to her and wrap an arm around her shoulders.

"You doing, okay?" I ask her. She looks up at me with tears in her eyes. Shit. I hate it when women cry, and honestly, I don't think I've ever seen Cali cry.

"Hey, Gunner is one tough son of a bitch. He'll be fine." I

try to soothe her.

She nods at me and takes a deep breath, putting back on the mask of confidence and power that I'm used to.

"I know he will. I just... he said he was just doing boring club stuff tonight, and I get a mysterious call from Doc saying Gunner was shot. Nothing more. I was still at work, and I nearly had a heart attack." She picks a piece of lint from the sleeve of her jacket. "I'm fine, I promise. Just hate this part of it all."

I can't imagine how hard this is for the women of the club. We signed up for this shit, knew exactly what we were getting ourselves into. They, on the other hand, didn't. I give her a squeeze.

"Yeah, I'll talk to Doc and remind him he can't just drop that on you without detail."

"No, it's okay. It's not his fault. It's Gunner's for putting himself in that position." She moves away from us and starts to walk toward the door. "Thanks again for your help tonight, Prince. I owe you." She waves to both of us as she struts up the stairs.

"No, doll. We owe you." He tips his head toward her and walks back to the conference room.

Why would we owe Cali?

Men file into Church as we sit in our designated spots. Only patched members are allowed tonight, seeing as how we may have a rat among us. Jax sits outside the door with a basket for everyone to drop their cell phones into while Knife takes his wand and searches the room for bugs.

"All clear," both of them say in unison.

Prince bangs the gavel and takes a seat at the head of the table. He doesn't talk at first, but leans back and lights a cigarette. Taking a deep drag, he stares up at the ceiling and then back down.

"Well, boys, tonight has proved one thing to me. The Reapers are not here to make peace; they're here for war. Nothing and nobody are off-limits to them, so tonight I want you all to make plans. I'm opening the clubhouse up to those of you who want to bring your families here. Keep 'em safe. Anyone wants to leave or has to go somewhere, make sure there is protection with them."

Everyone stays quiet and nods. I've already decided Jenna is staying with me until this shit is all taken care of. I don't care how long it takes. She's going to hate the idea; she already nearly blew a gasket when I told her she was staying tonight. I wish I could take her to my house. She'd be way more comfortable. It's nothing special—I bought it a few years back to have a place of my own but rarely ever stay there. But I haven't been able to set up a security system there, so we'll stay here.

"Otherwise, I want business as usual. We don't want those fucking Reaper scum thinking they've spooked us. Everyone goes to work and does their shit, but we keep a close eye out."

Prince looks to me.

"I know this has touched some people who don't exactly belong to the club, but if she stays, you better make sure she can be trusted."

I look around the room for a moment, looking each of my brothers in the face. I don't want to claim Jenna yet. She's not ready for that yet. But I need to make it clear that she's mine.

"She can be trusted," I say sternly.

Prince nods to me, and I make eye contact with Blaze.

"I'm not claiming her yet. Shit, I've only known her for a few weeks, but she's mine."

You could hear a pin drop in the room.

"Oh, look who's got his balls in a sling now," Jax jokes from across the table.

The men erupt with laughter, and the tense feeling in the room relaxes a bit. I deserve that. When he claimed Sierra, I gave him nonstop shit for settling down and being tied to one woman. Didn't see the point with all the ready and available pussy we have around here. Well, that was until a sexy teacher walked into my life.

"Fuck you," I say while flipping him off with both hands. A smile pulls at the corner of my lips.

"Alright, you two," Prince says like a father separating his kids.

"We gonna talk about the fact that we probably have a fucking rat among us?" Bear says from the back of the room. He's leaned back in his chair so the front two legs are suspended in the air.

"There's a reason we called an officer-only meeting, boys." Prince juts out his chin toward Blaze.

"We have a hunch that it might be one of the prospects," Blaze says.

"A hunch? What the fuck do you know?" I say in a pissed-off tone. If they knew something, we should have dealt with it by now. The thought of having someone unloyal in the club makes me see red. Whoever it is, is going to see why you never cross us or put the lives of us and our families in danger.

"Relax. We aren't sure. That's why we're going to feed each of them a different story as to how we're going to retaliate. If the Reapers make a move to attack, then we'll know who the rat is." A menacing smile grows on his face. "Then we'll deal with them."

It's a good plan, but it also means we have to keep the prospects separated for the time being. We only have three at the moment, so that won't be too difficult.

We devise a plan for what we'll tell each prospect and how it'll be delivered to them. The itch to figure out who the prick is overtakes me, I just want this done. I practically vibrate with anger. Every officer agrees on the plan. This will be done tonight, and we hope it'll lead us right to the dead man walking.

Prince stands, and we all give him our attention again.

"Remember, tonight you get your shit in order because tomorrow we figure out how to take these fuckers down." He bangs the gavel, and we all stand to leave.

Thank fuck. I need to get back to Jenna. I bet she's already fallen asleep and I want to wrap myself around her for a couple of hours.

I get two steps out of the Church doors when I feel a hand slap down on my shoulder. I turn back to see Jax.

"Prez wants us to go deal with the guy at the warehouse." He says as he heads for the main door leading to our bikes out front.

"Already planned on going in the morning," I snap back not wanting to deal with anymore of this shit right now. The guy isn't going anywhere and I am so worked up I'm not sure

I'm going to have the patience needed to do this interrogation well.

"No can do. Said it needs to be done now," Jax says as he opens a piece of gum and pops it into his mouth.

I roll my shoulders, trying to alleviate some of the tension. "Fine."

"Don't worry, lover boy. You'll be back soon enough." Jax slaps my back as I walk out into the dark night.

Chapter 20

JENNA

AXEL LEFT ABOUT twenty minutes ago. I am exhausted, but every time I try to close my eyes, I see that man staring back at me. Lifeless. Dead. Gosh, I really am not cut out for any of this. I roll over and decide to scroll through social media. Nothing quiets my racing mind quite like aimlessly doom scrolling.

Right as I'm about to put down my phone, a picture of Marley's face covers my screen. I answer as quickly as I can. She had texted me that she was on a plane back to California when we first arrived here, but I hadn't yet been able to get ahold of her.

"Marley!"

"Jenna? Oh, thank God!" Her voice sounds relieved. "I leave you for one day, and all hell breaks loose?"

I let out a dry laugh. "Yeah, try not to leave anymore, okay? I don't think I can handle this without you."

Once the words are out of my mouth, I hear Marley take a deep breath.

"I'm really sorry, Jenna."

"For what?" I ask, confused.

"For taking you to that party. For introducing you to the club. You wouldn't be in this mess if it wasn't for me," her voice cracks.

"Oh, Mar, stop it. You had no idea this was going to happen, did you?"

"No, of course I didn't," she says quickly.

"Then knock it off. I'll be okay, I just need some time to process everything." I look around. The moonlight is the only thing illuminating the dark room. It should feel strange to be in Axel's space, but I almost feel more comfortable here than I do in my own.

"Anyway, are you coming here to the clubhouse?" I ask, hoping that she is going to be stuck here with me. I can't be the only woman stuck here.

"Yep." I can practically hear her eye roll from here. "I forced Max to let me stop by the apartment first to pack a bag. Want me to pack one for you too?"

"Yes, please!" I almost shout. Not that I don't enjoy wearing Axel's shirt. Actually, I probably enjoy it a little too much. I pull the collar up to smell his scent like a weirdo. The thick fabric of his shirt rubs over my sensitive nipples, and a shock of excitement courses through my body. I shake my head, focusing back on the conversation.

"Will do. Where are you, anyway? Did they put you in a guest room?" she asks, genuinely curious, which tells me Blaze hasn't said anything to her yet.

"Oh, well actually... I'm in Axel's room." The words are barely out of my mouth before Marley's screams pierce my ears.

"What?! You are in Axel's room? Oh my gosh, tell me everything. And when I say everything, Jenna, I mean everything!" She pauses only long enough for me to hear Blaze in the background telling her to chill out. At this point, I'm full-on laughing. Marley definitely knows how to get me out of my own head.

"Have you guys had sex?" she whispers into the phone.

I feel my cheeks heat at the thought of what we've been doing. "I'll tell you everything when you get here, Mar, I promise. Just hurry up! I need my best friend."

"Oh, that was totally a yes!" she exclaims.

I ignore her. "Please don't forget my phone charger. Oh, and my favorite leggings and—" she cuts me off before I can continue.

"Yeah, yeah, I got it, Jenna," she says in a mocking tone.

"Thank you," I say as sweetly as possible. I am so grateful that Marley could talk Blaze into getting our things. I was going to be miserable, stuck here without any of my toiletries and my own clothes for however long Axel plans on keeping me here.

"Yep... Jen, I know I've already said it, but I'm glad you're okay! I'll see you soon."

"Sounds good, Mar. I'm going to try to sleep, so if I don't see you tonight, I'll see you in the morning, okay?"

"Of course. Sleep well! Bye!" she hangs up before I can respond.

I roll over until my face is pressed into the soft pillow. This bed could rival the fanciest of hotels. I take a deep inhale of Axel's heavenly spicy scent. I really need to stop doing this— it's not healthy. I turn onto my side so I'm staring at the large window across the room. Closing my eyes, I try to count backward from 100. That always puts people to sleep, right?

I recite my vows back to the minister. Axel's bright smile warms me as I place the ring on his finger. Looking back to the minister, he begins the same process again. This time, Axel is reciting his vows.

A large gust of wind comes from behind me as Axel's handsome face starts to fall. "Jenna, what's wrong?" he asks in a panicked voice. Reaching toward me, he goes to hold my elbow.

"Nothing, I'm fine. Keep going!" I squeak. Woah, that's weird. What's wrong with my voice?

"Babe? Jenna!" He is now holding me in place.

I feel shaky and start to shiver from the strong wind. Looking down, I see blood—dark, red, thick blood coating the ground around us.

I look back to Axel, worried he's hurt, but before I can ask him anything, I feel liquid dripping down my chin. I move my hand up to touch the foreign substance and pull it back to find more blood.

What's happening to me?

Panic floods my body as I try to move, but I can't.

I barely register Axel yelling in the background, asking for help. But when I look out to the crowd, no one is moving. No one is even batting an eye at us. Smiles cover the faces of our loved ones as they watch the tortured scene in front of them.

My knees buckle beneath me, leaving me with no choice but to sink into the ground. I close my eyes, fighting against the pain surging through my body. When I open them, I am cold, in pain, and alone in the sea of red blood that has pooled around me.

I shoot up out of bed, my chest heaving as I try to catch my breath. Gosh, these nightmares are becoming so vivid. Pulling the covers off my body, I move to sit on the side of the bed. Spending a few moments focusing on my breathing, I start to relax.

I don't remember falling asleep, but I rub my eyes and look around the dark room. Axel still hasn't returned.

I look at my phone: 3 a.m. He's been gone for hours, and I'm starving. In my periphery I notice something new, two pale pink suitcases now sit next to the door.

Yes! Marley dropped off my things.

I rush over and pull them back into the room. One suitcase is on the smaller side and is extremely light, and the other is a moderately sized case with some weight to it. I'm a bit confused as to what might be in the small suitcase, so I open that one first.

Unzipping the side, I start to see small scraps of lace burst out from the seams. Quickly, I realize Marley has shoved my entire lingerie drawer in this suitcase.

I gawk at the ridiculous amount of lace, leather, beads—you name it, it's there. I catch sight of a lime green post-it note on top of the pile. It reads:

Jenna,
You're welcome, go get 'em, tiger!
P.S. Who knew one woman could own this much underwear?!

I can't help but chuckle. This is my best friend, the woman who finds out I'm staying with a man, so she decides to pack me an entire lingerie store. I smack my palm against my forehead. Let's hope there is actual clothes in the next suitcase. I mean I love lingerie, obviously, I have so much of it I can barely contain it, but I haven't exactly had anyone to wear this for. I get a little giddy thinking of Axel walking in to me dresses in one of the outfits.

I run my hand over a royal blue sheer teddy. It's so gorgeous, and the stitching is to die for. I sigh, close the suitcase, and shove it under the bed.

Maybe I'll get some pieces out. I wonder if Axel likes lingerie? Who am I kidding—what man doesn't?

I rummage through the other suitcase and find a cute green bralette and matching underwear set. I slip them on and then look for other clothes. Pulling on a pair of leggings and zipping up a cream-colored hoodie, I'm almost ready to hunt for food.

I slip on a pair of white tennis shoes and run my fingers through my still damp hair. Perfect.

Grabbing my cell phone on the way out the door, I check to see if Axel has checked in. Nope. I continue to head out the door but stop when I remember that Axel always locks the room.

Not having a key, I choose to leave it unlocked. I shrug. I'll only be gone for a short amount of time.

Chapter 21

JENNA

Walking down the hallway, I can't help but notice that there isn't anyone around. It's creepy quiet up here tonight. I hurriedly make my way to the stairs and head down to the first floor, remembering that I saw a large kitchen behind the bar the night of the party. Surely, there has to be food in there. The moment my feet hit the landing; I hear a familiar voice.

"Jenna!" Sienna calls to me and waves me over to the table. She's sitting with Cali, Mia, and Marley.

Marley leaps out of her seat and practically runs into my arms when she sees me.

"Don't scare me like that again, okay?" She squeezes her small arms around my neck.

"I'll try, and we'll talk about the fun little package you left for me later," I whisper. Marley lets go and starts laughing so hard, I'm pretty sure I hear her snort. I shove her shoulder as I walk towards the other women.

"What's so funny?" Cali asks as I sit down at the table with them. A pile of nachos sits in the middle of the table, and my stomach growls loudly.

"Oh, nothing. I just left Jenna a little surprise up in her room. And she loved it!" Marley smirks at me.

"Sure. Can I have some of these? I came down here to find food. I'm starving." I look around the table.

"Oh, please do! We can't finish these alone," Mia says, pushing them toward me. I grab a loaded chip and fill my mouth. I sigh in happiness as the meaty, cheesy goodness explodes on my tongue.

Mia stands from the table and heads over to the bar. "Where are you going?" Sierra asks.

"To make us some margaritas!" Mia says in an obvious voice. "It's 3:30 a.m., and we all have had shit nights."

"Hear, hear!" I chant.

"Sign me up," Cali grunts from next to me. All of the women are in relaxed, comfy clothes. It seems like none of us can sleep.

"How's Gunner?" I ask Cali. I overheard someone talking about him getting hurt earlier when Axel and I came back.

"He'll be fine. The bullet went clean through. He was already up and complaining about not being able to ride for a while," she says, rolling her eyes.

Mia laughs from the bar. "Sounds about right."

Cali and Mia talk about some article they both read, and Sierra is busy texting, so I lean over to Marley.

"Where's Blaze? I thought you two were together earlier?"

I ask.

She finishes her bite before responding. "We were. He dropped me off and helped me get the bags up to our rooms. Then he said he needed to go help Axel and Jax with something. Said to not wait up." Marley shrugs her shoulders and grabs another chip. "Why?"

"Just wondering. Axel said he was going to be gone for only a short time. But that was around midnight," I explain.

"Hmm, must have got caught up," she says as Mia places the largest margaritas I've ever seen in front of each of us. Mia plops down in her chair and holds her drink up.

"To the amazing women of the HCMC" We all go to tap our drinks together, but Mia cuts us off.

"Wait, I wasn't done!"

Pulling our drinks back, we look around at each other with a slight giggle.

"And to Jenna spilling her guts about the mind-blowing sex she's having with Axel!"

"Cheers!" rings out from all the other women at the table.

I choke on the chip I just took a bite of and end up having a coughing fit.

"Oh, come on, Jenna, you have to spill. We've been so curious about Axel. He's never let us set him up with anyone and has never had a steady girlfriend. But here you come out of nowhere, and he's fawning over you like your vagina is made of gold," Cali says very matter-of-factly. "Spill!"

I take a healthy drink of my margarita. It burns my throat on the way down. I should have remembered from the welcome-home party, that Mia's cocktails are dangerously strong.

"To be honest, I haven't done anything special—well, I don't think." I study my nails for a moment, trying to put into words whatever is going on between Axel and me.

"Don't get me wrong, the sex is great—beyond great." The girls all cheer and whistle. I roll my eyes as I feel a deep blush burn my cheeks and continue.

"But there's more there. We are constantly being drawn together like two magnets. I feel safe and protected with him. I can't explain it, but it feels... right."

"Wow, sounds romantic," Mia says as she rests her head on her hands.

"But as romantic as it is, I'm worried. We've only known each other for a little over three weeks. These feelings aren't normal. We are supposed to go slow, right?" I ask honestly.

"Who says?" Sierra asks. "Because what I've learned from being around these men is that they love fiercely. Everything they do is quick. In this life, if you don't reach out and grab what you want, it will be someone else's a moment later." I watch as all the other women nod at the table.

"Don't overthink it, Jenna. We've all seen the way he looks at you," Marley states.

"And how's that?" I'm fishing for information here.

"Like you are a living, breathing angel." She slaps my arm. "He's obsessed!"

We spend the next hour talking and drinking. We talk about the men in our lives, our jobs, funny stories. I don't think I've laughed this hard in years.

We are all still sitting and chatting when a giant man with a scar running the length of his face approaches us. As he gets closer, I can't help but notice how gorgeous he is. Tall and muscular with soft, short chestnut hair. His brown eyes don't compare to Axel's, but they sure are nice to look at. I'm starting to rethink my whole idea about bikers—these guys are all smoking hot.

"Ladies," he says in the deepest voice I think I've ever heard.

"Hey, Motley," Mia says, a blush creeping up her cheeks. *Interesting.* I'll have to ask her about that later. "I'm sorry I didn't say hi on your birthday. You were busy, and I was stuck behind the bar." She continues.

"No worries, love. It was a crazy night," he says as he wiggles his eyebrows. He looks around the table at all of us.

"Sierra, you look good. How ya been?"

"Great, Motley. Still working at Axel's shop and trying to keep up with the grump that is my old man," she chuckles. Her face is now flushed from the tequila.

"Where have you been? We haven't seen you in months," Cali asks.

"Been up in Dalewood. Had a job to do with the charter in that area. Came back because I heard the boys had a little fun without me. Why? You miss me, Cali?" He bats his eyes at her.

"You wish," she says, rolling her eyes.

"Mark my words. One of these days, you're going to realize that I'm the big, bad biker you need—not that asshole you call an old man," his words laced with mischief.

"I'll be sure to tell him you think so when he's up," she laughs. He winks at her and then makes eye contact with Marley and me.

"Club girls?" he says to Mia as he moves to stand over me. She goes to respond, but he starts to talk. He puts out his hand. "Nice to meet you, gorgeous. I'm your biggest fantasy come to life."

I stare at his hand and then back up at him. "That's the best pickup line you could come up with?" The girls all chuckle as he cocks his head with a shit-eating grin.

"Oh, I like this one," he states. I shake his hand and laugh with the girls.

"I'm Jenna, and I'm definitely not a club girl. Whatever that is." I nod toward Marley. "That's Marley. Same goes for her." He winks at Marley and then brings his attention back to me. He still hasn't let go of my hand and is now staring at me as if I'm a difficult puzzle he wants to solve.

"Well, not-club-girl Jenna, why are you hanging out in a biker bar at 3 a.m. if you aren't part of the club?"

Suddenly, the front door slams open. Axel, Blaze, and Jax strut in with terrifying looks on their faces. Axel instantly makes eye contact with me, then his gaze travels up to where Motley is still holding my hand. His jaw ticks, a movement so small that if you weren't attuned to him, you wouldn't have noticed. I'm starting to realize that's his tell—the one that screams, *I'm mad as all hell.*

"That's why she's here," I hear Sierra giggle next to me. Motley drops my hand immediately like I have the plague and backs away with his hands in the air like he's been caught red-handed. The confident, cocky man who stood in front of me a second ago is gone.

"Shit, Ax, I didn't know she was with you. She just caught

my eye," he says as he shrugs with an unapologetic, smug look. I think he knew exactly what he was doing.

I can't stifle my laugh as I watch the three of them walk over to our table. Axel comes around to me, giving my head a quick kiss before resting his hands on my shoulders and kneading the tension I've been holding there. Having his hands on my body is messing with my mind, and I have to fight not to close my eyes and sink into the heavenly massage. I wasn't tired moments ago, but I feel like I can finally relax.

"Touch her again, and you'll be eating all your meals through a straw from here on out." His tone is calm and all alpha. I slowly look up at Axel, raising one eyebrow in question.

"Are you joking? Who says things like that?" I ask. I shouldn't like that he's threatening another man, but I can't help but get a little turned on by it. I want to grab him by the belt loop and drag him upstairs.

"I do. He shouldn't have his hands on you and shouldn't be looking at you like that," he says, looking down at me with a heated gaze—one that says this conversation is over.

I sigh and look over to Motley, who has the world's biggest grin on his face.

"Well, well, well. The mighty Axel has been snatched up, eh? Didn't hear anything about you claiming anyone, but I have been away a while," Motley states. Axel's hold on my shoulders goes still.

"Claim?" I ask, looking at Marley across the table. I laugh. "What the hell is he talking about?" But her face looks unsure as she looks around the table at the other women.

Cali shrugs. "It's their way of saying you're theirs. Once a member of the club claims someone at the table, it means you're pretty much married in the eyes of the club. It also means you have the club's full support and protection."

I blink a few times, trying to work through all this information. I've only known Axel for a few weeks, and although my feelings for him are strong, this seems pretty intense. The nachos and margarita churn in my stomach as reality is once again thrown right into my face. I really need to get home tomorrow and put some space between us. Get my thoughts together.

"Every guy does this?" I look up to Axel. His face is serious, and he stares at me for a moment before responding.

"No. Only those who want to make their woman their Old Lady," he states, moving his gaze across my face almost as if he's trying to read my expression.

"Hmm," is all I can say because I'm not really sure what to say. I have a million questions, but I'm having a hard time actually forming one. Everyone else at the table returns to other conversations, and I take a moment to think. I barely know many of the people at this table, including Axel, but somehow, I feel almost at peace—like this is where I belong. I sit up and shake the feeling away.

"I can hear you overthinking again." His breath smells like whiskey and smoke. I close my eyes and sink into the feeling of him around me.

"Yeah, well, when I hear talk of you 'claiming' me, I feel like that is something I need to think about," I whisper back. "This is happening too fast, Ax."

"We will talk about this upstairs, Angel. I'm not claiming

you yet." He brushes my hair back off my neck and starts to trail kisses from the base of my neck to my jaw.

"You think? I barely know you," I say with a low laugh.

"Dear Lord, take it upstairs, you two," I hear Cali say from across the table.

I feel my face heat as I sit up and look up to see everyone staring at us. I was so lost in Axel that I had completely forgotten we were with company. I look to Marley and mock-glare at her as she stares at me with an *I told you so* grin. I can't help myself and end up smiling right back at her.

I could get used to this—being with Axel, being a part of this group. But that little annoying voice in my head reminds me that something that burns this hot and bright is bound to fizzle out sooner rather than later. Looking up at Axel I take a moment to memorize his face. I need to remember that I am in control of this. We can slow down and talk about us later.

"How's Gun?" Blaze asks Cali, pulling my attention back to the conversation.

"Good, asleep when I left him, but I should be getting back." She stands and stretches her neck from side to side. "Bye, ladies. Let's meet in the morning for coffee? Seeing as we are all stuck here for a few days." She walks up the stairs as we all say goodbye.

"A few days?" I look over to Cali and then to everyone around the table. "What?" Everyone at the table looks at me and then to Axel. Seems like I'm the odd one out again.

"Well, that's our cue to leave," Sierra says pointedly. They all stand and head their own ways, and I'm left in my seat, confused.

Chapter 22

AXEL

Jenna straightens her shoulders and stands from her chair. I look down at her clothes; she's wearing leggings that hug her plump ass and leave little to the imagination. If only this woman knew what she does to me, the way I feel instantly drawn to her sexy as sin body. My hands move on their own, reaching for her to pull her close, but she takes a step back and crosses her arms over her chest. Her brow furrows, and she pops out her hip for dramatic flair.

I also love her sass but I really don't need this shit; I'm already pissed off that we didn't get any good information from that fucking Reaper. I do have to hand it to him, he was loyal to his club to the very bloody end. I run my hand down my face and stare at Jenna.

"Axel, I really don't like having to get information from other people. If this is going to be something"—she waves a hand between us— "then you have to communicate with me." God, she's so hot when she's all fired up. I level her with a hard look.

"Listen, if this is going to work, you are going to have to trust me to tell you shit when I'm ready," I say. "This is new to me, Jenna. I'm not used to having someone."

She softens her expression at my words. "I hear you, Axel. This is moving extremely fast." She pauses and looks at the floor. "Maybe too fast." I notice she rolls one of her small gold rings around her finger unconsciously. "This is all so new to me Dane; I just need you to keep me in the loop. Because I feel like I'm going crazy here."

Taking another step forward, I'm in her space before she can think about moving back. Her breath catches as I slide my hands up her body. "I'll work on it, babe."

"Good. Now tell me what all of this 'a couple days' business is." She actually uses air quotes.

"I want you to stay with me until we have the Reaper situation settled," I say, waiting for her to protest.

"Okay," she sighs. "I get it, I do. But we need to figure out what is happening between us. Because I think we might need to slow this way down."

My head spins at her reaction. I thought she was going to fight me on this decision, but she's willing to stay. The only thing I'm not too keen on is slowing anything down.

"That easy, huh? I thought you were going to give me hell for keeping you here longer than a night." I bend down and pick her up, her legs come around to wrap around my waist.

"Yep, I don't really want to go back to our apartment alone.

And Marley brought me all of my stuff... and more. So, I think I can stay for a bit." It almost hurts looking at her gorgeous face; she really is something else.

"I have one condition of this little lockdown. I don't want to be a prisoner; I am going to need to get out here and there. But I'll be safe." Lust fills her eyes as she digs her teeth into her bottom lip. I don't even know if she knows what she's doing, but it's working. Jenna's innocent look changes quickly into the vixen she is when she starts to grind her needy pussy on me. There's no mistaking the hard-on I'm sporting in my pants. Naughty girl. Wrapping her arms around my neck, I walk us up to my room.

"I hear you about needing to go and do your own thing sometimes, but while we are still on high alert, I need you to promise me you won't leave without me or one of the guys." She stops moving against me and pulls her head back a bit to look at me.

"Axel, that's a lot for you to ask of me. What if I'm just going to the store or going for a run? I'm not even a part of all this." she states. I have to remind myself that she has never experienced this life and doesn't realize that being with me puts a big target on her back.

"Babe, this is serious. I need to know you are safe so I can do my job for the club. Fuck, you being with me puts you at risk, and I won't be able to focus if you are off unprotected." I let out a heavy breath.

"If it means that much to you, I'll do it. But I don't like it. And the moment this is over, everything goes back to normal. And we date like a normal couple," she eyes me, and then sticks out her hand for me to shake like this is a business proposal.

"Deal," I say shaking her hand, even though I know we will never be a normal couple. This is far from your everyday situation. Jenna uses her arms, which are wrapped around my head, and pulls me in for a kiss. We make our way upstairs; I might blow my load before we even make it to the room. Her tight little body is grinding against me as I palm her ass. Getting to the door, I press Jenna's back against it and hold her steady with one hand. With the other, I unzip her hoodie to reveal a scrap of a bra covering her. I could see her rosy nipples through her sweater when I first walked in and had to actively fight to keep the drool in my mouth.

Pulling the scrap of fabric down, I release one of her firm breasts. Dropping my head, I suck and lick until her nipple is a sharp peak. She grasps the back of my head, pulling me against her as she arches off the wood.

"I need to get you inside before I fuck you right here in the hallway," I growl between laps. Reaching for my keys, I see Jenna reach down, and the door opens. We almost fall to the floor with the unexpected jolt.

"Fuck, Jen. Why is my door unlocked?" I ask. I trust my brothers to not move or take shit, but some of them always look for any open room to bring a club girl up and fuck, and I don't need that in my space. My room is my place to relax—and now — fuck my woman.

"Sorry, I didn't have a key and thought I was going to come right back up," she says as she kisses and licks up my neck.

Fumbling around, I find the light switch. Warm light radiates from the lamps on the nightstands. I gently lay Jenna on the bed, ready to devour her.

"Wait!" she says in a hurried voice. "I, uh… have something for you. A surprise." A blush creeps up her neck, and my curiosity peaks.

"Well, show me then," I say with a hint of humor in my voice. She leaps off the bed and crouches on the floor, pulling a pink suitcase out from under my bed.

"What are you hiding down there?" I try to look into the case when she sets it on the bed, but she swats me away.

"No, you have to wait." She pushes her hair over her shoulder and looks me right in the eyes.

"What's your favorite color?" She's so giddy, it's adorable.

"Hmm… black," I say without a second thought.

"Ohhh… okay!" Jenna grabs the small suitcase and dashes into the bathroom. I roll onto my back while I wait for Jenna to come out of the bathroom with whatever she has for me. A wave of exhaustion crashes over me, and I fight to keep my eyes open. Honestly with the fight at the club, I'm surprised Jenna is this okay. I remind myself she is probably going to break down at one point or another.

A few minutes later, I hear the faint sound of the bathroom door opening. I roll onto my side to see what Jenna's surprise is when my eyes catch on the hottest lingerie I've ever seen. She has pinned her long hair up and wears all black. On top, a see-through lace corset lands right above her belly button and cups her breasts so that there's a heavy helping of cleavage. Her matching thong and garter set leaves nothing to the imagination and showcases her long, smooth legs in a way that makes my mouth water.

I can barely think straight with the amount of blood leaving my brain and heading straight to my cock.

"Turn." My voice is huskier, darker.

Jenna slowly turns until I growl at the view of her perfect ass lined with the garter straps.

"Come here, baby." It's the last thing either of us says for the rest of the night. We take our time memorizing and worshipping each other's bodies. At the first sight of morning light, I draw the blackout curtains and settle back into bed. Jenna wraps herself around me, and we fall asleep.

Chapter 23

JENNA

Making my way to the bathroom, I step over the clothes we left strewn across the room early this morning. I try to be as quiet as possible to let Axel get some extra sleep. It's only 9:30 a.m., but I can't fall back to sleep.

Stepping onto the warm tile floor, I gently close the door behind me and flip on the light. I squint against the sudden burst of white light that momentarily blinds me. Last night, I moved my toiletries into the bathroom, so I feel like I can put myself together. This morning and hopefully have a somewhat normal day.

I turn on the warm water and lather my favorite face wash into my hands. I'm not the biggest fan of make-up, but a good skincare routine is like my own form of meditation. I gently wash my face and then apply the next few steps of my regimen. Feeling like my face is cared for, I brush my teeth and hair, use the restroom, and head out for a change of clothes. Before I leave, I can't help but look down at the large drawer still filled with female toiletries. I open it and inspect the products; all are too fancy to just be things he threw in here. Someone thought these out and understands high-end products. I know he wasn't ready to talk about whatever this is last night, but something about this feels off. Last night, the girls said he really hasn't been with anyone, but either he's really into female bath products or I'm staring at a giant red flag. I mentally shake myself; I feel like I'm going a little crazy. I barely know this man and I'm rummaging through his drawers and stressing about his secrets.

Closing the drawer, I turn off the light and slowly open the door. Axel is still lying on his stomach with his arm hanging off the bed. His light snores fill the room. I pause for a moment to look at him; he's so handsome, even while sleeping. I head over to my suitcase and rummage through the clothes Marley brought me. I put on my favorite pair of ripped black jeans and a green long sleeve shirt that makes my eyes pop. Sliding on a pair of boots, I head towards the door. I take one last look at Axel, then walk out into the hallway.

Mission: find some coffee and breakfast. I leave the door unlocked again. I know he wasn't excited about me leaving the door unlocked, but he's in there, and I really will be right back.

Chatter fills the hallway as I catch sight of a group of men making their way downstairs. I try to walk slowly to keep my distance and not get in anyone's way. I don't really know a lot of people here, and I don't want to be in the way. Also, many of these men have eyes that stare straight into your soul and look like they could rip someone's head off without a second thought. I smooth my hands down my shirt and continue behind them. About halfway to the stairs, one of the men turns around. I realize it's Jax, one of the guys who was in the car with us last night and Sierra's husband. I wave and offer a smile. He doesn't smile back but nods his head to the side, as if signaling me to catch up. I pause for a moment, and he realizes my hesitation.

"Get up here, Teach. We don't bite," he says. Now that makes the rest of them turn and look at me. I feel heat creep up my cheeks and make my way to Jax, who is almost perfectly in the center of the group of men. An arm wraps around my shoulders, and I feel knuckles rubbing on the top of my head like I'm a child.

"Not-a-club-girl! Nice to see you're still in one piece after leaving with that brute Axel," Motley says. I chuckle and then shove him off me.

"He always like this?" I ask Jax.

"Sadly." He glares at Motley over my head. I probably do look like a child next to these men. I'm not short, at 5'7", but these men are all easily 6'2" and above.

"You're up early. Sierra is still passed out," Jax states.

"I usually have to be up early for school, so sleeping in has become difficult for me," I shrug as I look around at the faces around me. I recognize a few but don't know any names.

"That's Bear, Shiny, Chuck, and Spider." All of the men nod at me as Jax says their names and points at each of them. I feel like I've already met so many members of this biker club, yet there are still people I don't know. How many of them are there?

"Nice to meet you all," I say as I nod to each man. Some smile, others just look at me and keep walking. "I was just coming downstairs to get some coffee and food for Axel and me. Know where I might find some?"

"We're all headed to get some grub now. You can come with us," Jax says as we make our way to the common area. Large trays of food line the bar, and a beautiful woman with long, curly salt-and-pepper hair comes out of the kitchen holding an oversized pot of coffee. My stomach growls in appreciation.

"Perfect timing, boys, just finished breakfast. Dig in!" the woman says. She goes to start filling coffee cups, but stops in her tracks when she sees me.

"And who do we have here?" she says as she sets down the pot of coffee and places her hands on her hips. Spider, who has a piece of bacon hanging out of his mouth, calls out over his shoulder,

"Ma, that's Axel's girl."

I almost go to correct him and tell him I'm not his girl; we really haven't put a label on this. But she drops her hands, and a huge smile covers her face. She rushes over and engulfs me in a rib-crushing hug. I don't have time to wrap my arms around her, so my arms are pinned by my side. She pulls back but keeps her hands on my arms.

"I'm so happy Axel has found someone. You must be so special!" she exclaims, and I honestly don't know how to answer her. I kind of want to change the subject.

"Um, hi... I'm Jenna," I say awkwardly as she lets go of me. "I'm not really Axel's girl, we have only started seeing each other." I choke out.

"Oh, pish posh," she says as she waves a hand in the air. "He's never brought someone back, and never once has one of the boys announced someone as his girl." A small smile pulls at my lips as I feel a blush creep up my cheeks.

"I didn't catch your name." I smile at her, hoping she doesn't mind the sudden change in conversation.

"Daphne, but everyone calls me D," she says as she points to the one called Spider. "I'm that one's mom and in-house chef."

I look toward the bar, seeing the resemblance between the two. Both have light brown wavy hair and bright amber eyes that radiate warmth and comfort.

"This all looks great. Mind if I make us some plates and grab some coffee to go?"

"Already taking care of him. I think I like you." She beams. "Of course, Sugar. And if you ever need anything, just holler. Us girls have to stick together."

With a wink, she is off talking with the men and women sitting around the tables that fill the large room. I look around and see three women seated at a round table in the corner. They are all dressed as if they are allergic to fabric. Honestly, I think I see more skin than clothes. But the clothing situation isn't what bugs me—it's the way they are glaring at me like I've ripped the head off of their favorite stuffed animal. It annoys me to no end, but I don't really want to start anything. The club is being nice enough as it is, letting me stay here.

I walk over to the bar and fill two plates of food for us. Daphne has given me a tray so I can carry everything in one go. I load up the coffee last and head back to Axel. As I leave, a few of the guys say bye and ask if I need help. I have to admit, for how scary they all are, they sure are sweethearts. I let them know I've got it handled and continue on my way.

Walking up to the door, I realize that I don't have a third hand to open the door. *Shoot, maybe I should have asked for help.*

Once in front of the door, I notice it's already cracked. *Huh, that's weird.* I push the door open further with my foot and make my way into the dark room. Expecting to find Axel in the same place I left him, I move to set the tray down on the small, round coffee table between the leather armchairs. The opening in the curtains gives just enough light to see around the room, but I have to focus hard to see the table under me.

Before I set the tray down, I see something move on the bed. I look up to steal a glimpse of Axel and see he's relaxed and peaceful. There is a medium-sized form under the duvet sliding down his body. I blink a few times, trying to make sure I'm not hallucinating. Surely, this isn't what I think this is. I stare at what's happening in front of me and forget I am still holding the tray. I feel it slip from my fingers but barely register the loud slap it makes, followed by silverware clinking on the plates and coffee spilling. Axel's whole body jolts up and he makes direct eye contact with me.

Instantly, I feel like an intruder, and a surge of anger runs through me. Not only because of what I just walked into but because I was stupid enough to go against my gut. I knew this was too good to be true. I had made that deal for a reason—men are assholes.

"What the fuck?" he looks confused and stares up at me from where he lays, still clutching the duvet as the form moves on top of him.

"Yeah, baby, you like that?" a gravely feminine voice purrs from under the covers.

"Jenna?" He looks at me and then down at the blanket in front of him. Ripping the blanket off the fully naked woman, until her ass stares me right in the face.

"What the fuck?!" he growls. Wow, I have to hand it to him—he's a great actor. The woman stops and turns to make eye contact with me. A devilish grin appears on her face as she nods my way.

"Want to join?" she asks as if this is somehow a game. I recognize her from last night—she was one of the women who had given me the death glares.

Frozen where I stand, I will my body to start moving to get anywhere but here. Axel jumps out of bed, his naked body on full display.

"No." I say in a firm voice, with my arm outstretched in front of me. I hold my palm up to signal him to stop.

"No, Jenna, this isn't—" Axel tries to speak.

"Stop. I don't want to hear it." Grabbing my purse, I sling it over my shoulder and turn to walk out the door. I make it a few steps before I feel him behind me. Every fiber in my body calls to him. He grabs my arm, gently holding me in place. Without a second thought, I wrench my arm out of his grasp and turn to him with a glare that is meant to keep him away. He's put a pair of briefs on in the time it took him to make it out the door.

"Leave me alone, Axel."

"No, I dont even know what the fuck is happening!" he says in his gravely morning voice.

"No, you don't get to do that." I point at him. "Fine, you told me everything I wanted to hear. Conned me into bed, into thinking you felt the same way. But now it ends." My voice is raising, and I can feel tears burning in the back of my eyes. I blink them back. He doesn't get to see me cry. I take a step back, pulling my shoulders back and my chin up. Doors start opening around us, and I choose not to be everyone's entertainment.

Lowering my voice, "Just don't lie to me. You owe me that."

"You think I'm lying to you? After everything I said to you last night?" he looks hurt, and I want to scoff. How dare he think that I'm that dumb? "Jenna—" he moves closer, but I take another step back. He drops his hand and lets out a frustrated sigh. "You have to believe me. I dont even know how she got in."

"I don't care." *Lie*, of course I do. "We were only hooking up and let ourselves get too wrapped up in whatever this is... was." I say the words with conviction, trying to also get myself to believe them. "So just let me go. This was only supposed to be a one-night thing, anyway. We don't even know each other."

"No," he practically growls at me. "This isn't over. I'm not letting you go." His soft brown eyes are now pools of black. The muscles in his neck are tense, and it's clearly taking all of his self-control not to pick me up and hoist me off like the caveman he is.

"You have no choice, because I've already made it." The words leave my lips as a whisper. I look behind me, seeing multiple pairs of eyes on us—one of them being Marley. "Goodbye, Axel."

"Fuck your goodbye, Jenna. This isn't over." He moves closer, but once again, I move back. "Fuck, babe." He says in a defeated voice. "Take some time if you need it. But this shit isn't what it looks like. And you know it."

"Axel, just go back to whoever it is you have in your bed. Stop acting like this means anything to you. We barely even know each other!" God, I'm starting to lose it. This time he moves so fast I don't have time to move back. He is standing so close I have to crane my neck to see him. His eyes swim with want... need and something else, but I can't give in.

"Just let me go." I say again, my voice betraying me by shaking. A lump is forming in my throat, and I'm having a hard time keeping my tears at bay. *Keep it together, Jenna!*

"Never." Axel says down at me. "Don't let this be your excuse for walking away." He kisses my forehead before I turn out of his grasp and walk away.

Chapter 24

AXEL

MY HEART FEELS like it's been ripped out of my chest. Standing in the middle of the hallway in nothing but my fucking boxers, I watch as Jenna practically runs in the other direction. Running my hand through my hair, I take a deep breath. *What just happened?*

One moment everything is perfect—*we* are fucking perfect—and now everything is crumbling around me. I'm not lying to her. I woke up to someone sliding down my body under the covers. I thought it was Jenna waking me up. She was the only one in my room, the only woman I've been with since I laid eyes on her. The moment I made eye contact with Jenna in my room, I knew something was wrong. Her beautiful face was full of disgust and hurt. I would do anything to take the pain from her.

I look up and see a few of my brothers and their old ladies

standing outside their doors, either glaring at me or looking at me like I've lost my damn mind acting like this over some chick. Well, fuck them all. Before I turn around, I see Marley standing with Blaze, her hands crossed over her chest, looking confused and pissed. Well, me fucking too.

Just then Sapphire waltzes out of my room as if she didn't just sneak in to ruin what Jenna and I have. I see Marley's eyes flash from me to her and then back. The look of utter betrayal and disgust rivals Jenna's. Turning to Sapphire, I barely register the blur that passes by me. Marley has Sapphire by her hair faster than anyone can see coming. Marley slams her face into the wall. We all hear the undeniable crunch of a broken nose. Sapphire screams and starts to yell about, "getting this crazy bitch off of her." Blaze grabs Marley and pulls her off, but she whips out of his arms to face me.

"You!" she jabs her finger into my chest. "Are an asshole. How can you do that to her?" she pants, still red from her attack. Sapphire is now sitting on the floor with blood gushing from her nose. Another club girl rushes over to help her.

"I didn't do shit. She must have snuck into my room. I thought it was Jenna," I say, keeping eye contact with her the whole time.

"So help me, Axel, if you are lying." Her chest heaves as she catches her breath, and Blaze comes up behind her. He gently sets his hands on each shoulder and kisses the top of her head.

"Easy, Tiger. How about you let me handle it from here?" Blaze says as she rolls her shoulders to get his hands off her body. She turns to Sapphire and kneels down in front of her.

"Is he telling the truth?" she questions. Sapphire stays quiet and just looks around at each of us for help. When she doesn't find it, she looks back at Marley with wide eyes.

"Answer me," Marley's tone is so quiet and calculated it sends a shiver down my spine. She may be small and looks like she wouldn't hurt a fly, but for her friends, I bet Marley would burn the world down.

"His door was unlocked, okay?! He's only been hanging out with that bitch since Knife's party. I thought he needed real company," she answers in a shrill voice. *What the fuck?*

Marley stands from her squatted position and turns back around. With a sigh, she pinches the bridge of her nose with her thumb and forefinger. "You need to deal with this, Axel." Marley goes to stand next to Blaze, who wraps an arm around her waist. "Jenna doesn't understand this shit. I don't even understand this shit. In the real world, random women don't just sneak into your room to wake you up with a happy surprise." She scoffs and they start to walk away. "Give her time."

Blaze stops a few steps in and looks at me. "This is what I was talking about. I know this shit isn't on you, but it's been less than a fucking day, Axel." With that, they leave, and everyone starts to disperse.

Squatting down, I look into Sapphire's bloodshot eyes. The blood has stopped running from her nose but is now matted all down the front of her body. Her eyes are empty. The fun, crazy girl looking for a good time who came to the clubhouse a year ago isn't there anymore. I feel bad for her—she is so desperate for attention that she will do anything for it. I should have found out what was wrong when I started to see a change in her. But fuck, this isn't my job, and I have so much other shit to focus on.

"Pack your shit and get out of the clubhouse." It's the only option. Her eyebrows shoot to her hairline.

"What?" she asks with disbelief.

"You're done. You knew I was with Jenna, and you chose to fuck with it. I know you have some shit going on, but this is inexcusable."

Her eyes well up with tears, but she nods. Standing up, I turn to see Bear. "Help her get her shit and see she has a place to stay. See what you can find out about what shit she is into. We can maybe get her some help."

I turn and walk into my room, slamming the door shut behind me. With my back pressed against the door, I feel a twisting in my chest and a rage I need to set free. Pushing off the door, I get dressed for a ride. My heart is beating so fast all I feel is the quick, rapid thuds in my ears.

Everywhere I look, I see Jenna. Her clothes are strewn around from the night before, her pink suitcase is open in the middle of the floor, and the bathroom counter has her products. I know that by the time I come back, it will all be gone—a memory. How can things go so wrong in a matter of minutes? I slam my fist against the wall, over and over, until my knuckles bleed and I see nothing but red.

As much as I want to go find her and drag her back here, I wonder if this might actually be the best thing for us. I knew from the moment I saw her that she was too good for me and this life. Maybe we just needed to be reminded of that.

I take off for my bike, the only one I can trust to not walk away.

Chapter 25

JENNA
PRESENT DAY

I idle at the last red light before my apartment and feel my car start to shake and make a disturbingly loud grumbling noise… again.

"No, no, no, no please don't give up on me now!" I say to the car, slouching back into the seat and wrapping my hands around the steering wheel. After my car was practically totaled at Tipsy, I needed to buy another car, but on a teacher's salary, I can't afford something new. My cousin Mark has been trying to sell his older compact SUV, and when I asked if it was still available, he gave me a great deal. The only downside is that something is wrong with it, and he definitely forgot to mention that when I bought it. I've taken it to two different mechanics, and each one said that it's probably cheaper to get rid of it altogether and buy a new car; everything needs replacing. But

I refuse to do that—I'm going to drive this thing until the wheels fall off.

Easing my foot down on the gas as the light turns green, the car slowly creeps forward, making a new horrendous grinding noise.

Ugh. That can't be good.

Fortunately, I make it to my apartment and internally do a happy dance. The car has lived to see another day! Opening the car door and stepping out onto the ice-covered sidewalk, I hold onto the car door handle for support. Snow covers the ground, and the slick ice makes the trek to my front door especially annoying. I gingerly place one foot in front of the other, hoping I don't slip and give my neighbors another free show of my clumsiest-woman-ever performance. Last week, I slipped and my feet flew out from under me, sending me backward onto a sheet of ice. When I finally caught my breath enough to stand, I looked up to see not one set of neighbors but three looking out their windows at me with amusement.

Once inside my apartment, I flip on the lights and rush to the thermostat to turn up the heater. Ever since Marley and Blaze moved in together a few weeks ago, I've had to get used to being on my own. I knew that Marley and I couldn't live together forever, but that fact became even more apparent when they got engaged.

I miss having someone here with me—to talk to and just have around. I rub my hands together for warmth, shake off the lonely feeling settling in my stomach, and decide to call Marley. The phone rings only once before she picks up.

"Hey," Marley says in a short tone.

Laying the phone on my bed and pressing the speakerphone button, I start to undress.

"Well, hello to you too, Sunshine," I reply, smiling at the bite in her voice.

"Sorry, I'm stressed about tomorrow. You're going to be up at 8 a.m., right? The makeup and hairstylist will be there at 8:30, and I want everyone to be punctual. And—" She's clearly anxious about her wedding; I mean, what bride isn't?

"Mar, I will be up and ready to go. The apartment is all set up for guests, and everyone will be here on time… I set it all up. Maid of Honor, remember?" I say through the thick material of my turtleneck as I pull it off. I slide on a silky pajama set and put on thick fuzzy socks.

A long sigh comes from the other end of the line. "Okay, good. I just don't… I don't know what the hell I was thinking rushing this wedding. A month?! I said we would get married in a month? Am I crazy?"

"Wow, no, you're not crazy," I laugh. "You're in love, and we pulled it off! So, stop worrying and just plan on enjoying the day tomorrow, okay?"

"But—" she tries to argue.

"Okay?" I say again before she can get any of her rebuttal out.

"Fine," she huffs. There's a silent pause between us, and I can hear her overthinking from here.

"What is it?" I ask.

"He's going to be there tomorrow, you know?" Her voice is low and sounds apologetic. I stop moving. This entire process has been happening so fast I haven't allowed myself to think about him. Well, that's a lie—I think about him at least once a day and then chastise myself for it. We haven't planned a traditional rehearsal for the wedding party to meet up, so I've been able to avoid him at all costs. My stomach twists at the thought of seeing him, but I blow out a quick breath and resume putting on my socks as if the whole situation doesn't make me want to hurl.

"Yep, I gathered that much when you told me he's Blaze's best man." My gut twists a little more thinking back to the last time I saw Axel. I was so mad and hurt, I walked away from him and forced myself to never look back. In the moment it felt like my heart had been ripped out and I had been so stupid to believe that the connection we had could happen so fast, be so perfect.

Later that day, Marley had found me cuddled up on the couch, mindlessly watching anything to get my mind off the situation. She told me that he was telling the truth, but by the time I was finally ready to talk to Axel, months had gone by and I didn't want to rehash the whole situation. Part of me knew he was telling the truth—but I think everything was happening so fast between us and I panicked. I saw my way out, and I took it.

I had just started to feel better. The thought of it all makes me queasy, and as much as I'd like to think I'm over Axel, my heart... likes to remind me I'm not.

I close my eyes and swallow down the thick emotions stuck in my throat.

"Think you'll be okay?" Marley rasps. I pick up my phone off the bed and start walking to the kitchen to make a cup of tea.

"It will be fine, Marley; we haven't seen each other in four months. I bet he's already moved on." I wait for her response with bated breath. I do this from time to time, wanting to know how he's doing but not wanting to actually ask. The line is silent, and then I hear someone speaking in the background.

"Hey, Jen, Blaze is here and he wants me to come see where everything is set up so we can make adjustments."

"No worries, get some rest tonight! I'll see you in the morning." I pick up the phone once more, my cup of chamomile tea in hand, and walk over to sit on the couch.

"Bright and early!" I hear my best friend say loudly. And with that, the call ends. I laugh at how excited yet stressed Marley is. She is going to be the most gorgeous bride tomorrow and really has nothing to worry about. I lean my head back to rest on the top cushion of the couch, remembering the day that Blaze told Marley he wanted to claim her to the club. Mar and I were sitting outside our apartments on a picnic table enjoying the small amount of sunlight we get here in Cranson Creek when Blaze drove up with Jax. Blaze had been working all day and was covered in grease and whatever else from his day at the mechanic shop. Up until that point Marley had been unsure about being claimed. She hated the term "claimed" and thought it meant that he was somehow above her in their relationship. She let him know that if he wanted to make it official, then they were getting married as equal partners in a marriage. And legally, not just in the eyes of the club.

"Max, I know this whole macho man bullshit is like a thing for you guys, but no way in hell are you going to "claim" me." She'd glared at him as she crossed her arms. "If you want me, then you better propose and only under the guise that we are partners, equals — not that I'm in some way your property."

Jax whistled under his breath as he and I waited for Blaze's response. *Go Marley, go!* I chant in my head.

"Marley, you know that's not how this works. In the club—" Blaze holds his hands out in front of him like he has no choice.

"No, I'm not doing this for the club and that's the end of this. If you want me, then you need to do it properly." She hadn't moved a muscle and looked like a goddess shining in the sun, putting him in his place.

"Can we talk about this later? Just the two of us?" Blaze had asked, looking back to where Jax and I sat at the far end of the picnic table. We both quickly turn our heads, looking at anything other than them. Acting as if we haven't been staring at their interaction.

"You were the one who decided to have this conversation out in the open." She stares at him and then huffs in frustration, sensing he needed to have this conversation in privacy.

"Sure, but you're getting the same answer. I understand that some other women might be okay with that but I sure as hell am not. I get that this is for the club and means something to you, but I'm not in the club. I need you to think about that." She takes a deep breath and lets her arms unfold and rest at her side. The two take a moment and stare at each other, not sure what to say next. Marley is tiny and looks as sweet as can be, but she is the most confident, self-assured person I know. Blaze stands in front of her, towering over her with his insane height and muscles. The vein in his forehead is pulsing. These big badass bikers really do not know what to do with a strong-willed woman. But they sure need them to keep them in line.

At this point Jax and I have actually turned away, allowing them some privacy.

"I love you, Max, but this isn't something I'm going to budge on." The silence is deafening as Jax starts to chat about the weather. I wave my hand at him to get him to stop.

"We shouldn't be listening to this." Jax says in a whisper to me.

"Yeah, well she's my best friend, and she's right." I stick my tongue out at him like an annoying child. He rolls his eyes at me and walks away.

"Fucking chicks, man." Jax scoffs as he heads over to his bike.

"I'm telling Sierra you said that!" I shout as he walks away. But Marley had to do this, she'd been open with him about this and he had to understand where she was coming from.

The next day, Blaze had called me to set up a surprise proposal at a sweet old gazebo. Very swoon worthy. Guess Marley had gotten through to him.

Melting deeper into the couch, I take a sip of my tea and flip on the TV. Some may choose to go out on a perfectly good Friday night, but me? I will be enjoying extremely dramatic reality television shows.

Beep, Beep, Beep... Beep, Beep, Beep.

My alarm sounds from the other side of the room. I

instinctively stick my arm out from under the covers and start to slam my palm against the nightstand, trying to turn the incessant noise off. After what feels like an eternity, I remember my phone is no longer next to my bed. I've started keeping it on the dresser across the room because it's too easy to turn off and roll back over when it's right next to me. Groaning, I slither out of the covers and practically crawl across the cold floor, clawing my way up the dresser and smacking the off button. The deafening beeping noise ceases as I squint at the alarm clock: 7:30 a.m. Perfect—just enough time to start coffee and take a quick shower.

Slowly making my way to the coffee machine, I hear a knock on the front door. Who's showing up this early? Moving over to peek through the peephole, I see the handle jiggle. What the hell?

I steady myself and take a calming breath. Over the last twelve weeks, I've been learning self-defense and even started beginner MMA classes. I don't know much yet, but I can put someone on their ass if they try anything funny. The handle jiggles again, followed by a familiar voice: "Jenna! Let me in. I'm going to pee my pants!"

Oh, thank God.

I swing the door open just in time for Marley to hurl her heavy dress bag at me. She races past me down the hallway and into the bathroom.

"Geez, took you long enough!" she shouts from the toilet.

"Sorry, I wasn't expecting anyone until 8. Why are you here so early?" I ask, walking her dress over to the window and hanging it from the curtain rod.

"I couldn't sleep. And Blaze has been in a cranky mood the last few days. Keeps saying something about getting all this wedding crap over with. How romantic, right?"

I giggle at her and then walk over, wrapping her in a hug.

"You feeling okay? Today's going to be amazing!" I pull back to make eye contact with her.

"Yeah, I'm okay—just slightly nauseous. I'm not going to lie, I'm nervous." Tears swim in her eyes, but a huge grin forms on her face.

"Well, we can always make a run for it," I joke. Marley slaps my arm and rolls her eyes.

"Never going to happen."

We link arms and head into the kitchen, grabbing giant coffee cups from the cupboard and filling them to the brim. Thank God Marley taught me how to set the coffee to brew in the mornings. It's the only thing that drags me out of bed.

Before we know it, the apartment is overflowing with bridesmaids, makeup and hairstylists, as well as family members. I've never been so happy for anyone like I am for Marley today. As I watch her laugh and enjoy her day, I can't help but feel anxiety at the thought of seeing Axel. I've purposely avoided the clubhouse or anywhere I might run into him. I know I shouldn't care this much, that he was never truly mine to begin with, but I can't control the constant pull I feel toward him. Whenever I'm around him, I can't stay away.

The last few months, Cal and I have been hanging out more, and he's truly become one of my best friends. It's easy to spend time with him. We talk about everything going on in my life, and he gives me all the details of his insane dating stories.

That man is a perpetual bachelor, but that doesn't stop me from trying to set him up on dates. Sometimes I wish it would have been him. He's so easy to love. But when I think of Cal, my heart loves him as a friend—a brother. I take a deep breath and straighten my shoulders. I'm lucky to have this new set of friends that are quickly turning into family.

"Oh my God!" Marley's mom's voice pulls me out of my thoughts.

"What?" Marley asks, alarmed.

"The baker just texted and asked when we were picking up the cake. I forgot to put it in the contract that they would bring it to the venue." She slaps her forehead with the palm of her hand.

"No need to worry," I chime in. "I can just go and quickly pick up the cake and meet you all at the ceremony."

"Are you sure? I can see if Blaze will have a prospect pick it up," Marley says, looking thrown off by the situation.

"I'm already ready—no need to search around for someone. The bakery is nearby anyway." I walk over to Marley and kiss her on the head. "You look beautiful, by the way. Relax and enjoy—I've got this handled!"

Marley mouths, "Thank you," to me as I make my way out into the Arctic tundra.

Chapter 26

AXEL

I CAN HEAR my phone buzzing, but all I want is for it to stop so I can go back to sleep. It's dark in my room except for the light peeking out the top of my blackout curtains. I should get up, but I was up late last night, and I need a few more minutes to shut the world out. The annoying sound keeps going and seems egregiously loud in this silent room.

When the buzzing finally stops, I roll over and try to close my eyes again, basking in the silence. But of course, I can't fall back asleep. Ever since Jenna left, I can't sleep at night. Something about having her next to me brought a calm I haven't been able to replace. I reach up, putting my hand behind my head and staring at the bare ceiling.

Fuck, I miss her.

The past four months have been hell. I pretty much go to the garage, get shit done for the club, and then come back here to pass out. Only to start it all again the next day. I still have a prospect tailing Jenna full-time; he keeps an eye on her, and it gives me peace of mind. With all the Reaper shit still going on, I can't have her out there unprotected.

Although today, I had to pull Shiny from her detail. She's with Marley all day anyway, so she's covered. Blaze keeps tabs on that woman like a psycho. But I guess that's what love does to you.

Dragging myself out of bed, I head to the bathroom and turn on the shower, making sure the water is hot before stepping in. The last few months have been quiet with the club. Too quiet, if I'm being honest. After the fight at Tipsy, the Reapers have seemingly vanished. They haven't even popped up creeping around town. Something's up, and it's leaving us all constantly checking our backs.

I close my eyes and lightly shake my head. This is what they want. They want us so fucking paranoid that we can't even see their attack. That's why I think today is a bad fucking idea. If we were smart, we'd have this wedding here in the compound. But Marley has to have the wedding at some fancy venue on the far end of town.

I've spent the last three days making sure we have proper security and prepping all of my men accordingly. Even with catching the club rat, I have a feeling we aren't out of the woods yet. Tex, one of the newer prospects, had been caught making calls to a number in Reaper territory. When Ace traced the call, it led straight to the snake himself, Red. I had to put an end to the treachery, so I took him out like the rat he was. Just the thought of that motherfucker makes my blood boil. He put this club in danger. He put everyone in danger.

I get out of the shower and check my personal phone; no notifications are there. I grab my work cell and see two missed calls—one from a local tow company and another from a random number. It's Saturday, and we're closed, so it sucks to be the sorry fucker that got towed to our shop. I toss the phone on my bed and head over to where D has hung up my suit. I get my pants and dress shirt on, only to hear my phone buzz again. Damn, someone isn't getting the hint. Before I pick it up, the buzzing stops, and a voicemail appears. I don't know why I feel obligated to open it. Shit, I couldn't even work today if I wanted to.

The dial tone beeps, and then I hear it—her silky voice. The sound travels straight to my heart, tightening in my chest. Her voice sounds a little shaky and unsure as she leaves a message.

"Hi, um, this is a message for the mechanic for Gears & Wheels Motors. My car broke down, and the tow truck driver said you're the best, so he brought me here. But I see you're closed, so I'm leaving the car here and will get it on Monday... Hope that's not a problem. My name is Jenna Waters, and it's the grey compact SUV. Thanks a lot!"

Before the voicemail ends, I'm already straddling my bike and ripping out of the lot. We might not be together, and she may have walked away, but I will always be there for her. Her being stranded at my shop alone leaves a bad taste in my mouth.

I drive through the quiet streets until I see my shop. As I get closer, I see the grey compact SUV, but no Jenna. She must have called for a ride. I drive up to the entrance just in case she's still here, and that's when I see her. Standing in the alcove in front of the front doors. She's wearing an olive-green floor-length dress which matches the color of my tie. It slips over her curves like running water. Her brilliantly red hair is pulled back into a low bun, and small curled pieces hang loose around her face, framing her angelic features. She's clutching a thin black piece of material around her upper body and has a phone pressed to her ear.

I take a moment to study her. She's even more beautiful than before—if that's even possible. I finally hoist myself off my bike and remove my helmet. Jenna finally turns to me, and her shimmering emerald eyes hold me in place. Her mouth drops open and then quickly closes.

"I'm g-going to have to call you back," Jen says into the phone. She doesn't move, just stands there and rakes her gaze over my body. I can't help the frown that forms on my face; her teeth are chattering, and her lips are almost blue.

"No, Mar, I have to go. S-see you at the ceremony." Jenna removes the phone from her ear and holds it at her side. We just stand there staring at each other for a minute, both not quite sure how to handle this. Finally, she breaks the silence.

"Did someone send you to help me? Because I have this h-handled," she says, waving a hand toward the car. The tips of her fingers are almost blue from how cold she must be. How long has she been here, and why didn't she wait in the car?

"I can see that," I reply. "Why didn't you wait in your car?"

"Answer my question first," Jenna shoots back, raising an eyebrow and crossing her arms.

There's my little badass.

"No one sent me," I say, shaking my phone in the air. "Got

a voicemail saying a stubborn teacher needed some help." I meet her eyes again, and this time they widen when realization hits.

"Wait, you're the mechanic the tow truck driver had me call?" She glances around at the shop. "I didn't know." Her voice drops to a whisper.

"Babe, now you have to answer my question." I close the distance between us and wrap my arms around her. She's ice cold and stiffens at first, but quickly sinks into me as I hold her tight. "Why didn't you wait in your car? You're freezing. Where's your jacket?" I pull my shop keys from my pocket, still not letting her go, and open the front door. Warmth spills out, and Jenna practically moans in gratitude.

"T-the driver left with the keys. I think it was an accident, and by the time I realized, he had already taken off. I tried c-calling him a few times, but the call kept dropping," she says through chattering teeth. Her body is trembling so hard I don't know how she's even standing. I'm going to have a word with whoever the fuck left her stranded here.

"I have a blanket in my office. You okay to walk with me and get it?" I ask, my voice low as I bury my face in her hair. The familiar scent of lavender and vanilla washes over me, and the tightness in my chest starts to ease.

"Y-yes, please," she stammers, still shaking, as we make our way toward the back of the shop. My office sits at the far side of the garage, with a large window looking out into the work area.

"I tried to get a ride service to pick me up, but you have the worst service h-here. None of my apps would open," Jenna grumbles. She looks down at her phone and then suddenly smacks her forehead.

"The cake." She turns abruptly out of my arms and starts heading back toward the entrance. Before she gets too far, I slide my arm around her waist and pull her back, grounding her.

"What?" I ask, searching her beautifully scrunched face.

"The cake! That's the only reason I was driving out here. It's in my car… but I don't have my keys. Oh God, Marley is going to freak!" Her voice pitches higher with every word, her panic rising.

"Can't do anything about it right now. Let's get that blanket first, and then we'll figure everything out from there." I turn us back toward my office. Jenna's hands grip my suit jacket for warmth, her trembling still constant.

As we walk, I can feel her putting space between us. It's like she just remembered we haven't spoken in months. I tighten my arm around her waist, unwilling to let her pull away.

I unlock the blue metal door and hold it open for her. My office isn't large, just big enough for a desk and two extra chairs for meetings. I grab a soft, plush black blanket from the basket under my desk. Sierra keeps extra gloves, socks, blankets, and other necessities for working in a cold garage during the winter months.

"Here," I say, draping the blanket around Jenna's shoulders as she sits in one of the chairs across from my desk. Unconsciously, I rub my hands up and down her arms, trying to warm her.

"Thank you," she says shyly as a shiver runs down her body.

I need to put some space between us, I need to talk to her about everything that's happened with us. I may not get another chance. I decide to sit in my chair, rolling myself forward until my legs are under the desk. Leaning forward with my elbows on the smooth wood, I rake my hands through my hair. Jenna glances at me quickly, then averts her eyes to look around the room, clearly trying to avoid the conversation hanging in the air.

"You need some pictures on the walls or something to make this space more inviting," she finally says as she rubs her hands together.

"That's what you want to talk about right now? How 'inviting' my office is?" I ask, not bothering to hide the disbelief in my voice.

"Axel…" Her gaze drops to her hands before lifting back to meet mine through those long lashes. Her green eyes are filled with sadness and something else—something that twists my gut. The color is starting to return to her cheeks as she straightens, pulling her shoulders back. "I'm really not sure what to say," she admits quietly.

"Let's start with you walking out four months ago, Jenna." I say with a little more bite than I intended. I gave her time and space to work her shit out, but months? The feelings I have for her are unexplainable and to think this thing might be one-sided, that she can just turn and leave, rips me open.

She glares at me, her face flushing red as anger sparks in her eyes. "Fine, you want to talk about this?"

She lets the blanket fall from her shoulders as she straightens further, raising her chin. I have to force myself not to get up and wrap it back around her.

"We both know me walking away was the best thing for us, Axel. This thing between us…" Her voice falters slightly as she starts spinning the thin ring around her finger. I've noticed this is a tick of hers when she's nervous. "It's not healthy."

She's lying.

To anyone else, she might seem calm and collected, like she means every word she says. But I know her better than that.

"Bullshit," I say, leaning back in my chair. Jenna slightly shakes her head and looks at me with surprise.

"What?"

"You heard me. Bullshit." I stay completely still, not giving her an inch. She crosses her legs and folds her arms across her chest, clearly trying to put a wall between us.

"I needed space," she finally says, her voice low. "I needed time to sort through all of this. Axel, the way I feel about you isn't normal."

There it is.

"Angel, I gave you your space because I know all of this shit is new to you. But I feel the same way. In this life, everything moves fast because tomorrow isn't promised."

"That's what scares me. This much intensity is bound to combust at some point." She uncrosses her arms, rubbing her temples. I don't know how to respond to that, because she's right. In most relationships, this kind of passion would burn out and leave nothing but ash behind.

But what she doesn't realize is that our relationship isn't like others.

"We should get back; the wedding is in a few hours." She

whispers, pulling me from my thoughts. I watch as she moves towards the door.

"Come here." I say in a low voice.

She looks back at me again but this time with longing, "Axel."

"Jenna, come here." I say again. This time my tone doesn't leave room for debate. We aren't leaving things like this. She lets out a huff and rolls her eyes, at me or herself, I'm not sure. I watch as her curvy body walks around the desk until she's standing between my legs. Fuck, I can see her nipples peaked under the silky fabric covering her. Her cheeks are flush and her breathing is uneven. She feels it too.

I move my hands up the side of her thighs, bunching the olive fabric to her hips. I rest my forehead on her stomach, taking a moment to revel in the feel of her in my hands. She runs her fingers through my hair and rests her hand on the back of my head.

That irritating voice sounds in my head again, reminding me that she is too fucking good for me. That she might be right and her walking away was the best thing for her. But I'm not a good guy, fuck I'm the guy people warn you about. She sighs and a calm feeling settles in my chest. She is my solace, my home. *Mine.*

"Don't run from this Jenna, that shit that happened back at the clubhouse… fuck it wasn't what it looked like," her body stills beneath my hold.

"I know you were telling the truth. Marley told me what happened after I left. But I couldn't come back. I hate the fact that when I'm not with you, other women are practically sneaking into your bed. I won't deal with that." She moves to step away, but my hold stays firm. "And the part that really hurt was that I felt as if I couldn't really be upset, because we were just hooking up. We never talked about what this actually was."

"That shit won't happen again." I say through gritted teeth. I'm not letting that stupid shit infect us more than it already has.

"I want to believe you, Axel." She says as she drops her head back to look at the ceiling. Her voice is laced with sadness and I can feel her getting ready to bolt.

"Believe it baby, because from here on out, it's only you and me. Even if that means we take this slow." Moving my hands to pull up the rest of the dress, I run my fingers over the soft flesh of her thighs. A moan escapes her lips as I trail kisses over her stomach and across her hips. She may not believe my words now, but I will spend the rest of my life proving to her that I am all in on her.

"Dane," she says in a breathy voice, "We need to go... the wedding."

I raise my head and stare into her eyes, rimmed with red, and her usually clear eyes are glassy and unsure. Fuck, I hate seeing her like this.

"Do you want me to stop?" I don't move, waiting for her response. Jenna calmly brings her hand to my face and rests her palm against my cheek.

"I want to try this again." My heart thunders in my chest. "But I'm scared."

I stand so that I can wrap my arms around her, my hand

traveling up around cupping the back of her head and pulling her to me.

"I can promise you that if we try this, it's you and only you. I don't know if I will ever deserve you, but I'm going to make it a priority to try and be worthy of you every day." Jenna's eyes soften and she rises onto her tiptoes; even in her heels I tower over her. Protectiveness surges through me as her smaller form melts into mine.

"Make me a promise."

"Anything." I reply quickly, my voice raspy.

"Never stop being honest with me. This Axel…" She pats my chest as she says my name, "is the man I fell for. I know you have to put on a front for everyone else. But with me, this is who we are."

"Deal," I shoot back with a wink.

Jenna's hands snake around my neck as I crush my mouth to hers. Our bodies molding into one as if finding our missing halves.

Jenna grabs the collar of my suit and pulls me with her as she leans her body back into the desk. I follow, letting her take the lead today. Whatever she wants, she gets. Her hand moves slowly as she undoes the buttons on my jacket, slowly sliding it off my shoulders. She raises her eyebrow when she sees my shoulder holster underneath. I remove my Glock and set it in the top drawer of my desk. Even though it's a special day, I won't go anywhere without it. She finally peels back my shirt until it's hanging from my arms. Her breath hitches as she catches sight of my new ink. She runs her fingers over it and then hums in appreciation.

"You know they say this is bad luck, right? The kiss of death actually." Jenna finds my eyes with a playful look.

A few weeks after the incident at the clubhouse, I needed to check in with Chuck about his security system at the tattoo shop. He's one of the older guys in the club and is one hell of an artist. When we finished our meeting, he mentioned his next appointment had bailed and asked if I wanted any new ink. I don't know why, but I immediately thought of Jenna. I ended up getting a small red J in cursive, right above my heart. It's the only color tattoo on my body and stands out just as much as my fiery woman does.

"Doesn't seem like it's bringing me bad luck right now." I roll the thin straps of her dress down from each shoulder. Jenna drops her hands allowing the silky material to slip down her body, pooling at her feet.

"Fuck, it might actually be my new good luck charm." I say as I gaze at her delicious body. She is wearing a thin see-through nude bra and no underwear. Fuck.

"You walking around with nothing covering this sweet pussy?"

When she doesn't respond I finally bring my gaze up to her. She's staring at me while chewing her lip.

"I didn't want panty lines." She giggles. "A happy coincidence, I guess."

All I can do is grunt back at her, she has no idea what she does to me. I quickly unclasp her bra and let it fall to the floor. Her full breasts release from the confines of the tight material, her rosy nipples at attention. A small whimper escapes her lips as I latch onto her. I draw light circles around her perfect peaks, licking and sucking, pulling sweet moans from her. She is my addiction.

I'm so lost in Jenna's amazing rack that I don't realize she's undone my belt. Her hand dives into my boxers, and I hiss as she makes contact with my swollen cock, lightly sliding her hand up and down my length.

"Don't tease me, Angel," I say gruffly. I wish her hair wasn't pulled into a bun and we didn't have somewhere to be after this so I could wrap my fist around her red locks. She removes her hand from my pants and steps back from me. In nothing but her heels, Jenna places her hands on her hips, eyes filled with confidence and lust as she stands like the goddess she is.

"Take off your pants," she commands. The demand makes my dick twitch under the suffocating fabric of my boxers. I don't say anything, allowing her to be in charge. I have to say, this is fucking hot. No one ever dares to speak to me as she does. I won't let it go on for long, but right now, yeah, it's working for me. I remove my belt, making sure to put on a show for her. A small smile appears on Jenna's face at the whipping sound it makes. I take note of her response—she enjoys being in control. Lastly, I remove my pants and boxers, allowing my cock to spring free. A bead of precum drips from my tip as I wrap my hand around myself, pumping my fist up and down while she watches.

Jenna steps forward and stops right in front of me. I reach out to pull her in, but she lightly shakes her head. A mischievous grin splits her face in two as she drops to her knees. She wastes no time and runs her tongue along the underside of my shaft, softly rolling her tongue around the head of my dick before wrapping her lips around me. Her magnificent mouth feels like heaven as she takes almost all of me down her throat. I let my hand rest on the back of her head, not moving, still giving her all the control. She grabs the back of my thighs and pulls me closer, my cock touching the back of her throat. Her eyes lift to mine as they water, and I nearly shoot down her throat at the sight. Her bright green eyes, filled with unshed tears as my cock is buried between her perfectly pouty lips, I've never seen anything sexier. But I'm not ready for this to be over—I need to be inside her. I pull out of her mouth and pull her up.

"Babe, I don't think you have any idea how fucking sexy you are," I growl into her ear as I kiss down her jaw, over her collarbone, and back up until my lips linger right above hers. Keeping her still, my hand slides down her body, memorizing every curve and freckle. The moment I slide my fingers through her slick folds, she whimpers against my lips. Jenna starts to grind into my hand, almost as if she can't handle going slow anymore. *Guess I'm in control now.*

"Damn, baby, you get this wet from sucking my dick?" I say into her lips, still holding her to me.

"Mhm, I love tasting you," she retorts as I dip a finger inside her. She arches her back. I remove my hand from the back of her neck and slide it down to the small of her back. Jenna lets her head fall back between her shoulders, her tits pushed out to me, beckoning me as she rides my fingers. I watch as she takes what she needs, unashamed of her pleasure.

"You have no idea what you do to me, Jenna." Pulling out of her, Jenna whimpers.

"Dane, please," she begs. I close my eyes. My name sounds

heavenly coming from her lips.

"Don't worry, baby. I've got you," I say as I lift her up and set her on my desk. Jenna lets out a yelp as the cold wood bites her ass. I set my hand on her chest, gently pushing her back to rest on her elbows. She eyes me as I step back and admire the view.

"What are you doing?" She asks as she starts to close her legs.

"Stop." I say sternly, "I'm enjoying the view."

I sit down in my chair, pulling Jenna's feet up to rest on the arms of the plush leather chair. I start by trailing kisses up the inside of her leg, feeling her squirm beneath me. When I get to the apex of her thighs, I can't help but run my tongue through the length of her soaking pussy. I slowly lick and suck her clit, taking my time devouring her.

She is now fully lying down, her back bowing off my desk. I won't be able to work here ever again without thinking of this moment. I plant my hand on her stomach to keep her where I want her. Jenna's legs start to shake around my head as she moans my name. I insert one finger, still using my tongue to pleasure her swollen clit. Jenna laces her fingers through my hair, holding me in place as she starts to rock into me. I growl into her as a primal part of me feels tied to her. I add a second finger and pick up my pace. Jenna's pussy starts to quiver and pulse around my fingers. I lightly bite down on her clit, immediately curving my fingers up into the spot I know will make her explode around me.

"Oh yes, yes, yes!" Jenna screams as she cums. I ride her orgasm out with her, slowing my motions and allowing her to catch her breath. I watch her the entire time, mesmerized by the way she falls apart. Standing up, I slide the fingers that were just inside Jenna into my mouth and lick them clean. My eyes stay locked on Jenna.

"You are one dirty man," she says to me with a content smile on her lips.

"Yeah, baby, but I'm your dirty man," I reply, grabbing the back of her knees and pulling her to the edge of the desk. Having Jenna splayed across my desk with her glistening pussy ready for me has my dick straining toward her. I glide the head of my dick across Jenna's clit.

"Don't tease me," Jenna says, throwing my words back at me from earlier. I can't help the grin that spreads across my face as I slam into her, calling her name as I bottom out. She's perfect. She starts to squirm under me, needing the friction just as much as I do. I begin to move in and out of her, keeping my eyes on where we are connected.

"You take my dick so well, baby," I praise Jenna as she takes all of me over and over. "Fuck, look at you, practically dripping for my cock." I lean down until my body covers hers and growl into her ear. "You were made for me, Angel. You are mine."

"Yes, I'm yours." Jenna grabs the sides of my face, pulling my lips to hers. "And you are mine, Dane… you are mine," she repeats as I pick up speed. Pounding into her, needing to feel her velvety walls wrap around me.

"Yes, baby. I'm yours."

"Dane, oh God, don't stop. You feel so… good!" she screams her last word as her walls start to throb around me, another orgasm taking her. I can't say I'm too far behind. Four months is the longest I've gone without sex, and damn, did I miss it.

My body tenses as I lose myself, my thrusts becoming erratic as I release inside her. Jenna grabs my neck and pulls my mouth to hers once more. Our mouths are ravenous for each other, sealing our promises to one another. I reluctantly pull out of her and gently pull her up as I stand.

"Well, that was…" Jenna touches her fingers to her puffy red lips. "Amazing," she smiles and looks up at me as I pull on my boxers and pants.

"Babe, that was better than amazing. And tonight, we are going to be doing a whole lot more of it." I lean forward and kiss her nose. She scrunches it and smirks. I wish we didn't have a wedding to go to, and I could take her home and keep her in bed for the next month.

"I like the sound of that," she says as she clasps her bra.

We get dressed and start to walk out of the office when I hear the bell above the front door ring.

Chapter 27

JENNA

AXEL'S HAND FINDS mine as we make our way out of his office, my mind a flurry of conflicting emotions. I fumble a bit while trying to secure my shawl over my shoulders, half-focused on the task at hand, half entranced by the beautiful man in front of me. His broad form is covered in a perfectly tailored black suit, and his jet-black hair is freshly trimmed. As he rakes his fingers through the dark locks, I take my time memorizing the tattoos covering his hands when I remember the new tattoo he has above his heart. Is he crazy? Who does that?

My core clenches as I picture him with my initial on his body, standing out against the others in bright red ink. Before I can get too lost in my thoughts, Axel quickly pulls me behind his body. I feel every muscle of his back tense under his suit jacket, I instinctively grab onto him. I haven't heard anything about the Reapers after the night at Tipsy, so I just guessed their fighting was over—unless there's a new enemy we have to worry about. I try to move and peek around him, trying to get a glimpse of whatever has set Axel on high alert.

"What is it?" I whisper as he pulls his gun from the holster under his jacket. Axel doesn't answer, instead pointing to a red, solid rolling case that stands about 4 feet high. I quickly understand that he's telling me to get behind it. I get ready to bolt when a loud voice bellows through the large garage.

"Axel! You in here, man?" My body instantly relaxes as Shiny steps in through the front doors. Axel lowers his shoulders and holsters his weapon, visibly relaxing as well.

"Fuck, Shiny. What the hell are you doing here?" Axel asks in an annoyed tone. "You're supposed to be on watch at the venue."

"Blaze sent me. Marley was getting worried about Jenna— she said her car broke down, but she hadn't heard from her in a while. I saw her car in the parking lot… then I saw your bike." He's smirking as he finishes his sentence. I decide it's time for all of us to get back to the wedding and step out from behind Axel. He quickly wraps his arm around me and pulls me close to his side as I try to walk past him to the front door.

"I'll call Blaze and get Jenna back. Go back to your post, prospect," Axel grunts in his direction. I glare up at Axel, letting him know I don't like the way he's talking to the younger man. Shiny nods towards us and then starts to say something, but quickly closes his mouth and turns to leave.

"Wait," Axel hollers out to Shiny. I look into his eyes and see something there that looks like curiosity wrapped in caution. "What were you going to say?"

Shiny turns back around to face us and shrugs his shoulders. "I'm just glad you two figured your shit out." He gives us both a huge cheesy grin that I can't help but return.

"Fuck off, prospect," Axel reacts. I slap his chest with my palm.

"Don't be rude. He was just being nice." I offer Shiny a small nod as he slowly retreats out of the building. Axel grabs the hand I now have rested against his chest and begins kissing each knuckle.

"You're too sweet, Angel," he says between kisses, wearing the sexiest smile I've ever seen. After he's satisfied with kissing my hand, he pulls me alongside him towards the entrance. Watching as Shiny starts to pull open the heavy glass doors, a glint of metal catches my attention. I don't have time to comprehend what is happening before I see a gun go off. The back of Shiny's head explodes all over the floor and wall. A scream tears itself from my throat.

Axel wraps his arms around me and dives behind a truck as gunshots ring out through the garage. I try to suck in big gulps of air, pleading with my body to relax into Axel's intense grip. But I can't stop the shaking that racks through me.

"Jenna, listen to me," Axel growls into my ear as the shots silence. "I'm going to try to distract them. You need to hide here until you see it's clear, then get the fuck out of here."

"No!" I panic and cling onto his suit. "You can't go out there alone." I look into Axel's eyes but only see determination and anger. I take another shaky breath and unwrap my fingers from around the thick fabric of his suit. "You better come back to me, Axel," I say as he rests his forehead to mine.

"Always," he says as he places a light kiss on my forehead.

"Ohh, Axel, I hear you have something I need. How about you come on out and we can discuss our situation," a loud gravelly voice hollers through the open garage. I watch as Axel pulls his gun out from under his suit and shoots me a quick glance before turning away from me towards the front of the vehicle.

"Red," he states, looking across the hood of the truck. He slowly rises into a standing position and walks around the vehicle. I don't move from my crouched position, but I dip my head lower so I can see under the car. Five pairs of boots line the room in front of Axel, and my heart begins to thunder in my chest. He's outnumbered. *Think, Jenna, think.*

I quickly grab my clutch from under my arm and swipe the screen open on my phone. I ignore the growing list of texts and calls that have piled up since we left and text Marley, hoping she is with everyone else by now.

Jenna: Help.

I hear footsteps moving closer to me, so I hit send and shove my phone back into my clutch, not wanting to draw any more attention to myself.

I turn my attention to the conversation between Axel and Red. I don't know what I've missed in my panic, but their voices are rising.

"So, you're the fucking rat," Axel snarls.

I hear a menacing laugh and then a growl of anger. "You had no idea, just went about business as usual. But you did have one thing right—Tex was in on it. He was just an idiot and got caught."

"I will kill you for betraying us," Axel returns, the pure hatred in his voice seeping into every word.

"Well then, it's a good thing you won't be seeing me after today. Reapers will tear your club apart, and I will be glad to stand with them as we watch you all burn."

My hands shake, anger and anxiousness coursing through my veins. I lean down a little more, hoping to get a glimpse of the man responsible for deceiving us all, for killing Shiny. But a blinding pain sears my scalp as my body is yanked up from the ground. I immediately realize that someone has grabbed me by my hair as the men and Axel come into view. Taking a steadying breath, I remember my training and stab my heel down into the attacker's foot while bringing my elbow up, smashing it into the nose of the man holding my hair. Blood splatters over my shoulder as I thrash around in his grip. The asshole doesn't let go but lets out a loud howl and then licks the side of my face as if enjoying my struggle.

I freeze when my eyes finally meet Axel's. He has turned toward us, turning his back on the others around him. His gun is drawn, ready to kill the person behind me, but in an instant, he goes down with a loud thud. The person behind him is holding a crowbar, Axel's blood glistening on the smooth metal. My heart stops, and I scream. I can't remember how long I scream, but I scream for him—to wake up, to fight back, to do something.

"Axel! No! What have you done?!" I look up at the man holding the crowbar, his blonde shaggy hair and short beard so familiar. A single tear falls down my cheek as realization stabs me in the gut. The first night I ever went to the clubhouse, he was working the gate.

"Why?" I ask, steeling myself and not allowing any more tears to fall. I can't let them see me crumble. I try to get a glimpse of Axel to see if he is still breathing, but the man behind me restrains my arms behind my back. I buck my head back in hopes of catching him off guard, but he holds my head steady. The traitor in front of me doesn't reply to my question. He just smirks at me as I feel a sharp pinch sting my neck.

I fight against the piercing pain, but my body won't respond. Panic like I've never felt before takes ahold of me as I struggle to move, but before I have time to process what is happening, the room begins to blur, and a heaviness settles over my body.

Chapter 28

MARLEY

"Bite me," I snap at Bear. We arrived at my wedding venue over thirty minutes ago, and there is still no sign of my Maid of Honor or Blaze's Best Man. The crowd of our friends and family is growing restless, but I don't care. This is my wedding, and I won't do it without my best friend.

"Marley, they are probably on their way and can meet you up there." Bear tries to reason with me as I pace back and forth in my small waiting room, but I glare at him in response. Bear huffs and holds up his hands up in surrender and walks out the door, probably to inform Blaze his bride is holding everything up. I was the one who wanted this wedding so I'm going to get exactly what I want. God, I kind of sound like a brat.

I pinch the bridge of my nose, trying to focus on my breathing. Jenna wouldn't want me to stress, but it doesn't feel right doing this without her here.

"Call Jenna again, please." I say to Mia, and she gives me a sympathetic nod. She dials her number and puts it on speakerphone. It rings a handful of times before Jenna's voice fills the room, *"Hi, sorry I missed you, but leave me a message and I'll get back to you when I can!"* I roll my eyes and let out a huff.

"Jenna, so help me... if you are not here in ten minutes, I'm sending a search party!" I say as I walk over and end the call on Mia's phone. I take a deep breath and try to reign in the bridezilla making her grand appearance today.

This isn't me, but something about professing my love in front of a room full of people makes me nauseous. I'm not getting cold feet; I know I love Max more than anything. But this is a lot to deal with, and without Jenna, I don't know how I will be able to do it. I don't realize I've started pacing at a rapid speed until my mom is next to me, guiding me to sit down on the plush golden couches lining the room. My bridesmaid, Malory, hands me a champagne flute filled to the top with rosy bubbles. Taking a large gulp, I allow the sweet flavor to relax my nerves.

"She must have got caught up figuring out her car troubles," Mia coos in a reassuring voice. I nod at her and take a deep breath.

"I know you're right; I just wish she would text or call to let us know she's okay." This whole situation doesn't sit right with me. Jenna's car breaks down, but she said the tow truck already picked her up, and she was going to be on her way back soon. That was over an hour ago.

I sigh as the door opens to the most welcome sight. My mom jumps up and rushes over to Blaze, shoving both hands in his face. "It's bad luck to see the bride before the wedding!" she screeches at him, standing on her tiptoes, barely covering his face.

His chuckle wraps around me, giving me a moment of reprieve from my all-consuming stress. He gently removes her hands from his face. "Lora, I don't believe in that. Let me see my girl."

Our eyes meet, and my breath hitches. I don't think I will ever be immune to how gorgeous this man is. His dark brown hair is pushed back and perfectly combed, and his bright crystal blue eyes shine with adoration and love. Max's black suit is perfectly pressed, and his watch glistens on his wrist. I can't help the small amount of drool that may have escaped my mouth. I can barely keep my hands off him when he's in his cut, but dressed like this, he is sex on a stick.

He makes the room seem small as he reaches me in only two large steps and drops to his haunches in front of me.

"You are gorgeous, Marley. More beautiful than anything I could have ever imagined," his minty breath wafts through the air between us. It adds to his usual delicious cinnamon and man scent, and I have to seriously fight off my current impulse to rip his clothes off here in front of everyone else. I shake my head and try to bring myself back to reality.

"You look really handsome yourself." I smile. We fought tooth and nail about the suits because he wanted to wear his cut. I get it's a tradition for them but it was a big no from me. I lean further into his space. "I think you should dress like this more often." Ending my sentence with a wink.

"Hmm, that might be able to be arranged." Blaze pushes

a strand of my hair back behind my ear. I decided to have my hair down and curled today. I know it's his favorite, and it's mine as well.

"Have you heard anything from Axel?" I question, keeping my voice low and away from prying ears.

"No, I sent a prospect to go search for Jenna. I told him she called you about some car trouble, so he's going to look at the bakery, her apartment, and the garage." Blaze is putting on a good front but I can see worry in his eyes.

"What is it?" I push, Max is usually so calm and put together that him being unsure has my worry meter buzzing off the charts.

"It isn't like Axel to not respond." He shakes his head and then collects himself. I watch as he straightens his shoulders and tries to act relaxed for me. "But if they both aren't responding, maybe that means he pulled his head out of his ass and they figured their shit out." The corner of his mouth raises in a small smirk.

"That would require Jenna to stop running from him and actually face her feelings." I chuckle. We've been letting them figure everything out on their own, but it's hard to let the people you love suffer because they are so stubborn. Axel refuses to go to her, saying he's letting her, 'have her time.' Whatever that means. And Jenna avoids the conversation altogether.

"I'm going to go talk to the caterers and ask them to go out and hand out champagne or waters to everyone in the crowd for being so patient. But we should begin soon," the wedding planner says as she struts out of the room. Both Blaze and I nod in acknowledgment of her statement, but keep our eyes on each other.

"I'm going to go and make sure everything is taken care of out there. You relax, and we'll sort this out." He stands, pulling me up with him. Max slides one hand up to cup my face and the other comes around my waist, pinning me to him. "I know you don't want to do this without Jenna by your side."

I place my hand over his, keeping his palm pressed to my face. "It's not that I don't want to do this, Max. I want this more than I've ever wanted anything else. I just...."

"Want her by your side when you do it." He smiles down at me. "I get it." He means it, and it makes my stomach fill with butterflies. I love him so much.

"Remember, relax. We will figure this out," he says as he walks towards the door. Once he closes the door, I return to my seat and lean back, chugging the rest of my champagne. Malory comes over and refills it with a large grin on her face and clinks her own glass to mine. She winks at me and lowers herself so that she is eye level with me.

"Does Blaze have any single friends?" she wiggles her eyebrows, making me giggle.

"Many, but be careful. They are a crazy bunch!" She's giggling now, already having met a few of his brothers from the club. We both hear a cell phone ping, and the room falls silent as I dash over to my phone.

"Oh, thank god!" I see Jenna's name light up on my phone. Ready to rip her head off for going M.I.A., I stop immediately, rereading the single word she sent.

This can't be real.

Jenna: Help

Chapter 29

JENNA

"Wakey, wakey, love." A man's voice pulls me from the comfortable darkness. A dull throb is all I can focus on, my pulse pounding against my skull. I peel my tongue from the roof of my mouth while struggling to open my eyes. Through small slits, I take in the room around me. Everything is blurry at first, just bits and pieces of light and walls coming into focus. *What happened?*

The garage, the traitor, Axel.

Remembering the events from earlier, I close my eyes and try to wake up from this horrendous nightmare. But I still smell the putrid scent of god-knows-what and know deep down that this is real, and I am in danger.

I think about Axel, the last time I saw him he was face down on the cement with blood trickling from his head. God, this is all so awful! The guys have to have found him by now, but will they find me? I try to move my arms but feel a sharp, immediate sting across my forearms. Slowly, I move my head so that I can look down at my arms. I'm tied to a chair with what looks like razor wire. The same material wraps around my ankles, ensuring I can't escape.

A slap comes out of nowhere, forcing my head to the side. Realization sets in that I'm not alone. I roll my eyes up, taking in the large form in front of me. I can't control my breathing anymore as my body begins to tremble. Death, the same man from that night so long ago. He flashes his yellow teeth at me with a disturbing smile.

"Glad to see you're awake, princess. I must say, after the night I saw you in that parking lot, I couldn't stop thinking about you." Death grabs my chin and holds my head in place as he leans down and whispers in my ear, "I can't wait to play with you. But sad for us, I'm not allowed to touch you yet."

The moment he loosens his grip, I rip my head from his hold and try to bite down on his hand, now in front of my face. I try to think of my self-defense classes and any move that I could possibly use to get out of this, but I can't think of one. Cal has been also training me here and there, he fights underground and I had mentioned to him I was trying to learn how to protect myself. Sadly, none of that is helpful at the moment.

"Fuck you," I say, and he chuckles.

I'm not sure where this newfound rebellion is coming from, but this man lives on fear, and I won't give him mine. I glare at him, trying not to wince as the throbbing in my head becomes overwhelming and my vision blurs again. All of this movement is messing with my ability to focus, but I need to push through.

He leaves me with one last smirk, "You'll learn to love me, princess." He says over his shoulder as he walks out of the room and closing the dingy door closed. The room I'm in is disgusting. The space is littered with trash and dirty clothing. The only furniture, other than the chair I'm sitting on, is a discolored, cigarette-burned mattress and a tiny nightstand missing its drawer. I feel anxiety settle under my skin as I get a glimpse of what looks like blood splattered across the brown carpet. Tears burn my eyes and start to spill over onto my cheeks. My breaths come in short and choppy as I finally allow myself to break down.

I take in large gulps of air, trying to calm myself. Death's words repeat over and over again in my head: *I'm not allowed to touch you yet.* That means they need me for something, and I need to use that to my advantage. I have to hope Marley got my text and that they find Axel.

The thundering pain in my head takes over my ability to think. My head falls forward, my chin resting on my chest. I finally let sleep take over, hoping that when I wake up, this will all have been a dream.

I don't know how long I've been asleep, but I wake to warm breath brushing over the side of my face and a hand wrapped around the back of my neck, supporting my head as I'm lowered down. The overwhelming scent of masculine cologne fills my nostrils, making my eyes fly open. That scent is one that has haunted me for the past year and is permanently seared into my brain. Jack.

Warm orange light filters in through the window, and I gather it is the sunset. I've been here for more than half the day.

"Hey, baby," he coos as he buries his face in my hair, taking a deep breath. Jack finally pulls back and leans against the wall, lighting a cigarette. His blonde hair is greasy and messy, and his usual bright blue eyes are bloodshot and unfocused. He's high or having a mental breakdown—or both. I let my gaze travel from his face to his torso and suck in a sharp breath as my eyes catch on his leather vest.

"You're a Reaper?" I say, almost in a whisper.

Flabbergasted that my prick of a businessman ex-boyfriend is now part of a motorcycle club, I wait for his response, but he just tips his head back against the wall and lets out a bone-chilling laugh.

"Oh, you have no idea who the hell I am now, Jenna," he says as his eyes rake over my body. I follow his gaze, watching as blood drips from the wire digging into the soft flesh of my arms and legs. He retied the wire around me after taking me out of the chair. Lovely.

"When you left…" He stares off into space for a moment before shaking his head and continuing. "I couldn't handle it. You were my life. My everything."

"I meant nothing to you," I spit at him, my voice coming out as a hiss. As quickly as the words leave my mouth, a knife presses under my chin, digging into my throat.

"Shut the fuck up. You have no idea what hell you caused, and now you are going to be a good girl and make everything right again." Spittle flies in my face as Jack spews his words. I may need to approach this differently. He clearly isn't of sound mind, and antagonizing him is only going to make this worse. I muster all the courage I have left and try again.

"I'm sorry, explain to me, please," I whisper, letting my body tremble in his hold. Fear that he will see through this tactic settles in my gut, but he relaxes a bit. This clearly pleases him as the knife leaves my neck and he starts trailing kisses along my jaw. I feel a bead of sweat slowly move down my neck, continuing between my breasts. A metallic scent fills my nostrils, and I realize he cut me. I take deep breaths through my nose, trying not to gag as I watch him lick the blood from my chest before licking his lips and smiling up at me.

"Mm, this is going to be so sweet, baby. You and I... we're so good together. I'm glad you finally came back to me." He groans as he backs away. Jack returns to his leaning position against the wall when the door opens. The man who betrayed Axel and his club stands before us with a smug expression on his face.

"Glad to see the reunion is going so well," he taunts as he nods to Jack. "Prez wants to see you. He wants you to bring Teach."

I snap my head toward him at the sound of my nickname— the name my friends use, not this slimy man. He doesn't so much as look at me again, but turns and closes the door, leaving me here with my psychotic ex. Jack lets out a heavy sigh and circles around me with his switchblade twirling in his hand.

"I guess we will have to finish our conversation later," he says, slowly sliding the sharp blade down my upper arm. I watch as it leaves a deep red line that starts to seep blood. I wince at the sight, trying to keep my breathing even. Play his game, Jenna. You have to make it out of here alive.

"Can't wait," I reply, flashing a grin that promises revenge.

This must take Jack by surprise because his brow furrows only for a moment before he recovers. The corners of his mouth curl as a smile spreads across his oily face. He grabs small wire cutters from atop the nightstand and slowly clips each ring of wire that restricts my legs. Another man walks into the room. *How many of them are there?* He isn't someone I've seen before, but he refrains from looking at me. As Jack fully removes the wire from my ankles, I visualize bringing my knee up into his face, but without my arms free, I'll just be a sitting duck. I wait as he frees the sliced skin along my forearms. Almost immediately, the man who entered the room grabs them and pulls me into a standing position. Without thought, I scream at the sting from his grip, making my knees buckle under me. He still doesn't look at me, his face unmoving, almost as if it is made from stone. Pulling my wrists together, he secures handcuffs to me. Jack stands off to the side, watching us. As soon as his buddy finishes putting on my handcuffs, he leans forward, placing his hand on my lower back. The room quickly goes dark as something is secured over my eyes.

"Time for you to meet the big boss, baby," Jack grunts in my ear.

Chapter 30

BLAZE

"Hello everyone! Thank you for being so patient. We are waiting for a few more people in the wedding party, and then we will begin. In the meantime, please enjoy a refreshment and mingle with the people around you!" the peppy wedding planner Marley just had to hire says into the microphone at the front of the room. I nod to her in agreement with her distraction plan for the guests as I walk around the room, checking in with my brothers to see if anyone has heard anything.

A hard slap lands on my shoulder. "How's Marley doing?" Prince asks as he shakes hands with the men around me.

"She's all wound up about not hearing from Jenna, but she's hanging in there." I let out a heavy breath, thinking about the look on her face when I'd told her I hadn't heard anything. "She's more stressed out than I've ever seen her, and I just want her to relax and enjoy the day. Fucking Axel. If we find out they are somewhere fucking while we're all running around waiting for them, I'm going to beat the shit out of him."

"We'll find them," Prince nods at me as he heads over to talk to D. He looks exhausted, and I know he's been working his ass off to make sure we're ready if the Reapers make a move. Their silence these last few months is unusual. We haven't seen one of them since the incident at the club. I know they'll attack sooner or later, but just sitting back and waiting is pissing me off.

Out of the corner of my eye, I see a flash of white charging toward me. I turn just in time to catch Marley, who slams into my chest. She looks up at me with glassy eyes and a look of bewilderment. Holding up her hand, the screen on her phone lights up to display a message from Jenna. I hold her shaking hand still as I read the plea Jenna has sent to her: Help. Realizing there's now a small crowd around us, I glance to my right and see Prince looking at the phone screen, too.

"Heard anything from Shiny?" I ask in a low voice. He shakes his head, no. We all know this has to be the Reapers. Our enforcer and his girl go missing, and all we get is a one-word text before radio silence? Not likely to be a mistake.

I look back down at Marley and cup her face in my hands. She's pale and shaking, her eyes unfocused, and I can tell her thoughts are racing. "Hey, Mar. Look at me, Babe." Her eyes lift to mine, and tears start streaming down her face.

"I've been sitting here worried about our wedding while my best friend is out there in danger," she whispers. My need to rip apart the people responsible for making her feel this way takes over. I'll do anything to ensure she never feels this way again.

"Stop that," Looking her right in the eyes. "You had no idea what was going on and couldn't have known. Understand?" She nods and wipes her tears.

"What can we do to help?" Marley asks, straightening her shoulders and looking as if she's ready to go to war.

"I need you to go back to the clubhouse and stay there until I call you." My voice comes out more commanding than I mean it to, but I can't have her fighting me on this.

"But—" Marley starts to protest; I shake my head.

"No buts, babe. I can't do what I need to do if I don't know you're safe." I can tell she wants to tell me off and jump into this headfirst, but her eyes soften, and she nods silently.

"Okay, but I need you to keep me updated, and if there's anything I can do, don't hesitate to call me." She reaches up on her tiptoes and crashes her lips to mine. Our tongues explore each other as if it might be our last kiss. My gorgeous girl is so perfect and understanding. I stare into her large brown eyes and wonder how I got so lucky. Marley leans back and gives a single nod, steeling herself. I call out to Spider, who's already at my side.

"Can you make sure the girls get back to the compound and take a few men with you to keep them safe?" I ask, already stepping into the VP role I know so well.

"Absolutely, Blaze. With my life." Spider nods and heads to Marley to lead them outside. All the women start to follow her toward the doors, and I turn to see Prince, Jax, and Cal checking their weapons. A chime sounds around the room, and Prince quickly answers the call, putting it on speaker for us to hear. I look around the room, realizing we're still in the middle of the wedding venue, but everyone is already gone. The only people left are my brothers.

"What do you got for us, Bear?" Prince hollers.

"Just spotted Shiny and Axel's bike at his garage. Jenna's car is parked near the back entrance. We just parked, heading in now. Oh fuck—" Bear stops, and then a heavy sigh comes through the phone.

"Shiny's dead," he states. I hear the click of him turning the safety off his gun.

"Fuck!" Cal bellows from our side.

"Do you see Axel or Jenna? Anyone else there?" Prince asks. There's rustling on the other side of the line, and then someone in the background yells.

"Axel's here!" My heart thunders in my chest as I wait with bated breath to hear if he's alive.

"He's breathing, but it looks like they knocked him out cold," Tank says in the background.

"Is Jenna there?" Cal asks. I know he and Jenna have developed a strong bond since the fallout with Axel. The look on his face has panic written all over it.

"She's not here," Bear replies.

I shake my head. "They had to have taken her. We're lucky they fucking left Axel alive." I stand straight and eye the men around me. "We're coming there now. Stay where you are, and I'll call Doc to meet you." I say, already halfway out the door.

Chapter 31

AXEL

A SHARP STING pinches my inner elbow, sending my fist involuntarily flying through the air. My fist connects with something solid, and my eyes shoot open just in time to see Doc staring down at me, holding his jaw.

"Fucking hell, Axel. Stay still," he says, grimacing. A needle hangs from my arm as a set of heavy hands pin me to the ground. I thrash my body, trying to get free and figure out what the hell is going on, but a deep throb of pain radiates from my head down through my body. The more I move, the worse the pain gets. I close my eyes and give in to whatever shit Doc is running through my veins.

"Axel, can you hear me?" a voice overhead says. My eyes stay closed, but I recognize the bite in his words—it's Blaze. His hands shake my chest lightly, like he's trying to wake me up.

"I can hear you, fucker. Quit shaking me," I groan, every word sending pulsing pain to the back of my head. Blaze chuckles above me.

"Yeah, he'll be fine."

I raise my free arm to rub my temples, trying to find some relief, only to be slammed in the face with reality. I start thrashing again, trying to pull out the IV from my arm and free myself from their hold.

"Shit, Ax. Stop!" Doc protests, but I can't stay here. They can't focus on me. *Where the fuck is Jenna?*

"Where is she?" I turn to Blaze, and by the look on his face, he knows exactly who I'm talking about. He takes a deep breath and lays a hand on my shoulder. My heart stops in my chest. Absolute terror and unfiltered rage surge through me.

"We don't know. Can you tell us what the hell happened? How did you end up here?" The sympathy in his voice pisses me off. I don't need his worry—I need him to fucking help me find my woman.

"Her car died, and she was towed here." I close my eyes, racking my brain for every detail I can remember, but the only thing I see is the look of terror on her face as Death held her up by her hair in front of me. I shouldn't have brought her into this. I shouldn't have let her become part of my life and put her in this situation. But I know I would never have been able to let her go, to live this life without her.

I'm not a good man, and for Jenna, I'll kill every man responsible for this. Protectiveness flows through my body, and I see it mirrored on the faces of my brothers around me. Murder is all I see. Those who dare to take what's mine will pay me back with their blood.

"It was the fucking prospect, Lee. He was the rat and sold us out to the Reapers. He was a goddamn plant, and now they have her." I look around the room and realize there are more than fifteen Hell Chasers gathered here. We're a larger charter, so it doesn't surprise me to see so much support, but it feels fucking good knowing we have this kind of manpower to get my Angel back. Each member in the club brings a special skill, whether it's from their time in the military, the garage, the fighting ring, or the tech business. They all have something valuable.

Prince pushes off the wall where he stands. I glance to his left and notice that Shiny's body has been removed, but the blood and brain matter remain splattered across the wall.

"I just got off the phone with Ace. He's running through the surveillance cameras from around the garage and through town. He says they took off in a black van, and she was with them when they left." Prince rubs his hand down his stubbly chin. "Right now, we know there are at least six involved in this situation, but we're going to have to be smart about this."

I nod at him and get to my feet, ignoring the onslaught of pain raging through my body. I start to sway, but Blaze steadies me with his hands on my shoulders.

"You have a concussion and really shouldn't be up right now," Doc mutters behind me. I turn and glare at him.

"I don't give a shit what I've got. I made a promise to her that I would keep her safe, and what did it fucking get her?!" I'm yelling now, and I know Doc hasn't done anything wrong, but I need to take this out on someone.

"Enough!" Prince roars. "We need to work fast, and this shit isn't helping. Get your shit together, Axel, or I'll leave your ass here."

I scowl at him, but I understand his words. I'm a liability right now. My connection with Jenna could put us all at risk, but I'm going to fucking be there to pull her out of this hell.

It's been almost four hours since I woke up. Ace had tracked the van to the edge of town and then it just disappeared from all cameras. That means they're hiding right outside Cranson Creek. Knowing the Reapers are behind this, we know the players involved, but no one has reached out to make contact. We don't know their angle yet, but we need to find out soon. Jenna's cell and purse were tucked under the truck where she hid, so we can't track her. I feel like I'm losing my mind.

"Jenna is a fucking badass. She's going to make it out of this," Cal says in a low voice next to me, no doubt seeing how close I am to losing it. It hasn't escaped me how intently he's searching or how invested he is in finding her. I know he and Jenna have become friends and spend quite a bit of time together. I don't blame him for getting close with her; Jenna is gorgeous and smart, but I'll break every bone in his body if he tried anything in these last four months.

"You're right, but she still shouldn't even be in this mess. She wouldn't be a part of this if I hadn't pulled her in." I state. Cal shakes his head and looks at me.

"You don't get it, do you? Jenna came back to you. She knew the risk she was taking when she fell in love with you, but she did it anyway." His voice carries a hard edge as he speaks about her and me. "She's not some damsel who needs you to shelter her from the world. Because you trying to save everyone leaves you with blind spots—like the one that let those fuckers walk through the door and take her."

He walks away before I can respond, but I know he's right. I should've told someone where I was headed this morning or asked for backup. I should've had someone watching my back in case something went down. But when I heard her voice on that voicemail, all I could think about was getting to her as fast as I could.

A buzzing sound pulls me from my thoughts, and I glance across the table at Jenna's phone. The number on the screen is unknown, so I take the chance and answer it. Maybe it's her.

"Hello," I say, holding my breath and hoping to hear her voice.

"Axel, Axel, Axel… thought you could take my girl from me. Tsk, tsk." The voice is familiar, it's that fucking prick from the bar. Jack. I put the phone on speaker and set it on the table.

"Don't worry. I've got her here with me again—safe, where I can make sure she doesn't get mixed up with you." Prince nods at Ace, who immediately opens his laptop and starts typing furiously.

"I swear, you lay a fucking hand on her, and I'll tear you apart, limb from limb," I snarl into the phone. The men in the room gather around the table, listening intently. Jack cackles, and then I hear the sound of a match striking, followed by Jenna's muffled screams in the background. I grip the table so hard I think it's going to snap in half.

"Every time you threaten me, I'll take it out on our girl here," Jack says, his tone smug and cruel. The line goes quiet for a moment, and I wonder if he hung up. "Her skin is so beautiful when it's red and coated in blood." His excitement is palpable, and it fuels my rage. He's enjoying this—hurting her. It's going to be satisfying to make him pay.

"What is this, Jack? You sad your ex-girlfriend left you, so now you have to fucking kidnap her?" I keep him talking, hoping to buy Ace more time to track the call. Blaze grabs his phone and starts texting at the mention of Jack's name. I did my research on the guy after the bar incident and found out he lost his shit when Jenna left him. The man spent time in a mental hospital after attacking a woman in a grocery store who looked eerily similar to Jenna. Seems he never got over his obsession, and now he's patched into the Reapers.

I hear another match strike, and my heart races. "What the fuck do you want?" I snap, desperate to keep his attention off her.

"That's more like it," another voice says in the background. Red.

"We didn't make any headway on our little territory proposition last time we spoke, so I thought we needed to give you a small incentive. I left you alive in good faith," he says in a calm tone.

I sneer at his idea of "good faith," but Prince steps in to take over communication.

"We can talk, but there will be retaliation for what you did, Red. This can't go unanswered."

"I understand. But that would mean we get to play with

the girl and then kill her. So, pick your poison. I want Cranson Creek, end of story."

"You want the whole fucking town?" Blaze growls from across the table. "That was never the fucking deal."

"Yeah, well, I've changed my mind. I want your answer by morning. We'll keep her alive until then, but mark my words—if you say no, I'll just kill her and find something a little more motivating." The call ends abruptly, and I feel the intense need to break something.

I punch the wall as hard as I can, over and over, until my knuckles are bleeding and the drywall crumbles onto the floor. A small buzz draws my attention back to Jenna's phone. Prince picks it up, and his face hardens with vehemence as he hands it to me.

I take the phone, my stomach churning as I see a picture of Jenna. She's handcuffed and kneeling in the middle of a disgusting room, covered in bruises and blood. Bile rises in my throat, but then I see her eyes. She's staring right into the camera lens, her expression defiant and full of fight. She's not broken. She's strong.

I read the message:

Unknown: "Tick Tock."

Slamming the phone down on the table, I level my gaze at every man in the room. "We find them now. We make a plan now. Let them think we're playing their game, but we will never let them win. We fight for her. Let's go get her."

The room erupts with shouts of fury and determination. Ace stands, and the room falls silent immediately.

"I've got a location," he says in a low, serious tone.

We're coming, baby.

Chapter 32

JENNA

LIGHT BURNS MY eyes as the blindfold is torn from my face, I barely recognize anyone in the room with me. Strong hands push me to my knees on the broken and tattered hardwood floors. Instantly my pain radiates through my bones as I try to move my body into a more comfortable position. The walls of the room are lined with an old crumbling floral wallpaper and the tops are yellow from all of the cigarette smoke. There are couches and chairs that sit around the room but no one is sitting, all of the men are towering over me as I am shoved to my knees. I try to mentally prepare myself for what is to come, reminding myself that they have orders not to harm me... yet.

I hear the distinct sound of a match lighting and look over to a dark corner of the room. A large man sits with a half-naked woman in his lap. I glance at his patch, trying to gather as much information about the situation as I can. The small rectangular patch says '*president*,' Prince has the same one. Underneath it is a patch that reads '*Red*,' in crimson lettering. He turns to me and I can see a distinct snake tattoo that wraps around his neck, slithering up to his fiery beard. He looks me up and down as if I'm more of an annoying gnat flying in his face than an actual human being. I glare at him, making it clear that I am not someone who will be swallowed by this situation. The facial expression earns me a malicious smirk.

"I can see why Axel is so drawn to you. Beauty and fire." He strokes his dirty hand down the arm of the woman strewn across his lap. "Death will have fun breaking you."

My facial expression falters for a moment as I try to regain my attempt to look strong. Out of my peripheral vision I see Jack shoot up to stand next to me, almost in a protective stance. His face is twisted in anger and worry, and I momentarily feel sorry for him. The man I once loved has turned into this lost and broken monster clawing to find a place in this world.

"You said she would be mine, that was the deal." Jack snarls at Red. One thing I've learned from being around the Hell Chasers is questioning your president or making a power move out in the open is frowned upon and usually ends in a few punches. Something about Red tells me he wouldn't stop at a punch. A large part of me wouldn't bat an eye at the thought of Jack being ripped limb by limb, but for some reason it feels as if Jack is somehow protecting me right now.

Quickly the woman who was in Red's lap is being thrown to the floor as he stands and wraps his gigantic mitt around Jack's throat, pinning him up against the wall. Jack's dull blue eyes widen in horror as his face changes from red to purple.

His legs and arms lash out in all directions, trying to be free of Red's hold. Finally, only when his body starts to go limp does the president let go and allow him to slump to the ground.

"Fucking junkie, we let you think you could keep her in exchange your information about her. She is our bargaining chip and nothing more. After we are done with the Hell Chasers, we have no use for her." He yells in his face and turns to me. I keep my shoulders back but don't say anything as he grabs my chin roughly and pulls me forward so my body is balancing against his hold. He looks down at me and licks his bottom lip.

"You are beautiful, I even thought about keeping you for myself. But I want to watch Axel and the rest of the Chasers suffer for what they've done. The men they have killed were our brothers and they must pay." He lets go of my face and I can't hold my tongue anymore.

"Fuck you, they will come for me and kill every one of you." I spit at him. The back of his hand comes down hard across my face. Momentary darkness takes over and I see twinkling stars dance in my vision. I slowly roll my head back towards him once more. I can't help the tears that start to fall down my face.

"Princess, you are strong now, but mark my words, you will wish you were dead when we are done with you." He turns away from me and sits back in his chair. Patting his lap for the woman to crawl back into.

"Well Jackal, make the fucking call. I don't have all day." He lights a cigarette and leans back against the dirty recliner. "Make sure she stays quiet; we don't need her going off." He points my direction as I scowl at him through blurry vision. A hand wraps around my mouth tighter than is comfortable. Jack stands next to me; he looks as if he has regained his composure but glances at me with an unsure look. He has been played by his own brothers, they used him for his connection to me and I know that must be eating him alive.

The room is silent as we all listen to his phone ring, my heart stutters in my chest as I hear Axel's deep voice answer. A sea of relief washes over me. *He's alive.* I don't listen to what they're saying at first, still reveling in the fact that he is okay, when Jack lights a match and heads my way.

"I swear, you lay a fucking hand on her and I will tear you apart, limb from limb." I hear Axel say from the other end of the phone. Jack lets out an ugly laugh and then stops in front of me with the bright flaming stick, he lights the end of a cigarette and smirks at me. I try to move out of the man's hold but I can't, a searing pain burns through my shoulder. I can't help the scream that escapes as Jack pushes the end of his cigarette into my skin. The smell of my burning flesh makes me gag against the calloused hand, the room growing fuzzy as the conversation continues. A few minutes later, the man behind me removes his hand from my mouth and backs away, leaving me alone again in the center of the room.

Jack moves to face me, holding his phone out in front of him, he eyes me almost apologetically and it infuriates me. He's the reason I'm here. My stomach churns with fear as I worry Axel won't get here in time. But I need to focus on getting myself out of this mess, I can't sit here waiting for him to save me.

"Smile for the camera, princess." Red commands from his

makeshift throne. I raise my head and glare at the lens. *Fuck you assholes.*

After our fun little outing to what I assume is the living room, the big guy who came in here with Jack blindfolds me and brings me back to the small room. They leave me in here for hours, and with each passing minute, the adrenaline rush starts to wear off. My head, neck, and ribs throb with pain. I can't help but think that only four months ago, I lived a very mundane and scheduled life. Now, I really don't even recognize the life I'm living. My cheeks heat, and something stings my dry, split lips—I hadn't realized I've started crying.

Allowing myself to emotionally purge, I take a deep breath and stare at the ceiling, willing my eyes to absorb any remaining tears. I think I've cried more today than I have in the last year combined. I need to stay strong; I need to figure out a way to escape because if Axel doesn't get here in time, I don't even want to think about what will happen to me. The woman who leaves this place will not be the same one I was yesterday.

When the brown-haired brute had brought me back to this room, he opted for zip ties instead of the god-awful wire that had held me in place earlier. What a gentleman, right? I look around the room once again, searching for anything that might help me. Realizing that in his panic to get me to the living room, Jack left his jacket strewn across the stained mattress. The moon is bright tonight, bathing the room in a soft white glow. The gleam of a blade catches my eye, and I let out a breath of both panic and relief. This might be my way out. The only problem is I might actually have to use that knife on someone else, and that thought makes the bile in my stomach churn. The chair I'm sitting on is placed close to the bed, but not close enough to grab the knife from the pocket. Okay, think, Jenna…

"Oh, kidnapper!" I say in a loud but sweet voice. I know there's someone outside my door standing guard because I've heard them talking on the phone here and there. The creaky door swings open, and the same man who walked me back to my room and tied my arms walks in with an annoyed look on his face. They either trust this man to guard me 24/7, or he's doing grunt work. I bat my eyes at him and try to place a smile on my throbbing face. I must really be putting on the charm because a scowl now covers his face.

"Brute, I need to pee," I say as he crosses his arms and leans against the doorframe. I've decided that if I can get him to untie me to use the bathroom, I can try to get to the knife before he notices.

"My name is not Brute," he replies with irritation.

Good. I want to get under his skin, to annoy him so much that he just lets me use the restroom.

"Well, I don't know your actual name, so Brute it is." I smile as he rolls his eyes and rubs a hand down his face. I study him for a moment and realize that he is extremely clean, unlike his other counterparts. It looks as if his hands are manicured, and his hair and face are perfectly trimmed and put together. I wonder who this man is for a moment and then quickly remember that he isn't anyone I want to know—he is the enemy.

"If I let you go to the bathroom, will you leave me alone?" he grinds his teeth as I nod sweetly at him.

"Scout's honor."

He struts over and kneels beside me, looking into my eyes as if we know each other. An apologetic expression covers his face for a moment as he looks from me to the knife. No, no, no! He knows my plan.

His head drops, and I catch sight of a rose tattoo under his right ear with the word *Lost* in cursive underneath it. I move my head to the side to get a better look at it. I've seen that tattoo before. He starts to untie the ties around my ankles and then leans in close to my ear. "Tell Jilly I'm sorry. I had no idea that they were planning on taking you, or I wouldn't have gone along with it." He moves back, and I can see regret and almost sadness in his eyes.

"W-what?" I manage to ask, not realizing he has freed my hands. I stare at him and realize that his strong face resembles my new friend's. It hits me in the gut like a ton of bricks—he must be related to Jill. But I shake the thought and hurl myself to my feet, race to the bed, and grab the knife. He doesn't move as I round the chair and hold the knife to his neck. He stays still, knees on the ground.

"Why aren't you trying to stop me?!" I whisper at him, not wanting to alert anyone that I'm up here freed from my restraints. He tilts his head, giving me a better angle to slice his throat. I rapidly blink, trying not to pass out at the thought. I stand tough, knowing that I need to do whatever it takes to escape. But the thought of taking someone's life is something I don't know if I can ever handle.

"Because this isn't right. Kidnapping an innocent was never in the job description." He looks me in the eyes, and I can tell he's being truthful.

Without another thought, I race to the door and pull it open, slowly sliding down the hallway with my back against the wall. I feel music pulsing under my bare feet as I make my way to a staircase.

Stepping on the first step, I place my foot as lightly as possible, trying to avoid any creaks. The old wooden step moves slightly forward, and I try to gain my balance as I realize all of the steps are coming untacked. Halfway down the banister, I hear a voice coming from somewhere below me. Moving slower, I try to keep my breathing even. My hand is shaking as I hit the bottom step and peer around me. No one is in the living room. I quickly shoot back against the wall as I hear voices again from the kitchen. Instantly recognizing Jack's voice, I strain, trying to listen in.

"He can't take her away. The deal was if I got her here, she was mine!" Jack growls. I can imagine his eyes popping out of his head as spittle flies from his mouth.

"Shut the fuck up. He has made up his mind. You can get better pussy at the clubhouse. Stop whining," another man says back to Jack. A grunt comes from Jack, and then I hear them scuffling. I stay as still as possible until Jack rounds the corner with his conversation partner right on his heels. His eyes bore into me, and immediately he leaps for me.

My head slams against the wall as I wrench back from his grasp. I can't contain my scream as my brain feels as if it's being sliced in half. I fling the knife out at him, nicking his arm. A hiss escapes his lips as he looks down at where the blade has broken his skin. He turns back to me, and I start to fight with everything I have against him when I hear loud pops sound around us.

Jack is in a fury, and I don't think he registers the sound because he doesn't stop. Grabbing my wrist, he digs his fingers into my veins until I lose my grip on the knife.

With my other hand, I shoot my fingers up to his face and dig my thumb into his eye, pressing until blood drips down his cheek and his scream rips through the house. He drops his hold on my wrist, and I scramble away from him, trying to grab my weapon again. Another hand grabs my throat as I stare at Jack, who is now stalking towards me with one eye swollen shut.

I feel my body leave the ground as the hand around my neck pulls me into the air and slams me back down into the coffee table behind me. The air is torn from my lungs as I fight to breathe against the pain in my chest. I close my eyes, grappling with the pain. I need to move, but my brain isn't working with my body at the moment.

The gunshots sound again, and the living room windows shatter around me. I open my eyes in time to see the man who threw me on the coffee table—Death. He looks down at me with a terrifying smile and I try to swallow down my fear.

Towering above me, he reaches down but stops when another round of shots comes through the window. Grabbing his neck, a dark stream of thick blood pours onto me. I roll myself away as his lifeless body slumps down onto the edge of the broken table. Landing on my hands and knees, I slowly rise, willing my broken body to keep moving.

I turn around to see Jack pressed against the wall, waiting for the shots to stop. He peers around the wall into the kitchen, unaware that I was able to get up. I look down and see that the knife I dropped must have been kicked in our fight and now sits halfway between Jack and me. I limp over to the blade, picking it up. The cool metal feels heavy and welcome in my hand as I wrap my sore fingers around it. Lifting my gaze from the knife to Jack, he still is oblivious to me, and I take a deep breath. This man was once my partner, the person I called when I was happy or sad, and now he is a stranger who takes pride in hurting me.

I start to move towards him as he finally turns his head in my direction. A loud bang hits my ears at the same time I plunge the knife into his abdomen. My stomach feels like it's being ripped open with a red-hot poker. I peer down and see my dress absorbing a pool of my blood. Stumbling back, I watch as Jack slides down the wall, leaving a large smear of blood behind him. A sound catches my attention, making eye contact with a man I met at the Chasers' clubhouse—Knife, I think his name is. I start to feel lightheaded, my body colder than it's ever been before. I watch Knife raise his gun and shoot someone behind me.

Turning my head, I watch as a man falls to his knees and collapses face-first onto the ground.

Knife looks at me with a worried expression and then hollers over his shoulder, "Oh fuck, Ax!"

My knees buckle under me as the knife slides from my bloody fingers. The sound it makes as it hits the hardwood floor rings in my head like a siren's song, pulling me into the darkness. I can hear the pounding of boots, doors being slammed, and voices... his voice. *Focus, Jenna. Focus on his voice. He's here. It's over.*

But I can't move. Breathing even feels like an unimaginable chore. Falling to the ground, my vision begins to tunnel. The only thing I can focus on are my bloody hands that I now hold out in front of me as if they aren't my own. They can't be mine. A stillness calms my body as the cool air numbs the pain radiating from my abdomen.

"Jenna!" he yells in a gravelly voice, as if fighting to keep tears at bay. It's the last thing I hear before everything goes black

Chapter 33

AXEL

It's been twelve hours since Jenna was taken.

All I can hear is the rush of blood pumping through my body. My focus is locked on making sure my trusted Glock is ready for war. I've already gathered more powerful weapons to take with me, but I don't go anywhere without my baby. I concentrate only on the task at hand and force myself not to ponder on all the fucked-up shit that might be happening to Jenna right now. If I let my brain go there, I won't be able to do what I need to in order to get her out of there. I'll be too riddled with the need to carve and slice the flesh from every one of those Reapers and then put it all back together to do it again.

Torturing each and every one of those disgusting fucks when I finally get my Angel out of there will be the sweetest revenge. It becomes my mission to hand-deliver the most gruesome torture I can to each of them, starting with Jack and ending with Red so he can watch all the monsters he created cry and plead for their lives. The bell dings above the front door of the garage and we all point our guns in that direction.

"Woah! Woah! It's us, assholes," Falcon, Spider, and Knife walk in with their hands up. I walk around Blaze and step out of the office.

"What do you have?" I don't have time for pleasantries, not when every moment away from her means she could be hurt, alone, and scared.

After the phone call from Jack, Ace managed to trace the call back to a small ranch outside of town. I'm familiar with the ranch, as many of us are. It used to belong to an old dairy farmer before he passed. He was never married and didn't have children, so the bank bought the land and let it sit vacant for almost ten years now. Many of us know the layout—just a house and barn on the property. But with how much time has passed, Prince sent a few men out to scout the area and report back with whatever information they can.

We gather around the makeshift table in the center of the garage as the three men relay everything they've gathered. During the hour of surveillance, four men guard the perimeter of the house at all times. They count at least ten to fifteen men coming and going from the house, including Red, but they never saw Jenna. Just hearing them say her name in connection to the situation puts an extremely bad taste in my mouth.

When Falcon, Knife, and Spider finish giving us the details, Ace and Jax step up to take point. Prince stands with us, letting his men shine where they're needed. Each of us carries special skills that provide knowledge in almost every facet imaginable.

You need anything tech-related? Call Ace. Military-related? Call Jax or Blaze. Mechanical or torture-related? Me.

Ace hands each of us a small, clear earpiece that fits comfortably in the canal of my ear. Within seconds, I hear a low beep, and his voice comes in quickly before going silent again. He then hands me thick, almost goggle-like glasses that fit snugly against my face.

"When we first pull up, we will park on the road and walk in through the woods surrounding the house," Jax says, mapping out the area and the best way to infiltrate. "These earpieces are how we communicate with one another. They also allow us to move quickly and efficiently. The sooner we're in and out, the less time we have for shit to go sideways. You got me?" He looks around to each of us as we nod in unison. "These are night vision goggles, and we'll need them to get into and out of the area easily." His lips thin as he makes eye contact with me.

"There are multiple places she might be, but the first places to check are the upper bedrooms. The first floor is too open, and they're probably not stupid enough to have her out in the open."

Prince moves to the corner and begins speaking. "This must be done with precision. She gets out alive, and we deal with these rats once and for all. If you can, I want Red alive." He adjusts his cut over his white button-down and sneers, an evil filling his eyes. "He's going to pay for thinking he can fuck with us, take one of our women and use her as a pawn."

The room goes silent as Jax continues to lay out each and every detail of how we'll approach and attack. One thing about the Hell Chasers is that we are meticulous, plan for anything, so no matter what, we always come out on top. It's what makes us so deadly.

After Jax and Ace finish, each of us straps up and checks our weapons one last time. We walk out of the back entrance and don't look back.

We take SUVs to be more discreet. The Chaser in me wants to be on the back of my bike, tearing into enemy territory without giving a shit if they know I'm coming. But I won't leave anything to chance. This needs to go exactly as planned so we can get Jenna out safely.

I sit in the passenger seat, continuously checking the mirrors to make sure we aren't being followed. We pass the last road in town and drive another two miles before pulling off onto a gravel access road that, to the untrained eye, looks like it leads nowhere. Halfway down, we park and get out, needing to go on foot from here to avoid drawing attention to ourselves. No one speaks but moves as if we've choreographed this mission.

Rounding the car, I make eye contact with Blaze, my best friend and probably the man I trust more than anyone here. His eyes are lit with fire as he flashes a wicked grin. It's as if the devil himself has been implanted into all of us, because right now, we are no longer men—we're killers who can smell blood in the air.

We spread out and make our way to the edge of the tree line surrounding the house. We're close enough to see what we need to but not close enough to be spotted.

I kneel down and stick the butt of my gun against my

shoulder. I look through the scope and easily make out two men walking back and forth in front of the house, each strapped with automatic rifles. I look up onto the porch and see five men sitting and smoking, laughing as if they don't have a care in the world. The top left bedroom window is the only one with the shades closed. My heart pounds in my chest, wondering if she's in there. Cal's voice breaks through my thoughts.

"I have eyes on two in back," his voice comes in low, steady.

"I have two in front, ready when you are." I take a deep breath, clicking the safety off my gun and wrapping my finger around the trigger, but I don't squeeze yet.

"When Axel and Cal shoot, we move. Everyone in position?" Jax's gravelly voice commands into my ear. Instantly, everyone fires back a quiet "yes." I hear Cal take a deep breath.

"Take the shot."

I line up my sight, so the crosshairs land directly between the eyes of one of the Reapers on guard. Steadying my body, I squeeze the trigger and watch as the back of his head explodes across the front of the house. I don't have much time to admire my work before I turn and do the same to the other guard, who's just watched what happened to the man next to him. I move quickly, keeping low as I make my way to the side of the house. A blood-curdling scream comes from inside, and I see red. That isn't just anyone's scream—it's Jenna's.

"Easy," I hear through the earpiece. It's Jax, and I'm halfway to the porch when he speaks again. "If you barrel in there now, you're as good as dead and no good to her. Keep your shit together, and we'll get her out."

I grip my gun until my knuckles turn white but obey the

command and slink down until I'm close enough to see the men on the porch. Moving almost invisibly, I reach up and slit the throat of the man who was leaning on the railing. Before I can exhale, Cal snipes the remaining two men on the porch in front of me. Blood splatters across my face, and I revel in the warm feeling.

I drop low again and continue moving as more shots ring out around me. The front window of the house shatters as another round of bullets tears through the glass. A Reaper jumps from the railing and lands directly in front of me, lunging forward with a switchblade. I dodge his movement, grabbing his wrist and shoulder, slamming the back of his elbow across my bent knee. His arm explodes in the wrong direction, and his scream is pure music to my ears. Gripping his blade, I slowly stab it into his neck, letting him suffer as he stares into the eyes of his killer.

Dropping low again, I round the house and head for the back screen door. A single shot echoes from inside the house, followed by another blood-curdling scream.

"Fuck this," I growl under my breath.

I catch sight of Jax, Knife, and Prince making entry into the house from the back. More quick shots fire, and I hear my brothers taking down the Reapers like the rats they are. I pick up my pace, flinging open the front screen door and rushing inside the small kitchen. Knife's voice cuts through my earpiece.

"Oh, fuck, Ax!"

I don't wait to hear more. Sprinting through the chaos, I round the corner and stop dead in my tracks. My eyes land on

Jenna at the bottom of the stairs, barefoot and covered in blood. Her once olive-colored dress is now deep brown, soaked in thick red blood. Jack is slumped against the wall, dead. Jenna's expression is one of grim satisfaction before her eyelids start to droop. My legs move on their own, propelling me forward just in time to catch her as she collapses.

The knife she's clutching falls from her hand, clattering to the ground. Cradling her in my arms, I start running my hands over her body, desperately searching for the source of all the blood. My heart pounds so loudly that it drowns out everything else. Pulling my hand back, I see it coated in her blood, dripping onto the floor. *This is too much blood. There's too much blood.*

My fingers find the small bullet hole in her abdomen, and my heart stops. I rip my shirt off and press it as hard as I can against her wound, my hands shaking.

"Get the fucking car!" I yell, my voice breaking. Someone sprints out the door, but I don't know who. My world narrows to her.

"No, baby, please open your eyes. Fuck!" I plead with her to open those gorgeous green eyes for me. "I've got you, Jenna. Just hang on for me." My words falter as my throat burns with unrestrained rage and fear. My angel, my everything, lies broken and bleeding in my arms.

A hand clamps down on my shoulder, and I glance up to see Blaze. His expression is filled with worry, but I don't have time for sympathy. My focus snaps back to Jenna. I see Prince and Cal rush into the room, their faces pale.

"No," Cal whispers, his voice cracking. He sprints toward

us and drops to his knees beside Jenna. "No," he repeats, his hands trembling as they hover over her.

"The car's out front. Knife's ready to go," Blaze says urgently. I scoop Jenna into my arms, careful not to jostle her. She feels too light, too fragile.

I push through the front door and rush toward the waiting SUV. Climbing into the back seat, I lay her down gently, keeping pressure on her wound. My forehead presses against hers as I whisper, "Stay with me, Angel. Please stay with me."

Her skin is icy, her lips pale, and deep purple rings circle her closed eyes. She looks like she's been dragged through hell and back. My stomach twists, bile rising in my throat.

"God, please open your eyes, Angel. Stay with me. Please," I beg, my voice breaking. Blood pools under her, soaking through my jeans and onto the car seat.

A roar tears from my chest as Knife slams on the gas, sending the SUV hurtling down the highway toward the emergency room.

Chapter 34

JENNA

DEATH IS CALM. Death is peaceful.

The moment I see Axel, I know I am safe. My body reacts before my brain can catch up, becoming numb, almost relaxed, as if it feels itself slipping toward peace. Allowing myself to settle into the comfort, my mind files through all of my favorite people and memories: my parents cheering me on at my college graduation, Marley with her crazy hair and sleepy face greeting me each morning, Cal and Sarah stopping by my classroom at the end of each day to check in and tell me about their day. And Axel—the man who forced his way into my heart even when I tried like hell to push him away. Each one imprinted in my mind as I latch onto every happy moment.

"No, baby, please." I hear it in the distance. It feels like I'm underwater and someone is yelling at me from above. Reaching through the darkness, I try to fight against the heavy weight surrounding me, trapping me inside. The harder I fight, the more tired I become, and I know I won't be able to break through. I settle back into the peace, allowing the darkness to swallow me.

"Beep...Beep...Beep..."

I quickly reach my arm out to slam the snooze button on the extremely annoying alarm, only to have it snap back into place as pain laces up my arm. What the hell?

Pulling the weights from my eyes and opening them for what feels like the first time in months, I stare around the dark space. Light filters in from under the door across the room, but the rest of the area is lit only by monitors to my right. Looking down, I see why I can't move my arm. There are more lines and tubes attached to me than I ever thought possible. Taking a slow, solid breath, I count to ten and try to recall the last thing I remember.

My heart rate picks up, and the monitor sounds loudly next to me. The sound of running water comes from the door where the light is peeking through, and I watch as it opens and Axel steps into the room.

He keeps his head down and turns off the light as he exits the restroom, not yet noticing me. I take him in: his disheveled hair, the way he runs his hands through it, his shoulders slumped like he has the weight of the world on them. The machine monitoring my heart hasn't relaxed, and I watch as he notices the change in pace. His eyes snap to mine, and I feel all the air leave my lungs. Great, here comes the tears again.

He freezes for only a moment, closing his eyes and muttering something under his breath before rushing to my side. Grabbing my hand, he peppers light kisses over my bruised and scraped knuckles.

"There's my girl," he says, his voice thick with emotion as he cups my face with his hand. "I am so sorry, Jenna." His voice is low and gruff. I lean my cheek into his palm and let his presence soothe my frayed nerves.

"I-" I try to speak, but my throat feels like it's on fire. Axel turns and grabs the small white Styrofoam cup off of the tray and brings the straw to my lips.

"Shh babe, you need to let your throat rest." Axel mumbles as he smooths my hair back. I take small sips and watch him look at me like I'm going to disappear at any moment. I can tell he feels guilty about what happened but honestly, I never would have been the target had I not been the center of Jack's sick delusions. It was the perfect storm, turf war and a crazy ex-boyfriend. I slightly push the cup away weakly and try to talk again. "It's not your fault," I croak, my voice weak and gravelly.

Axel's eyes narrow, his glare stopping me from continuing. "Are you joking? Jenna, you wouldn't be here if it wasn't for me!" He straightens his body and looks massive in this tiny room; I watch as his shoulders tense and he runs his hand through his hair again.

"God, I should have protected you. When I woke up and you were gone…" he stops and stares off above my head as if he's in a trance. After a few moments his Adam's apple bobs as he swallows his pain. "I didn't think I was ever going to see you again." He all but whispers.

"Axel," I say but he stays staring over my head like I'm not even here anymore. "Axel, look at me!"

This time I break through and his eyes flick to me. Darkness swirls in his deep brown irises, a rage and pain like I've never seen in him before.

"What happened was on the Reapers—on Jack. I knew exactly what I was getting into when I chose you. I tried to walk away, tried to let you go, but I can't." I take a deep breath and try to steady my nerves. Oh God, am I really about to do this?

"So, stop acting like you dragged me into this. I know you would never put me in harm's way intentionally." I reach for him, hoping he hears me. Axel sighs and slowly drops into the chair next to the bed. I run my hand down his cheek, to his neck, finally resting it on his shoulder. The gold necklace he always wears catches the light, and I trace the chain until I find the ring that hangs from it. I've seen it quite a few times, but being this close I can see a small but beautiful oval-shaped emerald. Surrounding it gold leaves and vines wrap around the gem, securing it to the thin gold band. I quickly realize that I've been entranced by the ring when his hand comes to wrap around mine.

Axel is still, he doesn't say anything but his eyes hold me in a way that makes my stomach fill with butterflies.

"I love you, Dane. I love you so much it hurts sometimes." I barely get the last word out before he crashes his lips to mine. A small wince as pain radiates from my mouth, but it is instantly soothed by the soft feel of his lips against mine. As quickly as the kiss started Axel is pulling away.

"No—wait" I try to pull him back in, but he isn't focused on our kiss anymore. Axel brings his hands behind his neck and unclasps the necklace. Slowly I watch as the ring I was just staring at slips off the gold chain and falls into his palm. It looks tiny in his large hand.

"What are you doing?"

"This was my mom's," he says in a husky voice. He stares at the ring for a moment, then wraps his hand around it and closes his eyes. A small smile appears on his lips as if he is remembering a happy memory.

"She gave it to me a few weeks before she died. I always thought I was never going to settle down, honestly, I didn't see the point. The club was my life and all I cared about was the shop and my club. But she knew, she knew I'd find you." My gut twists as I bring my hand up to cover my mouth. My vision becomes blurry and I can feel the hot tears burning the back of my eyes as I try to hold them in.

"My mom told me that one day I would find a woman that sets my world on fire. Someone so amazing that I couldn't picture living life without them. I thought she was talking crazy, but she was right, she always was." Dane slides the ring onto my left ring finger, a perfect fit. The corner of his lips curling into a smile as he peers down at my hand, rubbing small circles on my skin with his thumb.

"Jenna, I can't picture my life without you in it. I want your daily sarcasm and stubborn personality. I want to wake up every morning to your sleepy smile and fall asleep to you rambling about your day. I love you so much, babe. And I understand you think this all started quickly, but I think I knew from the moment I saw you that you were mine." Axel brings his hand up and wipes my face. I hadn't realized the tears I had been holding back had begun to fall.

"So, what do you say, baby? Will you marry me? Be mine to love, protect and cherish for the rest of our lives?"

I swipe at my face as fast as I can to gain some sense of composure and start nodding like a crazy person. This whirlwind of a man stormed into my life like a tornado and ripped everything I thought I knew to shreds. But he replaced it with more love than I could ever imagine.

"Of course, I will marry you!" I finally say pulling him into me, not caring that he is getting tangled in the cords attached to me. Almost on cue, a doctor flies into the room followed be a gaggle of nurses who quickly start to asses me. With a smile, Axel pulls away and lets them do their job. But he never once takes his eyes off me.

God, I love this man.

Chapter 35

JENNA

ONE MONTH LATER:

"MARLEY, YOU LOOK amazing! Blaze is the luckiest man alive," I whisper to my best friend as we stand in line, getting ready to walk down the aisle.

With my winning personality and a lot of Blaze's money, we were able to get the venue and all the vendors to reschedule the wedding. Everything is perfect, and Mar made me promise I wouldn't leave her side today. I'm still dealing with the physical effects of my injuries. Even now, bruises and marks that linger on my neck and shoulders, but everything is healing well. Thankfully, when Jack shot me, he didn't hit any major organs and recovery has been better than I could have hoped for. Emotionally, I'm still working through the trauma of being kidnapped by my crazy ex-boyfriend and used as a bargaining chip in a turf war.

As I smooth a rogue hair down on Marley's gorgeous head, I feel a familiar hand snake around my waist and pull me in tight. I look down to see Axel's tattooed fingers splayed across the front of my silky black dress. I opted for something a little more covering as I don't want to be bombarded with questions and concerned looks about my current appearance.

"You look amazing, baby. So good I could eat you right here." His eyes flash with lust and a hint of something dark. I can't help but giggle at his remark, knowing full well his words have ulterior motives. His silver wedding band stands out against his tattoos, and I intertwine my fingers with his, melting into his side.

Axel and I couldn't wait to be married and, unlike Marley, I wasn't dying to have a big, traditional wedding. Nothing about our relationship is traditional. We went to the courthouse a few days after I was released from the hospital. Luckily, both of my parents had rushed to be with me when they had heard what happened to me and have been staying in town since. My mom nearly had a heart attack when I told her we were going to elope and before we left the hospital, she surprised me with a gorgeous, simple wedding dress. Leave it to my mom to find me a wedding dress day-of. Marley came and did my make-up and hair and everything had been perfect.

A soft ballad fills the room as the large wooden double doors open in front of us. I turn to Marley and see her trying to peer around us, hoping to catch a glimpse of her future husband. The wedding coordinator stands off to the side, nodding to each pair of bridesmaid and groomsman, alerting them when it's their turn to walk down the aisle.

Finally, it's Axel's and my turn. But before we start walking, I hear the wedding coordinator ask Marley if she's ready. I smirk when I hear Marley reply.

"Absolutely."

So sure, so calm. She has found her person, just as I have found mine.

The ceremony and reception are gorgeous. Every detail screams tech wizard and biker, right down to the custom drinks—"Data Daiquiri" and "Whiskey." Marley had made a big deal about Blaze naming his own drink, only to have him choose the actual name of his favorite liquor.

I decide I need a break from the fun. Grabbing my thick coat, I make my way through the reception hall and out the large French doors. An open deck surrounds the building, overlooking a peaceful lake. I lean on the thick wooden railing that outlines the deck and peer out onto the water. The wind whips around me, filling my nostrils with the smell of winter frost. Thick fog settles against the water and forest, making it feel dark and unsettling. A chill runs down my spine, leaving goosebumps in its wake. On a night that feels so perfect, I hate that I still let my brain pull me back to that day. But something keeps nagging at me, and I can't let it go.

The man who let me go—who is he? Where is he? I asked Axel about him at the hospital and told him about what had happened. He had called Prince and Blaze, and they both confirmed that he wasn't left at the house. I didn't ask any further questions because I wanted to distance myself as far as possible. Thinking maybe he just had a change of heart and wanted to clear his conscious in that moment.

I tried getting into contact with Jill a few days after I got home from the hospital, but she hasn't returned any of my calls so far. Maybe I should go over to her house to see if she's okay.

The sound of clicking heels catches my attention, and I turn just in time to see Ace and a bridesmaid walking to the far side of the deck, the side completely encased in darkness. I don't think they see me, so I start to walk inside when Ace turns slightly and smiles in my direction. Stifling a laugh, I scan the room for Axel. My feet are killing me, swollen and sore from walking in heels all day, and the slight buzz I had from my earlier cocktails has worn off, leaving me tired, sore, and ready for bed.

Even in this room of enormous bikers all clad in the same leather vests, I spot Axel almost immediately. His broad shoulders and shiny dark hair stand out in any crowd. I gaze at him for a moment, enjoying the view of my handsome husband. The sexy, relaxed look on his face is quickly replaced with a scowl due to whatever the man next to him has said.

I realize it's Cal who's talking to him, and he is equally irritated. Both of them see me walk in at the same time and make their way to me. The group of people dancing in the middle of the reception hall part for them, and I can't help but laugh a little. Even at a club wedding, they have a way of letting their presence be known.

"We need to talk," Cal says before they come to a full stop in front of me. His face is flushed like he's just been riding out in the cold, and I can't help but touch his nose.

"Gosh, Cal, why didn't you drive here in a car? You're going to get frostbite."

"Jenna, focus. Remember that guy you told Axel about from the...house?" He whispers the last word and pauses, knowing I've been struggling with what happened with Jack and the Reapers. I don't say anything but nod at him, spinning the ring on my finger.

"This him?" I glance down at his phone and see the familiar man staring back at me, but he isn't wearing a cut like he was back at the house; he's wearing a police uniform. I'm stunned for a moment, unsure what to do with this information when I snatch his phone out of his hand and zoom into his neck. The rose tattoo is sticking up out of his collar, and I inhale a sharp breath.

"Yes, that's him." I stay frozen, staring at the screen. "Wait, if he's a cop, then what the hell was he doing in that house? Why aren't you arrested?!" I feel my chest caving and inflating rapidly. Axel presses his hand to the small of my back and pulls me into his side. Rubbing small circles with his thumb, he leans into my ear. "We can talk about this in the truck. We can't do it here. The club just needed confirmation that this is the man who helped you escape."

"Wait, Jill!" I whisper-shout at Cal. "Is she okay? I can't get ahold of her and haven't seen her since everything happened."

"Jill?" he asks, looking confused and quickly glancing between Axel and me. "Who's Jill?" He holds his hand out for his phone back, and I slowly hand it to him, trying to take in every detail about the man that I can.

"Let's talk about this back at the clubhouse," Axel says,

using a voice that tells me not to push it.

"Fine. Let me say goodbye to some people and then we can head out." Marley and Blaze left a while ago and the people still here will be heading home soon, so I feel okay leaving. I make my rounds, thanking everyone for being here and giving my parents a hug goodbye before I find Axel again and we make our way outside.

Chapter 36

AXEL

WITH THE WEATHER being so cold, all of the guys start driving cages instead of bikes. This is usually my least favorite time of the year because being on my bike used to be the only time I found any peace. But since I found Jenna, the transition hasn't been nearly as difficult. I still would rather be riding my Harley, but I can manage with the truck for a few months.

Jenna has been quiet since Cal showed her the picture of Mike, AKA Officer Stevenson. When I had Ace look into the guy who helped Jenna escape, I expected him to tell me he was just a member who probably felt guilty, but when Cal showed up and told me they'd found him and he's a cop who's been M.I.A. for over three months, I got a bad feeling in my gut. Something about this whole thing seems extremely suspicious. I reach over and rest my hand on Jenna's thigh, giving a light squeeze. She doesn't turn to look at me but instead just rests her hand on top of mine. I don't want to push her to talk, but I also don't want her to get stuck in her own head. These last few weeks since her kidnapping have been difficult for her, and I don't want this to slow her healing. I am so proud of her and her willingness to fight and talk about what's going on inside her head, but tonight I can see she's retracting, going back to keeping her thoughts bottled up.

Luckily, we pull up in front of the clubhouse a few moments later. Jenna swings open her door the second I put the car in park and speed walks inside. I half-jog to meet up with her at the door and press my hand to the cold wood, not allowing her to pull it open yet.

"Dane, let me open it," she says in a serious voice.

"Not until you look at me."

Jenna sighs heavily, finally looking at me.

"If this becomes too much, you have to tell me." I say making sure to look her right in the eyes. She sighs, closing her eyes, and I can almost hear her counting to ten in her head.

I can't control myself around her. I cup the sides of her face and run my thumbs over her soft, supple cheeks and lips. Her eyes flutter closed as I feel her start to melt into my touch. If I had half a mind, I would throw her over my shoulder and take her home, not let her be pulled back into this shit. But I know she needs this; she needs to get this out of her mind so she can move forward. I've seen the way she scans every room she enters and how jumpy she has become. Everyone has noticed. That's the only reason we are letting her in on this meeting.

I stay still as I memorize every curve and line on her angelic face. The way her long, inky black lashes fan across the tops of her cheeks and how rosy and pouty her lips are. The need to be inside her consumes me. I lean in and seal our lips together. She instantly grabs onto my cut, pulling me closer, deepening our kiss. Before she can protest, I pull her up my body so her legs are wrapped around my waist, pushing her dress up her thighs. Walking back to the truck, I swing open the back door and gently set Jenna down on the soft leather. With the truck being tall, the seat sits perfectly at shoulder height, giving me a delicious view of Jenna's already soaked lace panties.

Running my hands up her creamy thighs, the thin material of her dress bunches against my wrists until it settles at her hips. She shivers at my touch, and a trail of goosebumps rise where my hands have been. I want to take my time with her, fill her until she can't think about any of her worries, but we don't have the time. This will be hard and fast, giving us both the release we need before the shit show that's waiting for us inside burns through any peace we have left. I grab the scrap of light blue fabric covering her and tear it from her body, leaving Jenna bare to me. A slightly annoyed but lust-filled gasp leaves her mouth as she stares at the remnants of her underwear in my hand.

"Those were my favorite," she grumbles under her breath.

"I'll get you more. Hell, I'll buy as many pairs as you want. Because Angel, every chance I get, I will rip apart every pair of panties that stands in the way of me and this sweet pussy." My gruff response sends a flush across her cheeks and neck. I level my gaze at her. She's practically dripping down her legs, and I haven't even touched her yet. My cock hardens against my jeans, straining the trousers until it's painful.

"You really can be romantic when you want to be," Jenna's sarcastic remark is the last thing we exchange before I pull her hips to the edge of the seat and bury my face into her sweet pussy. She instantly arches her back, pushing her delicious tits into the air as I circle her clit in lazy strokes, savoring her taste. Jenna lays back across the backseat, and I slide a finger inside her hot, wet, waiting entrance. It only takes a few seconds for her walls to start rippling around me.

I push another finger inside her, curling them until I hit the spot that sends her body into a frenzy. She writhes beneath my mouth as I relentlessly take everything she gives me. I feel Jenna's body become languid as her eyes lock onto mine. A glimmer of satisfaction and desire sparkles in her deep green eyes, and my heart constricts in my chest. She is the most beautiful woman I have ever laid my eyes on, and she is mine.

"Mr. Romano, that was all good and well, but you have something else that I want." A gorgeous, relaxed smile spreads across her face as she slowly moves farther into the backseat.

I step up into the cab and close the door behind me. The truck is still warm from our drive, but the air crackles with the heat between us.

"And what would that be, Mrs. Romano?" I keep my response calm, although the need to bury myself in her makes my heart pound against my chest.

"Hmm… if you really don't know, we really need to work on your deductive reasoning skills."

A carefree giggle slips from her lips as I pull her into my lap, pinning her legs to the side of me and wrapping my hand around the base of her neck, holding her in place. Slowly I kiss and lick my way across her shoulders and down her chest, the car fills with her needy pants. Her pulse thrums exquisitely fast underneath my lips, reminding me of a hummingbird's wings.

"You're playing with fire, Angel. Undo my pants," I command as I hold her in place. Her delicate hands methodically undo my pants, then slowly pull my boxers down until I spring free, my cock jutting out and resting on her stomach. She moves without instruction, rising up onto her knees before sinking down onto me. She's so wet that she easily takes all of me, but she sits perfectly still when she is fully seated, adjusting to my size.

"Baby, you're going to have to move, or I'm going to fucking cum right now. You're so fucking tight," I growl at her, moving my hips to create some movement between us.

Her velvety walls tighten around me, and I let out a warning growl. I look at Jenna to see her with a mischievous smirk on her face.

"Move," I say again, trying to keep my voice calm when all I can think about is that I never want this to end. Jenna, relaxed and playful, gives me her full attention. This feeling is the best fucking feeling in the world. I don't know how the hell I got so lucky to have her, but I will try my hardest to make sure she is this carefree every damn day.

She starts to bounce on my dick in quick, rapid strokes, mixing in slow, deep movements. I slip the straps of her dress down her shoulders, which sends the silk cascading down to her hips to meet the rest of the fabric. The bruises that cover her skin make me want to burn the world down, to bring those fuckers back to life just to kill them again. Her delicious, lush breasts bounce with every movement. Rosy nipples taunt me as her head falls back with pleasure.

"Eyes on me, beautiful. I want to watch you come all over my cock." I barely get the words out when her emerald eyes lock onto mine. I love seeing her in control, but fuck, I need to watch her fall apart around me. Grabbing her hips, I take control of our pace. Jenna leans back, giving me an uninterrupted view of me slamming into her as her tits bounce uncontrollably.

"Dane... I... oh god... I'm going to—" Jenna's mouth falls open as I continue my unrelenting pace, pounding into her from below.

"Play with your clit for me, Angel." The moment her fingers circle her clit, she begins to clamp down around me.

"Cum now," I grit out.

Her eyes never leave mine as we both find our release together. Her body shakes in my hold as her orgasm slams into her. Our movements slow until the only sounds left in the car are our ragged breaths.

She pulls back, breaking our kiss, leaving us both panting for more. "I'm okay, I promise." Her words crash us both back to reality.

"Don't lie to me, Angel. I know you, and all of this has been weighing on you." I stare into her bright green eyes and see a flash of sadness. Jenna quickly puts up her façade of bravery once more. She moves off my lap, and I let her, giving her the space she needs.

We both get dressed again and exit the vehicle. I watch as Jenna smooths the front of her dress down with her hands and takes in a shaky breath. Any hint of relaxed, carefree Jenna is gone as quickly as she arrived.

"I'm okay, Axel. You have to let me do this. I can't not know who he is." She starts wringing her hands together again; it's a new tick I've seen her doing when she's nervous.

"I just… don't think I would be here without him… alive, I mean." Gut-wrenching anger bubbles under my skin at the thought of her not being here, but I understand her need to fully know what happened that night.

I step out of the truck, helping her out next before weaving our fingers together.

"I love you," I say into her hair and then take a whiff of her intoxicating scent. I let it seep into my nostrils, relaxing me. I tuck her under my arm as we make our way through the parking lot and into the clubhouse.

I spot Cal standing in the doorway of Church. He nods his head back, telling us a meeting is set up. I can feel Jenna's tense shoulders rise as she starts to speed-walk toward the door. Keeping a tight hold on her hand, we both place our phones in the lock box outside of the door and step into the room. I drop down into an open seat, pulling Jenna into my lap and securing my hands around her. She thoughtlessly wraps her arms around my neck, still focused on the men in front of us.

"Okay, we're alone. Tell me what you know," Jenna says immediately when the doors close, sealing all the club's officers inside.

Cal shoots me a look. He gave me a full rundown of what we might be dealing with earlier, but I have a feeling they found out a hell of a lot more. I nod at him, signaling that he can speak freely in front of her.

"Officer Mike Stevenson went undercover with the Reapers MC about nine months ago. He gained trust quickly and rose in the ranks just as fast. Within four months, he was a patched member." Cal pauses, grabbing his laptop off the table behind us.

It gives me a moment to digest this information. It doesn't make sense. It takes at least a year for someone to prospect, and even then, you have to prove extreme loyalty. Stevenson becoming a member in just four months seems unrealistic, and someone must have been pulling strings in the background.

Cal begins typing quickly on his laptop and then turns the screen in our direction. CCTV footage from Main Street is enlarged on the screen. Stevenson is off to the side, wearing a hoodie pulled close to his face. It looks like he's in a serious conversation with a short brunette. Her hands are flailing in the air, and then the woman slams into his chest for a tight hug before storming off in the other direction.

"Ace found this yesterday. It's from the day after we found Jenna and took out the Reapers." He looks at Jenna with a soft expression, trying to comfort her. She starts to speak, not taking her eyes off the screen or looking at any of us.

"That's her. That's my friend Jill. You can't see her face, but I know it's her," she says, pausing for a moment, almost lost in thought. "Right before he... or Officer Stevenson helped me escape, he told me to *tell Jilly he was sorry. That kidnapping an innocent was never in the job description.* Why wouldn't he have just called in backup when I was taken if it wasn't part of his assignment? Why aren't you all arrested? And what does Jill have to do with any of this?" The last part she almost whispers, looking around the room at all of us.

"That's what we're trying to figure out. It doesn't make sense that he didn't call it in unless he has gone rogue." Cal turns the laptop back to himself. "Can you give me more information on Jill? I'm assuming her last name is Stevenson?"

"No, her last name is Monroe—Jill Monroe. But I can assure you they're related. When I saw him, I instantly knew they were. Their facial features are so similar." She pauses for a moment. "They also have the same tattoo behind their ear." I watch as Jenna unconsciously rubs the spot under her right ear.

"Hmm, okay. I can start looking and see what I can find. Don't worry, Jenna. We'll find her and figure out what the hell is happening with the two of them. Can you tell me about the tattoo?" Cal types as Jenna describes the small rose with the word *Lost* written beneath Stevenson's. A look flashes over Ace's face, but he does well to right his expression. That tattoo is one we have all seen before, but it can't be the same woman. He shifts his eyes to me before turning the laptop around, displaying the woman Jenna described to us. I grip the side of the chair until my knuckles turn white.

At about the same time I make the connection, every other member in the room does too. The space becomes deathly quiet as I feel Jenna turn in my lap.

"Yeah, that's her! Wait… what's wrong?" she asks as she surveys the varying expressions on the men around the room. I pull Jenna into my chest as if anticipating what is about to happen. Heavy footsteps from the back of the room make their way next to us.

"Bear?" Jenna asks curiously.

"That can't be your friend," Bear says in a voice that would make grown men cower, but Jenna just peers up at him with a worried expression.

"No, Bear, that's—" Before Jenna can get out the rest of her sentence, the laptop flies across the room, shattering against the back wall.

"She's dead! What is this? Some sick game you're playing here?" He moves to get in front of Jenna, but I stand quickly, pulling her behind me.

"Don't you fucking dare," I growl. I stare into the eyes of one of my best friends and see nothing but pain and confusion. Without turning, I keep my voice calm as I talk to Jenna.

"Jenna, that woman we just saw on the screen isn't Jill Monroe but Macy Butler—Bear's supposed dead wife."

The End

ACKNOWLEDGEMENTS

Writing *The Lessons We Learn* brought me a reprieve during a time in my life where my days had become crazy. Any small time I got to myself I threw into writing and it gave me a little part of myself back. I cannot thank the people in my life enough for supporting and surrounding me as I decided to take a leap of faith and write my first book. I will be forever grateful that I have such an amazing group of people around me who are just as delusional as I am. When I mentioned that I was writing a book, none of them batted an eye or questioned it. I was met with, "Tell me more about it!"

I could probably fill an entire book with the thanks I wish to give each of them but will keep it short and to the point for everyone's sake.

First, my husband. The man who cheers me on and pushes me to jump in head first to anything I want to do. He jokes about being the inspiration behind my book boyfriends but he really is (I'm never going to hear the end of it after this.) I am so thankful to have found someone who not only is my best friend but is the best life partner I could ever ask for.

Next, my mom. My, "you can be anything you want to be," parent. I can't begin to summarize the support and guidance she has given to me. Not only with this book and my career as a writer but throughout my life. My mother has always backed my ideas and continues to be a sounding board for me throughout my adult life. I will forever strive to be as thoughtful and caring as she was with myself and my brother and continue to model the same unconditional love with my own children.

My social media and pr manager, Katie. I would be completely lost without you and am so thankful for you. I love our "Parallel play dates" so we can make sure we get our work done. Thank you for keeping me on track and pushing me to get out there.

Kristyn, my best friend who refers to this book as my, "sex book." Even though you don't read romance, you are always one of my number one supporters. I'm so thankful to have you in my corner.

My editor, Emily. I was terrified to let someone new read my writing but I couldn't imagine a better person to hand it over too. Thank you for making my first experience with editing so seamless.

Family and Friends is broad, but I have never been so blessed with the amount of people in my life who rallied behind me. In moments of doubt, I was met with more people than I can count lifting me up and telling me to get my shit together. Thank you to those of you who let me talk your ear off about characters and plots, who read my book, who brought me coffee while I wrote. I love you all!

With Love,
Chandler

ABOUT THE AUTHOR

Chandler Bean is a debut author, highlighting spice, danger and suspense throughout her small-town romance. You can expect to be entranced by strong characters and become immersed in their dangerous world. Located in Northern California, where the redwoods meet the ocean. She transitioned from teaching to being a full time Mom of two crazy, adorable toddlers. Chandler lives with her husband and two young daughters, enjoying everything this season of life has to offer.

She often can be found at the beach with her family and friends, or enjoying local coffee shops. When becoming a mom, Chandler quickly realized the value in quiet time and covets her early morning and late-night writing sessions. She is taking this time to pursue her dream of inspiring readers to live out their wildest fantasies!

Website: https://chandlerbeanauthor.wixsite.com/
chandler-bean-author
Instagram: @chandlerbeanauthor
Threads: @chandlerbeanauthor
BlueSky: @chandlerbeanauthor.bsky.social

STAY TUNED FOR:

The Secrets
We Keep

Hell Chaser's
Motorcycle Club
Book 2